THE DARK SIDE OF CHRISTMAS

AN ANTHOLOGY OF TWISTED WINTER TALES

REBECCA COLLINS   JUDI DAYKIN   ANTONY DUNFORD

LEWIS HASTINGS   ADRIAN HOBART   LINDA HUBER

LIN LE VERSHA   A B MORGAN   R.D. NIXON

BRIAN PRICE   S.E. SHEPHERD   KERENA SWAN

WENDY TURBIN   MARK WIGHTMAN

HOBECK

THE DARK SIDE OF CHRISTMAS

ISBN 978-1-913-793-55-5 (ebook)

ISBN 978-1-913-793-56-2 (pbk)

Cover design by Rebecca Collins

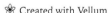 Created with Vellum

For everyone who has had their lives touched by homelessness

I will honour Christmas in my heart, and try to keep it all the year.

— CHARLES DICKENS

CONTENTS

FOREWORD

Maybe it's the crime writer's lot to find the darkness in the brightest of times, but as well as enjoying the festive period for all its worth I have always been drawn to the other side of Christmas. For every depiction of Father Christmas in his deep red robe, and silver beard, I would seek out a vision of Krampus with his horns, punishing the children who have misbehaved through the year. For every rewatch of *It's a Wonderful Life*, I would devour Tim Burton's *A Nightmare before Christmas*. And for every tale of loving families opening presents on Christmas day, I would read about Dr Seuss' Grinch stealing Christmas, or Ebenezer Scrooge battling his festive ghosts.

That was why I was delighted to be asked to write the foreword for this devilish collection of Christmas short stories. Within you will find dark tales of revenge, gruesome games, kindly thieves, twisted love stories, and even an insight into the trade union practices of Christmas Turkeys.

But much more than that, within these pages, amongst the murder and mayhem, you will find a true love of Christmas. It's all here. The traditions and humour, the personal rituals and anticipation, the nostalgia, and at times, the sense of community and kindness.

So why not pour yourself something festive, pull up a chair, switch the Christmas tree lights on, and enjoy these delightfully creepy yuletide stories from the Hobeck Team.

Just remember to check up the chimney before going to bed!

Merry Christmas,

Matt Brolly

CONTRIBUTORS

REBECCA COLLINS

Rebecca is a published poet and contributed to *Because We Never Said Goodbye*, a collection of poems about Charlbury in Oxfordshire, published by Wychwood Press in 2008. She is also the 'Beck' of Hobeck and an inspiring artist.

In Rebecca's own words: 'I didn't have any inspiration for my story at all. What I do have is a fascination with found objects which stems from my masters by research. Looking for inspiration, Hobeck author Harry Fisher suggested I write a story about a fish supper. So I did. The challenge was linking fish and chips to Christmas. The book that features in the story is a real book, it stuck in my memory.'

JUDI DAYKIN

Judi is the author of the best-selling Detective Sara Hirst series which is published by Joffe Books. Judi came to Hobeck with an interesting proposition which turned into *Wayland Babes*, a collection of interlinked ghost stories set in the Wayland Woods in Norfolk, published in October 2021 in time for Hallowe'en. There will be more to come from Judi!

Based on the sad story of the drummer boy of Hickling Broad, *Skating Away* combines a modern ghost story with the old East Anglian practice of holding speed skating competitions on flooded fields in hard winters. Jack French becomes a convert to the sport of his grandfather and is lured out to skate on the frozen broad with disastrous consequences.

ANTONY DUNFORD

Antony is the author of numerous short stories and *Hunted*, published by Hobeck Books, which was shortlisted for the 2019 UEA Crime Writing Prize and longlisted for the 2020 Grindstone Literary Novel prize. The sequel to *Hunted*, *Endangered*, is due out in early 2022.

In Antony's words, how the stories came about: 'The story "A Christmas Susan" emerged from the time-honoured tradition of adapting Dickens for nefarious purposes, borrowing inspiration from *The Pickwick Papers* as well as *A Christmas Carol*. Slap in some bad jokes, ask Ms Turbin to put in some good ones, cover in flour, bake for fourteen minutes and, hey presto, a completely credible police procedural. Ahem. Of course, given the collaboration with Ms Turbin, there needed to be a ghost pet. A rabbit led to Richard Adams, Richard Adams led to the South Downs, the South Downs led to Chichester, and Chichester led to the dark side (BogNoir). See you at BogNoir one day!'

LEWIS HASTINGS

Lewis Hastings is a pseudonym (even the Hobeck Cat doesn't know Lewis's real name) and nowadays he spends his days fighting crime and writing crime in New Zealand. Lewis is the author of the Jack Cade series of books which includes the trilogy, *The Seventh Wave*, and *The Angel of Whitehall*. *The Chemist*, the fifth Jack Cade novel, is due to be published in 2022.

In Lewis's own words: 'I worked in Nottingham, and lived just outside, for many years. It's what most police officers do. Never mix grape and grain, and all that. I was keen to introduce readers to Jack Cade, the main protagonist in my novels. I wanted to take the reader back in time to his early uniform policing days when he met a character who would remain a part of his life, and the Cade novels. I also wanted to focus upon loneliness – a curse of modern society. It might be the job I do, but I can't resist knowing a bit more about the man or woman sat on a park bench, or stood in a queue for a bus. Who are they and where have they come from?'

ADRIAN HOBART

Adrian Hobart is the 'Ho' in Hobeck, so he feels being published alongside the Hobeck team is both a privilege and a challenge. Adrian spends much of the year suggesting changes to manuscripts and tweaks to story arcs, so the tale that follows is an opportunity for the Hobeck authors to judge if their publisher can walk the walk too.

The inspiration for this story comes from Adrian's current fascination with industrial relations of the 1970s and 1980s – when, growing up as a boy in Cambridge, the sight of picket lines, braziers and placards seemed very alien, even though the battle for the future of industrial Britain was being waged only hours away up the A1 in the coal fields and car factories of the Midlands. So much has changed in modern Britain, and events in recent months suggest many have given up the will to fight, so let's return to 1979 in Adrian's story, *One Out, All Out*.

LINDA HUBER

Linda Huber, originally from Scotland but now based on the edge of Switzerland, has published two psychological thrillers so far with Hobeck (and many more books before that), *Daria's Daughter* (her tenth novel) and *Pact of Silence*. Both books published in 2021.

In Linda's words: 'I'm not sure what inspired my story. I was sitting wondering what to write and thinking vaguely Christmassy thoughts, when the picture of a little boy, about four years old with tousled blonde hair and wearing a red dressing gown slid into my head. His name was George, and he was standing at his bedroom window on the first floor, watching for Santa. I'm sure a lot of people stood at windows, watching for Santa when they were four. Fortunately, not many would have had the same adventure as George.'

LIN LE VERSHA

Lin lives and writes in Suffolk, where her new series is set. Lin is also the Director of the Southwold Arts Festival. Lin's debut novel, *Blood Notes*, published with Hobeck this November, described by Emma Freud as 'a wonderful, witty, colourful, debut'. The second book will be published in 2022.

The final line of Lin's story was the headline in a newspaper report of a murder trial in the 1990s. Thinking it would make a great short story, Lin kept the cutting for years but lost it when she moved to Suffolk. Steph and Hale, who star in her novels, appear in this fictitious version leading to the final killer line.

A B MORGAN

A B Morgan's wonderful creations, Private Investigating husband-and-wife duo, Connie and Peddyr Quirk feature now in two books and one novella with Hobeck Books. *Over Her Dead Body* published in early 2021 and *Throttled* in the summer. There is also a prequel novella, *Old Dogs, Old Tricks*, which is available to Hobeck subscribers. Alison (A B) Morgan is busy penning the third book in the series as this anthology goes to press.

As A B Morgan herself says: 'My story was originally generated by a group of cheese-and-wine-fuelled individuals. They were taking part in a "How to Plot a Murder" workshop that I had foolishly agreed to run in a local pub. The Christmas murder theme that evening resulted in a very inventive set of Secret Santa suspects.'

R.D. NIXON

R.D. Nixon is not new to writing, having numerous books under her belt before she came to Hobeck, but she's relatively new to crime writing. She's embraced it with gusto with *Crossfire* published by Hobeck Books in 2021 and the next in the series, *Fair Game*, due in early 2022.

R.D. Nixon's story *Double First* is a cat-and-mouse chase through an otherwise empty university building, where the bewildering layout could prove more than a mild curiosity. It could make the difference between life and death.

BRIAN PRICE

Brian Price, from the West of England, is the author of *Fatal Trade* which published with Hobeck in the autumn of 2021. The second book in the series is due out in the spring of 2022. Brian is new to crime fiction writing, but not new to crime, having been somewhat of a guru on the science of crime for many other writers for several years.

Brian was prompted to write his story having seen how professionals in caring roles can be ground down by uncaring managers who have no idea what their jobs entail, especially when the organisation becomes a company. Many such victims would like to take revenge – but perhaps not this far.

S.E. SHEPHERD

S.E. Shepherd has published one book with Hobeck so far, *Swindled*, and is busy already on the second book in the series. Sue (S.E.) Shepherd has written fiction before but recently decided to get in touch with her dark side and come to Hobeck.

As Sue herself says: 'I set out to write a Victorian story because I feel the Victorian era really epitomises a darker Christmas. However, it wasn't long before my love of dual timelines came into play, and I found myself writing from two contrasting perspectives. Hopefully, what I have ended up with is a Dickensian style story with a modern edge.'

KERENA SWAN

Kerena published three psychological thrillers before she came to Hobeck with the first book in the new DI Paton investigates series, *Blood Loss*, which published with Hobeck in 2021. Kerena is a juggler extraordinaire balancing her thriving care business with writing and looking after the new member of her family, Branston the dog.

Kerena was inspired to write her story by one of her daughters who regaled her with anecdotes about a game she played with her friend. Kerry found it interesting but, being a crime and psychological thriller writer, she got carried away with the darker side of storytelling and embellished it with a sinister twist. As Kerry herself says: 'I wonder at times whether I should write a flowery romance, but I'd probably end up with the boyfriend bumping off the heroine and framing the old lady next door, so perhaps I should stick to my chosen genre.'

WENDY TURBIN

Wendy's debut novel, *Sleeping Dogs*, was published by Hobeck in 2021. Wendy is a graduate of the celebrated Creative Writing MA course at the University of East Anglia. Wendy is currently working on her second book in her Penny Wiseman Murder Mystery series.

From Wendy: 'I was stuck for a Christmas story. "Bah, humbug!" I said to a certain Mr Dunford et al in a Norwich bar one rainy October day. Then Antony did his thing and wrote a speedy draft of *A Christmas Susan* which needed a character who could see ghosts. He sent it to me. I giggled through part one, nearly cried at part two, then I did my thing with Penny Wiseman and sent it back. This is the result of our shared madness. Merry Christmas, one and all.'

MARK WIGHTMAN

Mark Wightman's debut novel, *Waking the Tiger*, was shortlisted for the Bloody Scotland Debut Prize 2021 and longlisted for the Bloody Scotland McIlvanney Prize 2021. He was also selected to be one of the seventeen UNESCO City of Literature Story Shop emerging writers at the 2017 Edinburgh International Book Festival.

In Mark's words: 'I've always loved stories with a meta-fictional element to them and, in particular, found documents that tell a story within a story within a story, like a literary matryoshka doll, leaving the reader not quite sure where the truth ends and the fiction begins. However, I've never had the courage to attempt writing one and everything you read here is, of course, the plain, unvarnished truth (isn't it?).'

ARE YOU A THRILLER SEEKER?

Hobeck Books is an independent publisher of crime, thrillers and suspense fiction and we have one aim – to bring you the books you want to read.

For more details about our books, our authors and our plans, plus the chance to download free novellas, sign up for our newsletter at **www.hobeck.net**.

You can also find us on Twitter **@hobeckbooks** or on Facebook **www.facebook.com/hobeckbooks10**.

A CHRISTMAS SUSAN: PART I: THE GHOST OF CHRISTMAS PASTA

ANTONY DUNFORD AND WENDY TURBIN

DECEMBER 24TH, 2016

DETECTIVE SERGEANT SUSAN BROWN WOULD remember the Christmas Eve of 2016 for the rest of her life. To begin with, Richard Adams was dead at the age of only ninety-six. It was right there, online, bold as a headline. *The* Richard Adams. The author of *Watership Down*. The *Watership Down* that she had read without warning at a formative age.

She was only half-way down the first paragraph of Mr Adams' obituary when her morning was interrupted by a second shock. A hammering on the door. At this hour. On a Saturday.

She wasn't even on shift.

Fortunately, whilst this hour was remarkably early for the all, and still classed as night for many of the sundry, Susan was an even earlier riser and had showered and dressed two hours before the disturbance began.

She opened the door to her flat.

'Morning, Fifty,' said an insufferably cheerful voice. Susan's partner, Detective Sergeant Ian Feltpen, known to his colleagues as "Sharpie" for reasons Susan had never understood, pushed past her into the hall. 'Aren't you going to invite me in?' He surveyed her living room. 'Love what you've done with the place, really brings out the joyous spirit of the season.'

Susan looked around. Nothing in her flat suggested Christmas. Ah, of course. Susan wasn't very good at spotting irony, but several past incidents had led her to inquire why DS Feltpen sometimes stated the opposite of what he knew to be true, and he had introduced her to the concept. She still didn't fully grasp its purpose.

'Grab your coat you've pulled.'

She didn't move.

'We've got a case,' he clarified. DS Feltpen was absorbing as much as he could of her habitat whilst simultaneously trying to leave the flat. He almost tripped over his own feet.

'Fine.' Susan said, taking her coat from the closet and following him out of the door.

'Are you sure you haven't overdone it with leisure pursuits? One of the books on your bookshelf was only tangentially related to police work.'

'Where are we going?' Susan said, recognising the irony much more quickly, though this time, she suspected, it bordered on sarcasm.

'The Racton Ruin. There's been a murder.'

'The Racton Ruin? You mean the Racton Monument?' Susan said, at his heels along the corridor.

'Call it what you like, we locals tell it like it is,' DS Feltpen reached the lift and pressed the button.

'You're from Norfolk,' she said, opening the door to the stairwell.

'Always pedantic, Fifty. Loosen up! Hey, where are you going?' He hurried after her into the stairwell. 'My car's out front.'

'I'm taking my car,' Susan said. 'You can come with me if you like.'

His indecision stretched the silence.

Susan had once overheard a colleague comment on her driving. "You remember the way you were taught when you were seventeen?" he'd said to a laughing group of others. "Fifty drives *just like that*."

'I know there's a speed limit, but would it kill you to skip a gear once in a while?' DS Feltpen said.

'I am taking the B2178 instead of the A259,' Susan retorted. 'That will be quicker on a Saturday with heavy traffic forecast.'

'Put your foot down, Fifty. Did I mention there's been a murder?'

'You did.' Susan kept her hands in the ten to two position as she slowed down to let a tractor overtake.

Susan had studied the Highway Code. Rule 148 was clear: a driver must avoid distraction. If a passenger chose to bang his forehead gently on the dashboard, there was nothing she could do unless she first stopped and switched off the engine. As DS Feltpen had rightly pointed out, time was of the essence.

Susan drove on.

'Where have you two been?' yelled DI Squared from the top of the hill. 'You should have been here half an hour ago.'

'Sorry, ma'am,' DS Feltpen called back cheerfully as he walked briskly up the hill towards her, Susan hastening to keep up with him. 'Didn't expect you'd be here in person, or I would have driven.'

The DI's eyebrows raised, but she turned and stepped aside, revealing the inside of the ruined tower. Brightly lit by portable arc lights, the reveal was made all the more dramatic by the early morning mist that hung in slow-moving clumps about the hilltop.

Once, shortly after her transfer to West Sussex, Susan had asked the DI whether she should call her "DI Squared" or "Ma'am". 'Neither,' the DI had snapped, 'it's DI Icarus and don't you forget it.' Dawn Icarus, blessed with such convenient initials, had been gifted the nickname "DI Squared" as soon as she'd been promoted from Detective Sergeant to Detective Inspector. Susan never really understood the point of nicknames.

The lights illuminated the ground within the tower. Susan didn't look at what they were pointing at just yet, as she was trying to remember what she knew about the monument.

Racton Monument, or Racton Tower, known locally as Racton Ruin, was an eighteenth-century folly. It was four storeys tall, though as the stairs and floors had all been wood and had rotted away years ago, only the ground floor remained with a view straight up to the stars. It was an odd, triangular shape, festooned with unnecessary turrets. There'd been an illegal rave here a couple of years ago. Local ghost tours stopped here to recount several contradictory stories about murder victims and, peculiarly, an ethereal tractor. But, in the main, it was just a ruined tower on a hill where sheep grazed, and rabbits nibbled.

Susan observed the pathologist and his assistant at work. The body lay on its side, the arms and legs splayed in four different directions, the head back at an uncomfortable angle. Despite the mist drifting across the hilltop, the lights revealed the crushed skull, a heavy stone covered in blood and bone-matter lying next to it. Above, on the moss-covered wall of the tower, painted in glistening red, were the words "Help Me".

'Oi, Fifty, where are you going?' DS Feltpen said, running down the hill to catch up with Susan.

'Home. We're not on shift and it will be days before forensics can give us anything. You know nothing's as quick as on TV,' Susan said.

'Yes, but TV is right about the grumpy pathologist who can be sweet-talked into giving early insight into the likely results of long and complicated scientific tests. We just have to tell Conrad, that creepy old necrophiliac, he's the greatest thing that's happened to autopsies since the invention of death and he'll tell us all we need to know.'

'Don't bank on it, Sharpie,' said Conrad pushing past and disappearing into the mist.

'Oh,' said DS Feltpen, his crest well and truly fallen. 'I possibly shouldn't have made that jibe about necrophilia.'

Susan resumed walking to her car leaving DS Feltpen kicking the turf and muttering about him and his big mouth. She had just reached the vehicle when she heard running footsteps. It was the pathologist's assistant, Fleur something.

'DS Brown,' Fleur said, a little breathlessly.

'Fleur,' Susan said, opting for excessive familiarity to compensate for failing to remember the woman's last name.

'There are some preliminary observations I can share with you. Conrad, that is, I mean Doctor Unread, usually shares them with DS Feltpen, but Doctor Unread appears a little put out by DS Feltpen just now for some reason. So I thought I'd share them with you.'

'You should wait until the results are definitive,' said Susan.

Fleur's face fell. 'But if we do that any leads may go cold. Some of the genetic tests can take weeks, especially over the holidays.'

'But much better to be certain,' said Susan. 'A miscarriage of justice based on partially informed assumptions would be disastrous for us all.'

'But the murderer may get away with it.'

'It might not be a murder.'

'His head was crushed by a stone.'

'Which could have fallen from the tower.'

'It hit him three times.'

Susan admitted this made the likelihood of this being a murder slightly greater.

'Please, DS Brown, can I just tell you what Doctor Unread wanted to tell DS Feltpen? He'll be ever so grumpy if he hasn't passed on his terribly insightful observations to someone on the force.'

Susan considered. She could listen but then not act if there was nothing sufficiently compelling to act upon. Yes, that would work. Listen and ignore. Like DS Feltpen did when it came to the rules.

'Alright, then. What are your early speculations?' she said.

'Thank you, Detective,' said Fleur, with a smile. She pulled out a notebook and took a deep breath. 'The victim's name was Giuseppe Maronne. He was from Liverpool, now living in town. He was born on the twenty second of September nineteen eighty-three.'

'You got all of that from pathology?'

'No, from his driver's license.' Fleur waved an evidence bag. She continued. 'He was most likely killed by three blows to the skull from the stone lying on the ground next to his body. The blows came from an angle of seventeen degrees whilst Giuseppe was kneeling and the killer standing. The killer was therefore between one and three metres tall, and between twenty and two hundred kilogrammes in weight.'

'What? That's no use at all!' Susan blurted.

Fleur laughed. 'Only kidding. That's a pathologist's joke, you know, to see if you're paying attention.'

'But I was paying attention,' Susan said.

Fleur frowned. 'Yes, I realise that, Detective.' She muttered to herself. 'It always looks a lot more fun when Doctor Unread is telling DS Feltpen this stuff.' Then she shook her head and perked up. 'All we really know about the killer at this stage is they were staying at the Travel Inn.'

'How can you know that?'

'They dropped the key card to their room,' Fleur said, holding up another evidence bag.

'That could have been dropped by anyone at any time, including the victim, surely,' Susan said.

'No, the key card was in a shopping bag which also had two receipts, one from Waitrose, one from Screwfix, both with a date and time stamp yesterday between four-thirty and five-thirty, and the bag was on top of the body but spattered with blood. So either the killer left it, or it fell from the tower.' Susan thought she detected a hint of sarcasm in Fleur's last phrase.

'Is that it?' Susan said.

Fleur looked unhappy. Susan had no idea what to say next, but, fortunately, that didn't matter.

'That is magnificent,' said a voice from the mist. It was DS Feltpen. He emerged before them and enveloped Fleur in a magnificent hedgehog hug, which is like a bear hug but sensitive to the possibility that the recipient might not want to be hugged, or might be covered in spikes. 'Thank you, Fleur, thank you. Thanks to you the family of the victim may well now spend their Christmas with the small consolation that justice has been done, whereas without you they would certainly have spent it wondering what has happened to their poor Guiseppe. Can I borrow this?' DS Feltpen grabbed the evidence bag with the key card in. 'Thank you. Come on, Fifty.'

'You're welcome!' Fleur called after them, beaming. Susan tried to keep up with Feltpen as he raced down the hill like a rabbit.

❄

The reception at the Travel Inn was bedecked for the season by a solitary dusty artificial Christmas tree almost eighteen inches tall which sat on the countertop. Someone had draped a piece of tinsel over a light-fitting, though the draping was so artless it could have been merely displayed to attract its rightful owner, like a lost glove or a misplaced child.

'Hello. I am DS Brown, this is DS Feltpen,' Susan flashed her warrant card at the receptionist. DS Feltpen flashed his interpretation of a charming smile. 'We have found this key card at a crime scene,' she continued as DS Feltpen held up the evidence bag containing the key card and kept the smile on full beam. 'And will be requesting a warrant to require you to release information pertaining to the card, the room it opens, and the person or persons who have rented that room over recent days and weeks. Could you advise me where we should send the warrant once we have raised it? Do you process them locally, or are they handled at head office?'

The receptionist was a short man with a beard a barn owl could nest in. He stared at Susan.

'What?' he said.

'I shall repeat myself,' Susan said. And did so.

'What's she on about, Sharpie?' said the receptionist to DS Feltpen.

'No idea, mate. She lost me at "Hello". Can you tell us which room this is for and who rented it, the usual?' DS Feltpen held out the card in its evidence bag.

'Course, mate,' said the receptionist. He clicked something on the computer, then put the key card in its evidence bag on a magnetic plate. There was a beep. He handed the bag back to DS Feltpen. The receptionist scratched his mouth and a robin flew out of the thatch around it. 'That's strange,' he said, peering at the screen.

'It is,' said Susan, watching the robin fly away.

'What's that, mate?' DS Feltpen said.

'This card won't be issued until 2021.'

'Really?' DS Feltpen's eyes went wide.

The receptionist looked solemn, and nodded, then lost his self-control and grinned.

'Only joking, mate. Room 132. A party by the name of Bonnet. Checked in yesterday. Checking out today but hasn't been processed yet. Might still be in there.'

'Let's go,' DS Feltpen said, turning towards the lift.

'Just one moment, DS Feltpen,' Susan said.

'What is it, Fifty? We could catch him!'

'We have no official reason for assuming the murderer's in there. The key card could be unrelated.'

'On the other hand, we might be fifty metres from a murderer and five minutes away from having Christmas Day off after all.'

'Such a selfish consideration should not impact a serving police officer.' Susan stared at him coldly. He stared back by not looking at her, instead considering the ceiling.

'I know!' DS Feltpen said, as if achieving a dazzling insight. 'We compromise! I'll call up the station, get a couple of uniforms over here. We knock on the door of room 132. If the murderer answers we arrest him and have Christmas Day off. If he doesn't, we go to the pub for a rethink. Deal?'

Without waiting for an answer DS Feltpen pulled out his phone. Before he could dial the station, however, the phone rang.

'Fleur! How lovely to hear from you. Really? Arrabbiata, you say? Very interesting. How sure are you? OK, I see. That's brilliant, Fleur. Tell me, what are you doing later?'

It seemed to Susan that there was giggling at the other end of the line. DS Feltpen hung up.

'The words "Help Me" on the wall of the tower were painted in pasta sauce,' he said, as he dialled the station.

✳

Susan had a bad feeling. She stood in the corridor wearing a smock borrowed from the housekeeping staff as a disguise. She didn't think it was particularly effective as she'd simply put it on over her trouser suit, but DS Feltpen had insisted.

The two uniformed officers either side of the door were disguised as police in uniform, DS Feltpen had explained.

Susan was starting to think DS Feltpen might not be taking this entirely seriously.

DS Feltpen nodded to Susan. She approached the door and knocked.

'Housekeeping!' she said.

There was no answer.

Susan waited one minute, then knocked again.

'Housekeeping!' she said, and simultaneously held the key card in its evidence bag against the electronic lock. The light on the lock turned green and Susan turned the handle.

The smell hit them immediately, the heat only a moment after that.

'Arrabbiata,' DS Feltpen mouthed. Susan knew he was leaping to conclusions without bothering to go via the stepping stones of facts. No one could tell the difference between pasta sauces by smell at this distance, especially not in a room where the thermostat had been turned up to max.

Susan led the way, confidently, into the room. It was laid out like every other Travel Inn room in the country, with a bathroom too small for a rabbit to the left of the door, then the main room which seemed slightly smaller than the three-quarter bed that filled it.

On the bed lay the tears of a clown. Or, rather, the corpse of a woman, her face heavily made up but then smeared by the tracks of many tears. Oh, and she had been brutally slain, and was covered in blood.

Susan peered more closely at the corpse. She'd noticed something odd about it.

DI Feltpen slapped on a pair of latex gloves, leaned across the bed, and opened the window.

'Smell was making me hungry,' he explained.

The odd thing Susan had noticed about the corpse was, it was breathing. Another odd thing was the blood was, in fact, pasta sauce.

Susan stood up and felt her foot knock something on the floor. She looked down. It was an empty jar of Waitrose Arrabbiata.

The open window had allowed the cold December air to flow into the room. Out on the grass behind the hotel a winter rabbit nibbled its dinner. Inside the room, the sauce thickened.

DECEMBER 25TH, 2016

Susan wasn't particularly festive, but she had one tradition on Christmas Day which was to open the Christmas card from her mum. It was the last one her mum had sent her before she had mysteriously moved without leaving a forwarding address.

Susan sat on her sofa and took the card from the envelope, reading the familiar words that were carved on her heart.

"To Susan. From Mum."

She sat there contemplating the meaning of everything, as well as whether or not to have another cup of tea, when there was an unexpected hammering on the door. Again.

For the second time in twenty-four hours, it was DS Feltpen, this time wearing a Christmas jumper and false reindeer antlers with fairy lights twinkling all over them.

'Merry Christmas, Fifty. Just popped round to let you know we got a full confession. The pasta sauce woman admitted to

doing Giuseppe Maronne's bonce with the rock after he accidentally gave her the sauce he meant to take home to his wife rather
than the,' DS Feltpen paused to check a notebook, 'chrome,
gravity-pumped, bath filler he'd promised her for Christmas.
Turns out she and he had been having something of an extra-
marital affair inspired by their mutual love of DIY.'

'Why were they at Racton Monument?' Susan said.

'For atmosphere,' DS Feltpen replied. 'The Christmas spirit
and all that.'

They were both silent for a moment or three. The lights on
DS Feltpen's antlers were the only thing that moved until he
looked about the flat, his gaze lingering on the Christmas card in
Susan's hand.

'Not going home for Christmas dinner?' he said.

Susan shook her head.

'Would you like to come to my parents? They'll be having a
goose. So I am told. I'm not going, obviously, as they disowned
me years ago, so there'll be plenty to eat.'

'They disowned you?'

DS Feltpen couldn't keep his face straight any longer.

'You really must learn to lighten up, Fifty. That's settled then.
I'll pick you up at two thirty. Wear something wholly inappropri-
ate. Like a suit jacket with only two buttons. See you then.'

And he was gone.

Susan went back to sit on the sofa. She looked at the card
from her mother again before placing it carefully on the coffee
table.

She smiled to herself.

She settled in to wait for two thirty, picking up a book
analysing the finer points of the law regarding fly-tipping to
while away the time.

GOODBYE, AND CHEERS FOR ALL THE LIMBLESS COLD-BLOODED VERTEBRATE ANIMALS WITH GILLS AND FINS – A CHRISTMAS STORY

REBECCA COLLINS

Room 107
The Golden Lion Hotel
8–10 King St
Stirling
Scotland
FK8 1BD

24 December

MY DARLING S.

I normally like to start my letters with 'I hope this letter finds you well'. But that won't do. We have been apart for over a decade now and you are not remotely well. Besides which, you will never read this letter so I could start it with whatever I like and it doesn't matter.

You may ask me, why are you writing this letter, what's the point? My answer is simple. I need to confess something to you. I am in my final years now and I want to feel better about what happened. I want to get it all off my chest. If I put what is in my head onto paper and address it to you, then I will feel better even though you'll never read it. That's why people write journals, isn't it? Pouring their thoughts, their misdemeanours and misadventures onto paper to wash their bad feelings away, at least to a small degree.

Can you believe I am writing to you on the anniversary of our last day together? Ten years have passed and here I am again, back in the same location. How could I not keep up the tradition? Despite what happened, I still had to keep it up. I could never let it go.

Anyway, I decided it is time I told you the truth. Ten years seemed an appropriate milestone. I'm older now, and tired, and want to tell you my side of the story. Before I confess, I want you to know that from the start, I was genuine. Our story was real. I did love you. I still love you, even after the end. I don't quite know what happened, how or why. Things did change, in some part for me at least.

From the moment we first met, we shared a spark, and that was good and that was real. It was more than good, it was the best. Our story begins so well, yet the ending, what can I say about that? It is interesting, though, don't you think, that what brought us together also tore us apart. I would call that ironic. I'm sure you'd correct me. It isn't irony, you'd say, just a plain old coincidence.

Our coming together will remain one of the highlights of my life. Why wouldn't it be so? Surely meeting the love of your life is anyone's highlight, alongside giving birth, I imagine.

I was very young when we met. You were young too I see now, but you seemed old to me at the time. In those days, five years was a really big age gap.

Remember, we met on an ordinary day, ordinary for me. It happened to be Christmas Eve, so perhaps not so ordinary. I was happy to work that evening, as I had nowhere else to go. It was a

Friday as you know. We were expecting a busy night of course, one of those nights when you are always fighting the tidal wave of customers, especially the drunken end-of-night ones wanting chips with curry sauce. Christmas in the shop is always busy. I was just starting my shift. I hadn't been in the shop for long when we met. It was a hot, sweaty evening to be behind the counter. It was hot in there all year round of course. Winter, at least, was bearable. You got used to it. I was young then and I could cope. We were allowed to work in vest tops, and aprons. So long as we were clean and decent, we could get away with it. I kept my hair tied up. It was luscious and long in those days. Strands of it would keep falling out, and sticking to the sweat of my face and neck, something which you later told me you found irresistible but at the time just irritated me. I always looked like I was in a sauna, winter or summer. Looking back, perhaps I should have just cut my hair all short. I'm glad I didn't. You might not have found me desirable then. You adored my hair.

You were the third or fourth customer that evening. I think it was early. My memory may have fogged up a little over the years. I only remember three other groups before you though. The first customer I remember was Creep Face as we called him, his real name was Cliff but we knew him as Creep Face. He sported this awful mullet, fancied himself as Richard Marx no doubt. It was a Friday like I said and Creep Face was always first in on a Friday, irrespective of the time of year so Christmas Eve was no exception. I assume he came straight from work with his Friday wages to get his fish supper. I don't think he ever missed a Friday, until his last. Whatever happened to Creep Face, I don't know. On that night, Creep Face did his usual: push the door wide, swagger over to the bar, stand opposite me, lean forward, attempt to flirt, joke about being rebuffed (again) and comment on how he wouldn't be able to wait around for me for ever. He then placed his order and moved to the back of the shop to wait, leaving the front counter with a wink. He was harmless enough.

The girls of today wouldn't tolerate it. Not even the flirting. But he never touched me, just used to leer a lot, creepy. I often wonder how he would have reacted if I'd taken him up on one of his many offers. Run a mile. Not that I can imagine him running that far, he wasn't exactly fighting fit. This Friday I'm talking about, the one when we met, he had brought a wilting sprig of mistletoe with him, no doubt pinched form his place of work on the way out. He had no chance.

As Creep Face stood waiting, rebuffed once again, for his large cod and large fries, second to wander in if I remember rightly was a group of local teenagers, buying the most they could afford and the least they could get away with. They dominated the shop, as they always did, flirting and poking each other with wooden forks. They'd come in bringing their usual waft of sweat and cheap aftershave, Old Spice or whatever. I was only a few years older than them at that time but I felt decades away. They were like scrimps to me. Having a real job really does make you grow up quickly. They were dressed in their best going-out clothes. The boys sporting pulling shirts, on the shark no doubt. The girls in short skirts and tinsel, complete with enormous bauble earrings. One boy had a can of silly spray which he plonked on the counter for me to see as he dithered between a small chips or a medium. I eyed him with caution. That was enough.

Just before you came in, the next customer to enter the fold was Book Woman. She also used to come every Friday. She was a strict chicken and chips lady. Every week, she'd order her chicken and stand demurely at the far end of the counter where Creep Face would still be waiting, where we put the local papers for people to peruse. There she would wait, almost invisible, while we prepared her chicken, reading a folded over paperback. She had a different book every week. I never found out what she did for a living, but I guessed she worked in a rather dull office doing rather dull things. She looked the type – fishtail skirts that were so fashionable then and court shoes. I bet she filed and typed up memos all day. Reading seemed to be her big pleasure, that and her Friday night chicken and chips. Did she ever move on? I don't remember.

Then, after her, in you walked. I raised my head at the door's tinkle and there you stood, hovering over the threshold, the lights from the shop's Christmas tree flashing echoes of colour on your face. You looked lost. This was unusual enough for me to keep looking at you. Most people walk confidentially into a chip shop. It is such a British institution, what's not to understand? Yet, you were different. You paused, blinded by slight confusion. You were a new face to us and we were new to you. Like I said, you just looked like you didn't know what to do in a fish and chip shop. I smiled at my thought that you had been beamed from the Starship Enterprise or something. I looked at you, embarrassed for your awkwardness. The school kids, happy with their chips, wanted to get past you, to get out. You didn't notice immediately. They jibed at you and you broke out of your thoughts and then you moved aside.

You eventually approached the counter. I waited patiently for you to order. I remember you had the bluest eyes I had ever seen. They were as blue as the ocean, as corny as that sounds, but I'm not the one good with words as you know, but they really were. They were deep, again, cheesy, I know. I almost couldn't look into your eyes for fear of drowning in them. I wish I knew how to describe you like those romance books do. You were like that to me then.

Then, you broke my revere by asking me the strangest of questions: Do you sell fish fingers? I remember giggling. Firstly, because who asks for fish fingers in a chip shop? Secondly, you were American. What an accent! If the eyes didn't have me then the voice certainly did. I remembered where I was and what I was supposed to be doing and righted myself. You were the only person ever to have asked me that question in all my years behind the counter. Even if I hadn't fallen in love with you, I would always have remembered this exchange. We settled on the closest thing to fish fingers, two fish cakes (and a medium chips). I felt sorry for you.

Despite those amazing eyes of yours, like I said, you were awkward that first time we met. At first, I thought you were just quite shy, someone who needed to be brought out of their shell. You weren't shy, just a fish out of water in this odd environment. I'd never seen anyone your age dressed like you were: tweed jacket with patches on your elbows. You gave off a faint hint of pipe smoke and paper as you leaned on the counter squinting those eyes at the menu above. You were different. I felt an immediate pull. I was hooked. This could not be our only encounter, I decided. I wanted a taste of that difference. As you know, I didn't expect to see you again.

As with any common love story (and really all love stories are as common as salt, aren't they?), we did manage to break beyond the purpose of our initial exchange and find out a little something about each other. That lead to a date, between Christmas and New Year, at my local pub, the Dolphin. You told me that you were a researcher at the university in town, a leading expert in electric fish (who knew there was such a job?). I told you that I had worked in the chip shop since leaving school. I wasn't academic, my love was for water not words, I explained to you. I told you about my previous lofty ambitions to pursue a career swimming. But lack of money, lack of parental support, lack of water except at the local baths, put pay to that. So I worked in a chip shop. Glamour, eh?

You know the rest of the story of course. We fell in love. We married. We got on reasonably well despite our differences. We were together, albeit with your frequent trips to middle America, until your untimely demise, which of course is the main subject of this letter. We didn't have any children. It just didn't happen for us. We went through a period of trying. We found out that your swimmers weren't strong enough. But that was ok, eventually. We grieved, we came to terms with it, we moved on.

We were very different creatures, you and I. You generated electricity. I lived off your spark. You shone and I absorbed. It was always that way. It seemed to fit though. We were different but we complemented each other. You existed on a plain above me, well above my horizon. Your mind flitted here and there, always hungry for more. You loved words. No, you adored words. You never gave up learning. You had an incredible thirst for knowledge and a constant desire to make waves. You just had to know more. Whereas I was content with what I could see and feel. I often wonder what our children would have been like, more like you I expect. You were never able to accept that we knew it all. There was always something unexplained, something you hadn't quite worked out yet that you needed to work out. What was it? You were always searching for the final answer. It is such a shame you never got there. It was just a few strokes beyond you. I, on the other hand, accept the world as it is. It is just what we see. It is made up of various elements and those elements are made up of the same thing. That's what I think. We sometimes used to row about it. You'd call me passive and unimaginative. I'd tell you that you were exhausting. After a while, the constant sparks flying was too much for me. Call me fickle, but it's true.

One thing we did have in common, is our sense of romance. I'm not talking flowers and champagne. We both agreed that was all utter rubbish. But we wanted to mark our first meeting. That is how we started the tradition of a fish supper every Christmas Eve. It was meant to be romantic. We ended up having a fish supper on the same night every year. We didn't miss it once. When I say fish supper, I mean two fish cakes and a medium chips to share between us, it was tradition after all. Those fish cakes were awful, but it was what you wanted. Every year we did this, until that day. Do I regret what happened that day now? Yes, of course I do.

After a couple of years together, once we had married, you took the romance up another level. I loved that about you. By then we could afford it, we started taking our Christmas Eve fish suppers to the hotel rather than at home: The Golden Lion in Stirling. It was where we had stayed on our honeymoon, of course. We became such regulars there that we'd book the room as we checked out after Christmas every year for the following year. The staff came to know you as that famous fish man. Everyone who met you loved you. I think they, as I had done, felt endeared to your social awkwardness. I was just the rather dull fish wife. But for a long time I didn't mind that.

The years passed, every Christmas Eve we marked with a fish cake and chips fish supper at The Golden Lion hotel, without fail. I loved that place. We used to joke that Agatha Christie must have stayed there once or twice. It had the feel of the 'golden age'. It glowed inside. We always stayed in the same room as well, room 107, where I am now writing this. I don't know why it was that room, except that that was the room we stayed in on our honeymoon. I think now how lucky we were to be able to keep that tradition.

So let me end this rather self-indulgent nostalgia trip and return to the purpose of this letter: to confess. I confess, darling S., that my thoughts towards you were not always pure. I loved you, with all my body and soul, but it was so hard sometimes living with someone who had achieved so much, who was so good with words, who was so loved by all. You could have been content with that, yet you never were. You were always seeking more. Yet, there was me, I hadn't been allowed to achieve what I wanted to achieve, and I'm not blaming you for that, and I had to be content with my lot to allow you to be the unsettled ambitious one. I blended into the background. Nobody cared about my ambitions, my needs. I hardly swam at all after we met. It just wasn't possible. Academia doesn't pay well and we had to travel so much, so I had no time due to work. That was tough. I bore it very well for many years of course. I convinced myself I didn't need anything else besides to be your support and to be loved by you. I was loved by you. That never waivered, at least not to my knowledge. It wasn't as if I was a battered wife, you were always gentle and loving. That's not the point of this story. But in the end, all that, what we had wasn't quite enough for me. I'm sorry. I just thought, warped perhaps, in that moment and just in that moment that it was your fault I felt like that. When the opportunity to change the course of our future arose, I blamed you. There, I have said it now. I did, I blamed you for my life, in that one single moment. I didn't want to take the lime-light from you but it was like suddenly a door was opened for me. So when the opportunity arose for me to take control, I really wish I had an explanation, other than, I took it.

It really was a 'moment of madness' they'd say that led me to make that split-second decision. I guess you could argue that I decided to be inactive rather than active. It is the Christmas Eve of your demise, and we found a new fish and chip shop to try. The old one had closed, sadly. This new one was posh. The fish cakes were really posh. They were made of real fish. The chips were triple cooked, whatever that means. I had never eaten anything like it. Cheap and cheerful, it was not. Delicious, it really was. Such a shame it was to be our last. The cod in the fish cakes had been cooked to perfection, you know what I mean, with steaming flakes falling apart. In that moment we were happy, and then it turned suddenly very sour. How was I to know that you'd pick up the tiniest of fish bones in your first fork full? How was I to know that on this particular occasion, when for so many people this turns out to be a harmless occur-rence, easily swallowed, the fishbone would get lodged in your throat? How could I predict that you would stumble into the bathroom to run some hot water into the sink to try to relax your throat? Why didn't I suggest you eat some of the bread left over from the lunchtime sandwiches? That has worked for me in the past. The thought flashed through my mind. I dismissed it. I am sorry, my love. The words were stuck in my throat. I could not have known that the steam in the sink wouldn't be enough, so you decided to run a hot bath instead to calm your throat. Who was I to try to stop you, knowing that earlier I had left my phone charging balanced on the side of the bath? How many times had you told me not to leave my phone charging in dangerous places? Oh if only I had listened to you. How was I to know that the phone would slip into the bath, as you had warned might happen just a few hours earlier, and just as you climbed in, in your distress. No, I had no idea. I just let it happen. I left you to flounder until you turned silent. Silence. It was strange. It was an accident. All an accident, I told them. It was all just a series of unfortunate events. It wasn't my fault. What could I have done? I just sat and watched from afar. I was frozen. I was inert, I told them, shocked and frightened. Was it ironic, the circumstance of your death? No, you would say. It was just a coincidence.

You still get letters about your book you know, from all over the world. The fish academics just want to feel that they have communicated with, touched in some way, the famous fish professor. Before I reply with the bad news, even after this much time, I read all the letters. They are very amusing and sometimes quite moving. You are, you were, much loved. Nobody knows or knew as much as you did about fish. We were the golden couple of the fish world. Were. I am now, a lone swimmer. Yes, I took up swimming again. Somehow, losing you unlocked my swimmers' block, as I call it. However, sadly, it was too late to do anything with it. I just became an old woman who swam regularly.

For now, my darling, I will end. I have confessed. Can inaction be said to be action? I don't think I can go to prison for that, can I? For now, the sea is calling me. I will leave this hotel room tomorrow early, travel to the coast, and go for my first Christmas Day swim in over fifty years. I feel the pull of the ocean. I haven't had a Christmas Day swim since my youth, since before I met you. It seems the right time to return.

Yours, always in love,

W.

Letter found by cleaner at The Golden Lion Hotel, Stirling, on the morning of 26 December 20xx, inside a copy of The Shocking History of Electric Fishes, *by Stanley Finger and Marco Piccolino, Oxford University Press, 2011.*

Room 107 had been occupied by Professor and Mrs Finger every Christmas Eve from 19xx until 20xx and thereafter by Mrs Finger from 20xx to 20xx. No bookings were made after that.

SKATING AWAY

JUDI DAYKIN

As he walked through the village to catch the bus to Norwich, Jack French saw the skies thick with low, solid, grey clouds. One more day of college, followed by a shift at the coffee shop, and it would be half term.

The ground was rigid with the sharp frost that had descended last night to make the edges of Hickling Broad crackle with thin layers of ice. If this cold snap kept up for long, the ice would deepen in a way that Jack had not known in his eighteen years. His father, Freddie, on the other hand, was gleeful at the prospect.

'Maybe we'll be able to skate again,' Freddie had said this morning after inspecting the rim of frost. 'Like in the old days.'

'Maybe.' Jack had replied. He doubted it would ever get that cold for long enough these days. Global warming had messed with the weather, and they rarely seemed to have the kind of cold snap that enabled the races they'd had when Jack's grandfather had been Fen Skating Champion of 1959.

Jack finished his shift at the coffee bar in Norwich at six o'clock. Now he had the rest of the half term holiday to himself, and he was looking forward to some downtime. The last local bus eventually got him back to the village. He trekked along the lane past the few neighbouring cottages. It was bitterly cold. Flakes of snow drifted around him.

The smell of his mother's cooking filled the house. She had been baking. Jack smiled with anticipated pleasure. He brought in some logs from the large pile by the back door, and stacked them in the basket by the log burner. It threw out both warmth and cheer. The television burbled in the corner.

'Just in time to make Valentine's Day even more romantic,' said the weather lady on the local news. 'From tomorrow, we will see the Beast from the East return. The Beast Mark Two, if you will, and it looks like it's going to be a big one.'

His mother was looking through the kitchen window. Snow was falling heavily. The wind driving it into piles in the back-yard and on the road. When his dad's van pulled up outside, she sighed with relief. Their cottage was the last house on a narrow lane that ended almost on the shores of the Broad. Their nearest neighbour was several hundred yards back towards the village.

'Reckon I'm going to be the last one in,' he said, dumping his work bag on the kitchen table. 'It's really cold out there. That stuff is already freezing on the roads and more falling on top.'

The snow had settled on the window ledge as Jack lay on his bed watching the skies. He listened to the wind shift and twist in the chimney. Snowflakes span out of the dark against the panes, only to dance away out of sight. Downstairs his father whistled between his teeth as he tamped down the fire. He heard his parents settle down in their bedroom.

As he drifted in and out of sleep, Jack heard another whistle. Bright and sharp, it flew with the wind up the lane from the water, so piercing that Jack was instantly awake. Tumbling off the bed, he hurried to look out of the window. It must be someone calling for their dog. But who would be stupid enough to be out in this and at this hour? A glance at his mobile told him it was after midnight. He could feel panic rising, clogging his chest and shortening his breath.

'It must be some visitor,' he muttered, straining to look into the dark. Jack opened the window a crack. Cold air rushed in as he put his ear to the gap. The whistle came again, a confident sound with no edge of fear. As he wondered what to do, there was another whistle. This one sounded different, as if from a deeper voice.

'There must be two of them.' Jack closed the window with a grumble. He pulled off his damp T-shirt and closed the curtains before heading back to his bed. 'Good luck to them. Idiots.'

By the next morning, they were cut off. The lane outside was deep with hardened snowdrifts. The television news said the region was shut down, and Norfolk had settled into a state of siege. After breakfast, Jack shovelled a path across the yard to the shed and around the log pile. The air was laden with ice which hurt his lungs. He carried on until he managed to clear the garden path to the lane.

'How do you fancy a walk?' his father asked after lunch. Freddie was an outdoor man who wouldn't enjoy being shut inside all day.

No one had been past their cottage. There were no tyre tracks or footprints. Jack thought about the dog walkers last night. They must have come back this way. There was no other route unless you had a boat or swam. The snow must have covered their tracks. Jack and his dad struggled to the corner, where they could make out a tractor about half a mile away. It was coming along the lane, making slow progress, but heading in their direction.

'That will be Mr Nicholls,' said Freddie. 'From Stubbs Farm.'

They waited, stamping their feet to keep their toes warm until the tractor grew nearer. The driver was using the front dozer attachment to push and scrape at the snow, reducing the level of the drifts. When Freddie waved, the engine rumbled to a stop, and Mr Nicholls opened the door.

'Earning my money for once,' he said to them. 'Council pays me every winter to clear these lanes if it snows, but I haven't had to do it for years. How you coping?'

'All right, so far. Got a minute?'

Mr Nicholls climbed down from the cab, and the two men settled in for a chat, a prospect Jack didn't fancy. He set off back through the snow to the cottage. It was getting dark when Freddie got back to the cottage. The tractor had worked its way past their place, then turned round and gone home an hour ago.

'Where have you been?' asked Jack's mum. With a wide grin, Freddie didn't reply. Instead, he climbed into the loft with a torch. They could hear the muffled thumps and bangs as he dragged stuff around, searching for something.

Eventually, he brought down a very old-fashioned looking pair of ice skates and handed them to Jack. 'Here we are.'

'What do I need these for?' Jack turned the skates over, examining them.

'I'm going to teach you to skate.'

'What? How?'

'I'll tell you where I've been,' said Freddie, winking at his wife. 'I persuaded Mr Nicholls to set us up an ice rink in one of his fields at the edge of the Broad. Opened the dyke and let the water in. It should be ready in the morning.'

'But I've never been skating. I don't want to get hurt.'

'Don't want to fall on your backside and make a fool of yourself, more like. Give it a try. It might even be fun.'

His father had spent much of the evening rubbing waterproof dubbin into the old leather of the skates until it stopped creaking and became supple again. Jack was feeling cautious after breakfast on Sunday morning as his dad led him down the lane to the frozen field. Mr Nicholls had opened a sluice in the dyke wall, and now there were more than four inches of solid ice covering the saturated land. Someone else from the village had beaten them to it. The visiting couple from the holiday cottage were twirling around, hand in hand. Mr Nicholls stood on the bank watching them.

'Asked me as soon as they saw me,' he said in greeting. 'I checked it was solid right down, and off they went. I think they've done this before, don't you?'

After spending some time falling on his bottom or doing belly flops, Jack began to get the hang of it. It seemed as if he still had some muscle memory to help him. He'd had roller skates as a kid. By lunchtime, he was speeding around with only the occasional mishap. His father explained how to go faster, using that bent-over arm-swinging stance that he'd seen in the photos of his grandfather.

More people arrived, some driving tentatively down the lane in cars. Word had obviously got around, presumably on social media. Stiff from the unusual use of his muscles, Jack flopped onto the bank where his dad stood talking to Mr Nicholls.

'Perhaps we could organise a few races,' suggested Freddie to the farmer. 'You could open the farm shop café for a few days. Make a bit extra.'

Mr Nicholls watched the skaters as he considered the idea. The farm shop stayed open in the winter, but the café didn't as there was rarely enough trade. 'I can hardly charge them for getting into the field. But I'll ask the wife about opening the café for a few days. How would we let people know?'

'I can do that,' offered Jack. 'Social media and a message to the local radio should do it.'

'Do you think the weather will hold?' asked Mr Nicholls. 'Or will people go down to the Broad instead?'

'Radio said the cold will last for at least ten days. Might even snow some more, although they seem to be getting the roads more manageable now.'

'Could people skate on the Broad, Dad?'

'No, and we shouldn't encourage them. You can only do that when the ice is thick enough on a big body of water like that. It hasn't frozen that hard since the 1980s. Did you enjoy yourself?'

They were walking back to the cottage, the skates dangling from Jack's hand. 'It's fantastic. I've never moved that fast before, even when I was running.'

'It's an amazing sensation, isn't it? Now, let's hope your mother has some hot chocolate in the house because I'm perished.'

Mr Nicholls rang Freddie after teatime. 'The wife thinks it a great idea to open up the café. Could your lad let people know?'

Freddie had agreed on Jack's behalf. Jack didn't mind. It was something to do. They sent announcements across social media, while Freddie found email addresses for the local radio station. 'That should do it. You going to enter?'

'I might have a go,' agreed Jack. After all, there wouldn't be that many people who knew more about it than he did. Battling down his natural competitive streak, Jack tried to convince himself that it was only a bit of fun. 'I'm going to need more training.'

Outside, the snow had begun to fall again, although the flakes were large and drifting gently. The wind had dropped too, leaving the cold air to re-freeze any dampness from the day. His parents were sat watching television as Jack pulled on his warmest coat, collected a torch and slipped out of the kitchen door. He stretched his aching legs. He needed to get some of this lactic acid out of his muscles if he was going to try again tomorrow. Just as far as the Broad and back.

The snow in the lane was packed hard where the tractor had skimmed the worst away. Frost and fresh flakes made it almost as slippy as the ice rink. Jack stepped cautiously along the centre, grateful to be outside. The torch beam lit up the floor and the hedges around him. It was slow going, but he made it to the end. Climbing over the stile, he began to follow the footpath that ran along the bank next to the water. The track was trodden down by the feet of daytime dog walkers and not difficult to follow. He wouldn't go far.

The sky was clearing, and stars glittered through the streaming clouds. The moon was young. It didn't give much light. Where the path met the Broad's edge, Jack stopped to carefully poke at the ice rim with his foot. He expected it to move or crackle, but it didn't. Shining his torch, he could see that the ice reached several metres out before it met the dark ribbon of water. He searched on the bank until he found a frozen clod of earth and reeds. Jack took it back to the rim and threw it as far out as he could. Expecting it to break the surface, he grinned when the heavy lump skidded across the ice until it fell off the edge with a splash into the distant water. Another night of these cold temperatures, and he might dare to bring his skates with him.

Having barely made the decision, a sharp whistle cut through the air. It sounded from the opposite side of the Broad, beyond the reed beds that fringed that bank. Jack wanted to believe it was those stupid visitors walking their dog again, but there was no footpath on that side and no access. He waited, his breathing shallow until the whistle came again.

'Hello?' Jack called, trying to train the torch onto the far bank. 'Are you all right?'

There was no reply. The beam from his torch didn't reach far enough for him to be sure the bank was empty.

'It's dangerous over there. You shouldn't be there. Do you need help?'

There was still no reply. Jack waited, his nose growing colder by the second. Maybe it was standing still that did it, but he began to shiver. He tried again, shouting as loudly as he could.

'Hello?'

A cold breeze ran past him, ruffling his skin and making it pop with frost. To hell with them, he wanted to get home. Looking forward to a warm drink, Jack walked back to the lane.

The next day was bright and clear, the sky a sharp blue. The roads were clearing, and rows of cars filled the lane. Mrs Nicholls opened the farm shop café, which, by early afternoon, had run out of soup and hot chocolate. The ice became so crowded with children flapping and falling that Jack gave up in disgust. After their tea, Jack waited for his parents to settle down in front of the television. Then dressing up warmly, he took his skates and went to the field. The moon still made little impact, but he had taken the head torch from his dad's toolbox. It would be enough to see by.

There were lights on in the café. Jack could see Mrs Nicholls hard at work, preparing for another busy day tomorrow. The temperature hadn't risen above freezing all day, and it was more than cold enough to keep the ice hard. He had barely sat on the bank to pull off his trainers when Mr Nicholls appeared along the lane. The farmer whistled to his two dogs, who obediently trotted behind him.

'What are you doing, young Jack? Not thinking of going out, are you?'

'I wanted to have a go while it was quiet.'

'Well, you can't. I've just been down to open the sluice.' Mr Nicholls pointed along the bank. Jack listened, and sure enough, he could hear running water. 'I wanted to top it up so it could freeze overnight again. Your dad explained how to do it. You'd best get off home.'

With a disappointed nod, Jack gathered up his skates and bid the farmer goodnight. Then wandered back down the lane. The trouble was that in a couple of days, Jack had become a convert. He was desperate to skate now, even if it was only for a few minutes. There was no need to sneak past the cottage. His mum had drawn the living room curtains before teatime. They didn't know he was out and wouldn't be looking for him.

In a matter of minutes, he was crouched in the frost-covered vegetation on the side of the Broad. He poked the ice with his foot. It seemed solid enough. Using one skate, he hammered on the surface a few times, barely making a dint. Inching carefully forward, he took a few steps out from the side, and it bore his weight without a creak. It was enough. Sitting on the bank, he laced on the old skates, turned on the head torch and launched out onto the ice shelf.

Surely, if he stayed close to the bank, he'd be fine as the water wasn't very deep anyway. Even if it did give way, he wouldn't fall more than a foot or two. That was ridiculous, and Jack knew it. Within inches of the edge, the water plunged deeply. It was the nature of the old peat cuttings that had created the Broads in the first place. Jack didn't care. He just needed a few minutes.

Now he was flying along, keeping a couple of feet out from the bank. Here and there, reeds or vegetation poked up through the crust, making him swerve and twist. His handling skills were definitely improving. The skin on his face was beginning to freeze, but his grin was growing warmer. Turning an elegant loop, he pushed back towards where he thought the lane end would be. His thighs began to burn as he increased the effort and bent into the rhythm and momentum. The virgin ice cut beneath the blades with a sinuous swish. He flashed past his trainers on the bank and headed in the other direction. In seconds Jack was beyond the limit of the path and onto the Broad proper. He flew on, the exhilaration was beyond anything he had ever felt in his life.

Even so, Jack had to acknowledge it was too dark to see this far out. He had left all trace of the village or walking path well behind him. Reluctantly slowing, he turned another elegant loop and headed back, sliding to a halt next to his trainers to recover. Leaning back in the dead grass, he star-gazed as he waited to get his breath back. The ground was cold under his back, the air crisp with new frost. 'It's wonderful. I'll go again in a minute,' he murmured.

Jack wasn't sure when he became aware of footsteps in the dead grass. If his dad or Mr Nicholls found him here, they would go ballistic. He sat up to pull off the skates, his fingers reaching for the laces when he heard the whistle. The beam from his head torch skittered across the ice as he looked up in surprise.

The sound was high and clear. It carried across from the far bank straight towards him. It was mournful, perhaps even full of longing. Jack paused at that thought. When had he become so romantic? He stood up, bending forward to keep his body level with the reeds where he couldn't be seen. The whistle came again.

The reply came from behind him. Jack fell forward in shock, scrabbling at the dead vegetation to stop himself from falling too hard. His legs began to weave their own pattern. Out of control, he clattered and scratched across the ice shelf. Whoever was whistling had virtually called over his shoulder. Unable to stop any other way, Jack dropped to his knees, then crashed down onto his chest, forcing the air from his lungs in a rush. The strap on the head torch unravelled, and it flew away to spin on the ice out of reach. The whistle came again, sailing over his head, sending a freezing blast up his back and raising the hairs on the nape of his neck. Scudding out on his knees, Jack retrieved the torch. The ice held his weight for now. Clutching it, he tried to turn back as another sound came.

It was a steady drumbeat from the far bank. It vibrated over the dark water, caught the near bank and returned as an echo. Another whistle answered. The reeds rustled with footsteps, heading towards the water behind him. The whistle mixed with the drum, the echo, the footsteps and, now, the swish of ice skates. The sounds became a noise, became a cacophony. Jack slapped his hands over his ears. Panic rose in his chest, and he suddenly yelled. An inarticulate noise. A shout of terror. A creak of the ice.

Something warm ran down his fingers. As he lowered one hand to look, in the gloom, he saw a flash of red. The drumming was closer now, the rhythm was getting faster, the sound of skates closing in on him. He could feel the presence of another person almost on top of him. Jack threw himself flat on the ice, waiting for the collision. It never came.

Instead, the ice began to crack. Jack felt it move under his belly. Felt it rise, one section higher than the other. Levering himself up, he looked around. He was much further away from land than he had ever intended to go. Some ancient instinct told him that he shouldn't stand this far out. Scrabbling on his hands and knees, he aimed for the bank. Thank God! Someone was there, waiting for him. Holding out their hand to help him up. Nearer safety now, Jack pushed up onto the blades, skating a few steps with his companion. The shadowy figure that pulled alongside Jack. Someone who was certainly younger than he was. A drum was hanging from a thick strap at his side, and he beat a tattoo on it. Even in this light, his long jacket was bright red. The new skater didn't look at Jack but stared intently at the figure on the bank and whistled.

The sound was deafening. It roared in Jack's ears, jarred his brain, caused him to falter and fall onto the ice. Lifting his head Jack watched the blades of the newcomer flash away in the darkness. The ice creaked. The ice cracked. The ice broke into a hundred pieces. Water rushed up, and Jack knew he had made a desperate mistake. There was a shout of anger from the boy with the drum. A crash and a splash and the creak of ice coming back together. A scream of terror rose from the figure on the bank. The world slipped away from Jack.

Jack was freezing when he woke up. The head torch clutched in his hand shone a single line of light across the ice towards the reeds. His cheek was stuck to the ice. There was barking on the bank. Men's voices were shouting. His dad was calling to him to stay still.

'Help's on its way,' yelled Mr Nicholls.

Jack's eyes came back into focus. How long had he been lying here? Not long enough to freeze to death, obviously. His knees ached, and he was generally damp. But not wet enough to have fallen through the ice into the Broad beneath. With a groan, he tried to kneel up.

'Jack, don't do that,' screamed his dad. 'I'm coming.'

Now there were more people on the bank. That ice skating couple from the holiday cottage were two of them. Twisting his neck, Jack could see his dad creeping out on the ice, tethered by a length of rope. The farmer and the visiting man were holding the other end. He tried again and, this time, managed to get to his knees. His head dropped to his chin after the effort and his gaze into the floor. The head torch clutched in his hand; its beam fell through his thighs to the ice.

Gazing up at him with an expression of longing, a pale young man's face bobbed. The eyes were wide, staring at Jack, the mouth open as if he was trying to speak. The boy was trapped. With the flash of a red coat, the body drifted out of sight under the ice.

Tears started into Jack's eyes. A howl formed on his lips. Then his dad was there, putting his arms around his son and the night terror began to fade.

There were mild frost burns on his hands and a cut on his face, which caused an argument between his parents. His mum wanted to take Jack to the hospital. Mr Nicholls had offered to fetch his big 4x4 to drive them there. His dad said there was no need.

'The boy just needs to warm up and get a bit of cream on that lot. I used to get that all the time.'

His mum snorted as Mr Nicholls held out his own hands, which were covered in dark patches. 'Like this. I get chilblains all the time in winter. You get over it.'

His dad won. Jack was cossetted, then packed off to bed. Unable to get a word in edgewise, he never mentioned the drummer boy in the red coat. A night of good sleep, and Jack was ready to get back on his skates, strictly in the farmer's field only.

The cold weather lasted over the whole of half term. On Sunday, they held some informal races, which Jack didn't do too badly in. Afterwards, as dusk was falling and everyone was heading home, Jack sat on the bank, changing his skates for trainers.

'Shame it's going to warm up again,' said Jack to Mr Nicholls, who stood beside him watching the last of the skaters leave. 'This has been fun.'

'I've enjoyed it too,' said the farmer. 'Been nice to see people at this time of year. The missis has done well in the café.'

He eyed Jack for a moment. 'Can I ask you something about the other night?'

'I'm so sorry, Mr Nicholls,' began Jack, but the farmer held up a hand to stop him.

'I know you didn't mean to upset anyone. No need to apologise.'

'Thank you.'

'I just wondered.' Mr Nicholls paused as a late car rumbled past them. 'When you were out there, did you see or hear anything unusual?'

Jack looked down at the grass on the bank where he sat. 'Why'd you ask that?'

'It's just that we would never have gone looking for you but for the drumming.'

'Drumming?'

'The dogs went mad, scratching at the door to get out. I thought it was an intruder or something.'

'It wasn't?'

'They shot off down the lane. When I followed them, I could have sworn I heard a drum. On the Broad. Did you see him?'

'Him?'

'You must know the story.'

'Yes, of course,' confessed Jack. 'But it's just a story to get the tourists in.'

'Young, they say. In a red coat. It's just that I've always wanted to see him, and I never have. Though I've lived here all my life. I followed the sound of that drum and found the dogs going crazy on the side of the Broad. That's how we found you. Good job we did. You were out way too far and unconscious as far as we could make out.'

'Under the water,' said Jack. He looked at the farmer, who nodded his encouragement. 'He was floating under the ice. No more than sixteen, if you ask me.'

'And his coat?'

'Bright red.'

'You're a lucky chap,' said Mr Nicholls. 'I reckon that drummer boy saved your life.'

They parted company, the farmer to help his wife count the takings at the café and Jack heading home. As he reached the garden gate, a sharp, high whistle echoed past Jack and vanished down the lane.

THE DRUMMER BOY OF POTTER HEIGHAM

In the winter of 1814, a few months before the battle of Waterloo, a young regimental drummer was visiting his home in Potter Heigham on leave. As is the way with young people in times of war, the drummer boy and a local girl fell madly in love. Their desperation to meet was driven by the refusal of the girl's father to have a son-in-law with such a lowly job and, no doubt, by the knowledge that the boy could die in battle. It was a bitterly cold winter, and the water of Hickling Broad froze solid, a rare occurrence at any time. The couple began to meet at night, the boy skating over the ice-bound Broad to meet with his lady love on the far side. He would beat on his drum to tell her that he was on his way. But in the centre of the Broad, a channel where the wherry working boats usually ran was melting. The drummer boy fell through the ice and drowned as his distraught lady whistled a warning signal. They say that only his ghost came to meet her on the far bank. Now people claim to hear the drum beating and the whistles between the lovers on February evenings, around Valentine's Day, as the pair still try to meet two hundred years later.

HOME ALONE, TOO

LEWIS HASTINGS

'I'M GOING OUT FOR A WALK.'

'Good idea, lad. You'll learn a lot more about this noble profession on foot. Give it a few weeks and trust me, you'll know all the best places to hide. From the rain, who to talk to, where to find information, and importantly, and never forget this, where not to go. There should be no such thing as a no-go area around here, but now and then, there are a few you wouldn't want to be alone in. Remember that and you'll be fine. It's time to cut the apron strings.'

Bob, who was an absolute doppelgänger for the actor Robin Williams, had what he considered to be a lantern jaw and was a few years older than me. But in our world, that equated to ten, and in the last few months, he'd taught me all he knew, and then some. Ten long years of knowing all those aforementioned places, and for Bob, the most important one was where you could find a good cup of tea when it was raining. If the householder happened to tell you something about the neighbourhood, that you didn't already know, then that was a bonus. Bob never drank tea at number twenty-three, the house with the pebble-dashed frontage on Wilford Grove.

'Last time I went there, the old girl brought me a brew in a jam jar.' He feigned being sick. 'I ask you, a bloody jam jar, it still had some jam in it, the pips stick in my teeth – have these people no breeding?'

In many ways Bob was already becoming a facsimile of the past. The job was changing rapidly, if you didn't want to change with it then move on or find yourself creatively moved.

I didn't know how to answer his comments, but made a mental note never to visit number twenty-three.

'And don't go to twenty-seven, he's a miserable old bastard who spends most of his time in drink. I've never managed to get a single word out of him. Forever letting himself get burgled. Now there's a challenge, get him to talk and stop him being a victim. And kid, watch out for Annie across the road. Five kids, three dads. All with one thing in common. None of them live with either of them. Three in care, two inside. All five better off.' He took another sip of his fifth tea of the shift.

'One stray glimpse down her cleavage and you'll be hers. She has what might be called a penchant for young men like you and many a good man has gone before you. They are like breasts of alabaster. A siren by a different name. You've been warned, kid, and before you ask, you'll just know.' He carried on drinking his tea whilst putting yet another pile of paperwork into some semblance of order.

'And the bloke at twenty-seven, watch out for his...'

It was too late, I stepped out of the Victorian red-brick building with its blue-brick trim and resident pigeons, turned right, walked past the central railway station and headed off into Old Meadows. There was a new one, but it was best described as an architect's wet dream; from the seventies, when far-sighted design meant building as many small blocks of flats, and what they lovingly called quarter houses, into a square acre – all the same colour. They had the same windows, same doors, same leaky gutters, rotten window sills and a permafrost of misery, and fog like a familiar shawl that drifted off the nearby River Trent and wrapped itself around the place, and not just in the winter.

But in the winter, it was much worse.

It was December, and therefore worse than normal. Cold, the sort that creeps up on you and stabs you in the back, twisting the knife just a little further. The penetrating unsympathetic wind that blows across a river whipping up yet more misery. They said, whoever they were, that heading out for a walk on a day like this was akin to madness. Bob's words were at the fore-front of my mind: *Give it a few weeks lad and you'll know all the best places…*

It was raining as I walked along Sheriff's Way. The sort of rain that makes its intentions known quickly, seeking out the slightest weakness. I was fine, and I needed Mother Nature to know this. I'd only been out on my own for a week. I was dressed head to toe in black and blue, dark navy at a push. Black hat, a decent waterproof black coat, trousers, boots. Well-pressed, the trousers were tailored, just-so, and the creases were sharp enough to cut through the sarcasm that soon came from the shadows, the abandoned doorways and the headless voices from afar, yelling cowardly obscenities. They say you became hardened to that too. I was fine. Despite what the cowards shouted with such conviction, I knew both of my parents. Those sarcastic voices only showed themselves when they had safety in numbers, goading you to follow them further down a passageway to God alone knew where and more importantly, what.

I'd soon be picking up a few knocks and scrapes. The toecaps of my boots would get scuffed. And by the next day they'd shine once more, a podiatry beacon on a street full of gloom. At night it was worse, the locals locking themselves away whilst the pack animals gathered on street corners whiling away the hours. I was approaching Wilford Grove, once a proud street, all hanging baskets and polished brass door handles, freshly painted steps and a relic of the past, a metal grate where the working men would clean their pit boots and allow the rain to wash away the filth. Every thirty or so paces were Victorian cast-iron street lamps, lighting the way home. But that was then, and now, only one bulb stood sentinel, defiantly standing the test of time and the well-aimed rocks of the misspent youth. It was outside number twenty-seven.

I caught a glimpse of myself in a shop doorway. Actually, to be more accurate it was once a shop – now just a grubby window with faded sign-writing and an empty room occupied by glimmers of the past, from a time, about twenty years ago, when the community was just that, a melting pot of black and white, miners from the local pit, good men with better women at home. White, black, they said it didn't matter when you ventured below ground as you were all the same beneath the coal dust. What mattered was how hard you worked and whether you'd carry the man next to you to safety. It was the same in my job. The big difference came in who you supported, every Saturday, on the pitch. Those glorious men in black-and-white stripes or that lot in red south of the river.

A young black boy waved to me, he was all of four. I waved back. He smiled an innocent smile. His mother ushered him in and closed the door before he had chance to be influenced. His was the generation I needed to work with, the current one almost too far gone to ever recover. I sometimes wished we could press reset on the world for his sake as well as mine.

The house next door had an unadorned Christmas tree that hadn't moved in years. The mantra being that it would soon be time to get it down from the loft, so why bother putting it away? Soon, the owner would drape a set of fading lights around it and hope they lit up, casting some cheer in the room behind the tatty and greying net curtains. Two older boys walked towards me, sucking air through their teeth, one spat on the ground.

'Alright boys, how's it going?' I asked, full of naïve hope that someone might actually talk to me.

'We don't have to answer you.' They stared at the pavement, slightly out of breath, one shuffling from trainer to trainer, they looked new, almost too new.

'No, you don't but it wouldn't hurt, would it? Where are you off to?'

'Anywhere. Nowhere.' He rubbed his hand, the palm of which was bright red.

'That looks painful. What did you do?'

'You're new round here, eh?' he said, skilfully, redirecting me.

'I am. Why do you ask?'

'Because you're asking lots of questions and smiling. Anyway, we can't be seen talking to you. Watch your back yeah?' They wandered off down an alleyway.

I thought I'd try again. 'Nice trainers. Where did you get them from?'

Someone whistled, loudly. They ran, I chased them. I had no idea why. Someone shouted 'Pigs'. Another whistled again. A distant shout of 'Babylon' met with cackles of laugher as the hyenas gathered.

The alleyway narrowed. Ahead I saw a group of three or four, all with hoods up and scarves across their faces. It was cold, I'd give them the benefit of the doubt. I passed tall wooden gates of post office red and signal green, dustbins, with their shiny aluminium lids, rare moments of colour in a monotone street. Brick courtyard walls with broken bottles set in concrete sent a message, often only felt by the errant, lost and desperate to escape. There he was. I called him Red Shoes, identity was always an issue when you were chasing and providing a commentary, so you picked something memorable. I was alone and chasing four people, on their patch.

I turned left and right and they were gone. The air was frigid, the vapour from my lungs, filling the alleyway with mist, I could hear my heart beating and my legs starting to pound. The kit I was carrying was never designed for sprinting, not like name brand training shoes were anyway. I had no idea why I had chased them. Instinct, I guess. It wouldn't be the last time I would run towards a fight. We were unofficially taught that you ran to a fire and walked to a fight. The truth was, you ran towards anything that needed controlling, protecting life and property. That's what we swore an oath to do.

As I recovered, allowing myself to breathe slowly, I smiled. Foot chases were a combination of fear and excitement. An old lady watched from a first-floor window, stood behind the lacy nets. I waved. She shook her head, waving back awkwardly, another one that didn't want to be seen. She was from a time gone by. I pitied her and I think the feeling was mutual. They were right, this was the best and worst job in the world and often all at the same time.

It was nearly Christmas and I was chasing young guys down a dark alleyway, without any thought of what I mind find. I was feeling invincible. I knew I'd make it home after every shift, if you worried too much, you'd never leave the station. Like one of the older officers back in the station, they called him the Olympic Torch – he never went out.

Moments later the first call announced itself. It echoed in the alleyway, a ginger cat hissed, arched its back and ran off, clearing the nearest gate without a pause and skilfully running along the glassy wall tops, without so much as a scratch.

'Uniform One, you receiving?'

'Go ahead.' I managed to control my breathing, Breathing, running and talking were often required and not always in that order.

'Can you visit number twenty-seven Wilford Grove, go and see a Mr Francis. He's come home from the shops to find his back door kicked in and his video recorder stolen. Second time this week apparently. Apparently only happened about five to ten minutes ago. Over.'

'Received. Number twenty-seven. Any descriptions?'

'Negative. And watch out for...'

It rang a bell. The miserable bastard. I was heading there straight away, no time like the present, especially at Christmas. I wrapped a ribbon around my own joke. It was the only beacon of hope in the entire bloody street. I stepped neatly around something left by an earlier canine visitor, then avoided a large puddle, I didn't want to ruin that shine. I walked south for a while until I reached Wilford Grove. A long road that joined new to the old, not unlike the stereotypical view of back-to-back Britain. The Grove ran in a perfectly straight line all the way to the river.

I arrived and realised that there was no way I'd get an answer to the front door. It resembled the entrance to a strongroom: solid black metal with three locks, in the centre, a letterbox which channelled mail into another steel box. He had his reasons. Three fireworks and a bag of something unpleasant to stamp on as the fire took hold was memorable enough for him to never get caught again.

On the door was a brass number two and the sun-bleached outline of a seven, where the second number used to reside. I nodded to the Indian shopkeeper who ran the nearby food store. He nodded back, eyebrows raised. His single movement spoke volumes. He knew something but valued his livelihood. His look said good luck.

I walked past two wheelie bins, into an alleyway and reached an impressive metal gate. It was almost medieval, handmade by the looks of it. I was about to try to open it when a neighbour, two doors down, who happened to be in his back garden, whistled.

'I'd wait if I were you, youth. Give it a minute and he'll let you in. He'll know you're there.'

'OK, thanks,' I said, slightly confused and grabbed the handle.

'Mother Christmas!' I yelled as I fought to let go of the bloody thing.

I looked up and down the alleyway, on a nearby roof two old pigeons were fighting over a postage stamp-sized piece of bread. Good, no one had seen me. My growing reputation in this tough area was paramount. Then I heard a click, followed by a buzz.

The neighbour called out again. 'Has it buzzed?'

'It has.'

'Then you're alright to go in.'

I entered the small back garden. I say garden, I mean a featureless flagstone courtyard whose only colour was a mane of tall grass growing out of a gutter. I saw what was left of the back door. I tapped more out of sympathy than anything else. 'Hello, Mr Francis?'

'Come in, the door's open,' a sad resigned voice with just a hint of silver humour lining the clouds.

I cautiously stepped over the shattered wooden frame and before I'd taken another step, I called my control room. 'Thanks, standard-sized wooden door, will need boarding up as soon as possible. Thanks Al.' Alistair was my control operator and the voice of calm. He'd forgotten more than I would ever know. He too had grown up policing the same streets. It was considered one of *the* places to learn. If you could police there, you could police anywhere. It sounded picturesque. It even had a Crocus Street. Floral, it wasn't.

'Everything you need to know is on that bit of paper.' He pointed to a worn sheet of blue-lined paper with torn holes along the margin. It sat on a cabinet that held a decanter and crystal glasses, only one of which was ever used. On the cabinet was a photo of a young woman holding hands with a boy, dressed as a soldier. Next to it was a more recent image. The same smiling face, this time in a uniform, holding a rifle.

The proud face of a young soldier between his equally proud parents, only weeks before his first tour of Northern Ireland where the boy would become the man. A foot away was a dusty Notts County Football Club mug, full of pens, and a comb, and an unchecked yellowed lottery ticket. Next to it was a growing pile of advice leaflets from the police. Each with a unique number written on the front. Crime prevention at its best.

I looked around the room. The ceiling had a plaster cornice around a light fitting which only had one working bulb. There were paintings on the wall. All the classics, *The Hay Wain* and something colourful by Turner. A tiled fireplace housed an electric two-bar fire with fake logs that glowed orange and kicked out little heat. The carpet was old but had been a considered purchase, some forty years ago. I looked at the corner where the television once sat, four clean marks were all that remained. Underneath was another gap where the video recorder had once lived.

I knelt down and looked for 'prints. It was dusty, which contrary to public opinion didn't help me. I went through the motions. Then stood up and looked at the man, the victim, the one we called without much compassion, a repeat. I was damned if I was going through the motions a moment longer. I put my pocket book away and pointed to the sofa. 'Can I?'

'Fill your boots, kid. Just give me one of your pamphlets and I'll add it to the others, my insurance company won't pay up anymore, so I keep them just in case.' He snorted a laugh. 'In case of what? Christ knows. Anyway, I guess you've got plenty to do?'

I thought about my answers. There were two possible responses. Yes, with some caveats, or no, with none. 'Actually, Mr Francis, I'm not that busy and until this radio bursts in to life I can sit and have a cup of tea with you – would you like that?' I looked at the former soldier. His date of birth didn't correspond with his looks. He was forty, forty-five at best. He'd walked the streets of Belfast in his teens. He looked sixty.

'It's Christmas in two days, kid.' He snorted again, a resigned tone that said he'd given up. There was a familiar smell, an unwashed man and a two-day old scent of alcohol. 'Christmas. What have I got to celebrate? I can't even watch Ma'am's speech. It's the highlight for me, that and *The Great Escape*. I watch it every year and every year they capture Steve McQueen. You think he'd learn, silly bugger.'

'Or at least build a ramp.' It seemed the right thing to say.

Suddenly the old soldier laughed. It lasted a while and I found myself joining in. 'I mean why wouldn't you, or find a different way around the wire?'

'Aye, or build a glider out of the motorbike?' he offered.

'But he'd never surrender, would he?'

'Never!' He stood up. 'A soldier never surrenders unless he's run out of options.' He was a little unsteady on his feet. 'Sorry mate, I'm a little bit pissed if I'm honest.'

'Well honesty doesn't seem to be a virtue around here.'

'Unfair. He pointed a steadfast finger at me. 'You're new around here. There's plenty of good people around, youth. You've just got to find them.' It was a phrase I had become used to. It was a term of endearment for someone younger than you. 'I mean constable, my apologies. I didn't mean to offend.'

'No offence, but your punishment is to put the kettle on. Come on, I'll help you find it.'

'Cheeky beggar. I know where the kettle is. Not so sure about the milk though.'

He was right. It was more like yogurt. 'I'll nip next door and get some. Do you need anything else?'

'Most kind. A back door if he's got one going spare. His name is Sunny.'

As I walked the short distance from his home, I couldn't help imagining what the place had once been like. Half way up the front wall of his three-storey home was a decorative plaque – it read Lucerne Villas. Very grand, although sadly these days not so.

I returned to his home, tapped on the gate, waited for the buzz. Then entered to hear the familiar whistle of the kettle. It was turning colder outside; we'd need to get that door boarded up before the darkness returned. It would provide warmth and reassurance.

'I'd offer you a biscuit but…'

I handed him the carrier bag: butter, eggs, milk, bread, strawberry jam and biscuits – ginger nuts. Everyone liked ginger nuts.

'What's this?' he said gesturing towards the plastic bag.

'Call it an early Christmas present. Now, what are we going to do about these people and their mission to strip your home of everything you cherish?'

'Firstly, thank you, no one has been so kind since…' he stared upwards trying to recall when a gesture of kindness and empathy had last visited Lucerne Villas. 'Not since my days in the army.'

'I saw, impressive figure of a man there.'

'Not so much now.'

'Well, you said it, Mr Francis. What changed?'

'You mentioned that there wasn't much honesty around here, so I'll correct you and I take my hat off to you for having the balls to ask such an impertinent question.' He winked his approval.

'That changed. It changed me and who I am, it made me leave behind the man I was.'

He pointed to a growing collection of empty scotch bottles sat neatly beneath a photo of three young soldiers, smiling at the camera with no idea when they'd next see home.

He sighed; his eyes reddened. 'That was a long time ago. I miss it terribly. Look at me, constable, I'm forty-odd with a stack of bills and an equally high stack of crime prevention notices. I've let my guard down, let the hyenas into my home. They're just kids half of 'em. There was a time, when I came home on leave, at Christmas, that I'd walk the streets, shoulders back, head high and I knew everyone – and trust me, they knew me.'

'Regiment?' I asked, genuinely interested.

'Intelligence Corps.'

'Nice.'

'Some say Dave Francis and Intelligence is an oxymoron.' He smiled comfortably for the first time since the hyenas had kicked his back door in. He sipped his tea, skilfully dunking a ginger nut, waiting just long enough so it didn't break in two and sink to the bottom of his mug. 'Any plans for Christmas?'

'Me? No, I doubt it. I volunteered to work, so the family men can spend the time with their kids.'

'That's good of you. You seem like a decent bloke. I'm glad you came. Some of your colleagues are not so empathetic. I get it, they've been there, seen this, got the frigging T-shirt, just another door kicked in by those little darlings from the next street, but they get to go home at night to a warm home, your colleagues, they live in a decent area. Like this one used to be.'

'Do you have any family, Mr Francis?' I asked, genuinely interested in this man, sat on his worn chair with his large hands wrapped around his favourite mug. 'Could Victim Support help?'

He ignored the question, perhaps seeing it as a sign of weakness.

'They've all moved on, flitted here and there. I've a sister a few miles away, though she may as well be in New Zealand. My parents are both gone. That's me mam there on the photo.'

'Good looking woman,' I offered.

'Steady, she'd eat you for breakfast. Pure class my mother. Not like Annie across the road. She's as slack as they come and twice as wise. She can empty a drunkard's wallet of his dole money before he's barely through the door, at which she has a constant stream of men. No pride at all.'

'Annie?'

'Annie Adams. I went to school with her brother. He joined up with me, lasted six weeks.'

'Marvellous. Takes all sorts, I guess. What was in the box?' I asked, pointing to a well-known sports brand with a tick.

'Training shoes for my nephew. I'd been saving my benefit money for months to be able to get them. He's a good kid, lives up on the Clifton Estate. My sister's lad. Haven't seen them for a long time. I know he's fourteen now, trying to get fit to trial for County. Would be the best thing for him, that or the army.'

'Do you regret leaving?'

'I had no choice kid, but yes, of course. It's a long story. Senior officer decided I'd done something wrong and before you know it, I was facing time at Colchester Barracks or a straight-forward dishonourable discharge. Or both. For something I never did.'

'What did they say you did?'

'A story for another time. If you ever come back. I won't be replacing the telly or the video, so I doubt it.'

I changed the subject. 'What colour were the trainers?'

'Odd question?'

'Not really. I'm guessing they were nicked along with the video?'

He leant down and opened the box. 'They were red. Bastards! How did you know?'

'Call it a coppers ABC. I was taught well. Accept nothing, believe no one, confirm everything. Leave that with me. You say the kids that target you live on the next street?'

'They do. But I can't prove it.'

'Names?'

I spent another hour with Mr Francis. Listening to his tales of military life, forming my own opinion of the real persona behind the grumpy old bastard from Lucerne Villas. He was younger than many people realised, far more experienced and I'd made him my mission – whether he liked it or not. I was going to turn his life around, steering him along a different path, call it patronising, call it naïve.

The team arrived to board up his door. 'You're going to have to use the front door for a while. I think it will be good for you, let them see you, shoulders back, head high like the old days. Anyway, when you are feeling a little steadier there's a couple of lightbulbs in that bag too, and a bar of chocolate – let's see if we can swap one bad habit for another.'

'I'm not with you.'

'The drinking. When did it start? I think I know.'

'Then you'd be almost right.' He made a quiet noise, somewhere between a laugh and a sigh. 'I guess I'm not strong-willed enough to stop.'

'You didn't answer my question.'

'Am I under caution?'

'No, but I can if it helps.'

'It happened around the time I left the army.'

'Has anyone ever tried to help you? You know, really tried to help, set you some achievable goals?'

'No, I guess not.'

'Then how about we try. If you truly want to cut back.'

'It's a deal. I want to stop altogether. I'll try not to disappoint you.'

'Try to think of it as your next chapter, Mr Francis. You know what they say about eating elephants, bite-sized pieces to start with. Polish that photo frame on your cabinet, let that proud mother of yours see how her son is turning his life around. Anyway, I've got somewhere to go. I'll try and pop in and see you tomorrow. If not the next day.'

'Christmas Day? You'll be having a slap-up breakfast if I know your lot, sat in the warm praying the radio doesn't burst into life, then home to your wife and family. I'll be fine. You look after yourself.'

He stood and watched as I walked across the street, settling that iconic policeman's helmet down onto my head, checking in the reflection of a nearby window. It was still new, so the leather trim inside hadn't quite worn to the shape of my head. I was proud of it, the shiny silver-and-blue badge with the distinctive ball-top that set it aside from other county police forces. Inside, my 'collar number' was written in indelible ink, a common thing to do, it helped find it in a hurry among the others when a shout for assistance came in. It also stopped the less than scrupulous coppers from other areas nicking it!

I looked back. He was still stood, looking up and down the street and trying to avoid the lustful gaze of her from across the road, with her breasts of alabaster. I waved and rounded the street corner, walked a hundred or so paces and turned left again just before St Faith's Church. Mundella Road. There was something I meant to ask him, but it had slipped my mind before I left.

On one side the same two- and three-storey properties, one had a Villa name, now long-faded. Opposite, there was a row of white stuccoed properties, whose roofs almost reached the first floor, giving the appearance of a lop-sided triangle. I walked along the road until I reached the fourth house. It had ground-floor windows that were whitewashed, cheaper than curtains, I guess. A little dog barked at me indignantly.

I opened the battered wooden gate which sat between two hedges, one smartly cut and clearly loved, the other unkempt – like the family that probably lived inside. It was best described as a dump. It had an overgrown garden with a long-abandoned lawnmower still in situ, barely visible, some borrowed wheelie bins, a bike, another with no wheels and a pushchair that was full of free newspapers that should have been delivered months before. But they had a satellite dish, and they recycled their countless empties, so their priorities were incontestable.

I knocked on the door with a familiar tone – a musical rat a tat tat, delivered with a black leather-gloved hand, loud enough to wake the dead and exactly as I'd been taught. I left the occupants under no doubt I was there and I was staying until they came to the door. A woman answered. Her brown hair needed cutting. It was what she clearly thought was an attractive length for a woman of her age, when in fact it made her look anything but. Dirty, where it had once shone, and a hint of a former curly perm, it draped across an equally grubby oversized T-shirt that she was wearing as night attire during the day. I stood and looked at her and realised that no matter what time of the day I knocked, Maggie O'Shaughnessy would look the same. Unless she was heading to the pub, in which case she would have done something with her hair and adopted a pair of black stretchy leggings. I shuddered at the thought. It was cold and that would be my excuse.

'You comin' in or what?' Five little words to make my skin crawl. It was the way she enunciated. She had what my dear English teacher would have called a certain economy with words. That was what met me, that and the sight of her stood in the doorway, leaning nonchalantly against the worn wooden frame, cigarette perched precariously on her bottom lip and two obviously protruding nipples vying for my attention. It was cold, that much was certain. I wished my radio would crackle into life, sending me anywhere soon.

I stepped in and felt the carpet clinging to my boots. I'd remind myself to wipe my feet on the way out. 'Sit down, duck.' She pointed towards a sofa that had at one time offered support, its shiny red velvet arms and a dog blanket reminding me why Bob never sat down in such a home.

'I'm fine. I'm here to see your Patrick.'

'What's the F has he done now? Honestly you lot are always

'round 'ere picking on him. "Es out any road. No idea when he'll be back.'

'That's fine, Mrs O'Shaughnessy. I'll come back.' I heard the floorboards upstairs. I knew he was in. The tell-tale sign at the door betrayed him beautifully. 'And I'll be taking these back to where they belong. And that video recorder that is sitting suspiciously on your kitchen worktop, that can make its way back to its owner – by tomorrow evening, or I will be back here to arrest Patrick and anyone else who gets in my way.'

'You're new 'round 'ere aren't ya?' Again, that speech rankled.

'I am.' I left it at that. I opened the door, thanking my lucky stars I was wearing gloves. The little dog came sniffing around my boots again so I discreetly shooed it away.

The matriarch followed me outside. 'Can I 'ave a word officer?' she whispered.

'Go on.'

'I'm not admitting to owt, but if I were to get that video back to the miserable bastard at number twenty-seven, would you leave my Paddy alone? It's Christmas, it's the least you can do, i'nt it? Don't be such a bloke like that Scrooge bloke was from that book... I don't want the Five-O 'round 'ere in their Scooby Doo's when we're trying to celebrate the Lord's holy day.' She almost said please. She also needed to take a walk up the street and confess her forty-year absence to the vicar of St Faith's.

I had no idea what she'd said, but figured it out as I reached the garden gate, with my fingers metaphorically in my ears trying to shut the gate but not pull it off the hinges.

'Tomorrow by the very latest. I'll be checking and if it's not back with its owner – an ex-soldier by the way, who your son should show some respect to, then I will be arresting him on the stroke of midnight Christmas Eve. And there'll be no turkey for Tiny Tim where he's going. Deal?'

The curtain twitched upstairs. I knew he'd heard. I stood

there just long enough for him to see the red training shoes in my hand.

'Who's Tiny Tim? Is 'e one of them drug dealers what my Paddy has been threatened by? I didn't see you lot coming to help him when that happened.' She pushed her breasts up with her tattooed forearms.

'My sergeant told me that if you play with feathers, you get your arse tickled, Mrs O.'

'He what? What about my son? Don't think you can come to my 'ouse and throw your weight around – I'll press charges. You just watch me! Isn't it enough that he got a bad 'and?' It was what all the mothers of people like Patrick O'Shaughnessy did, nice to your face, then pushing out their ample chests at the garden gate, but only when you left, they had to save face in such a tough community. If you learned to play the game you'd survive. And it was the survival of the fittest in the urban jungle.

'Tell me, what happened to young Patrick's hand, Mrs O'Shaughnessy?'

'It's dead nasty. Says he did it ironing.'

'Ironing?' I asked, trying not to appear shocked. This family clearly had never ironed, never seen one, never contemplated owning one, let alone burning a hand on one.

'Well, in future perhaps he'll be a bit more careful, ironing can be a shocking business.' Again, he was listening at the window. I quietly hoped his hand was really stinging.

I decided I was going to like my time here. I adjusted my helmet and winked to a nearby elderly neighbour, who'd heard it all as he swept the falling snow from his path, I could also hear the hideous tone of Mrs O screaming at her little Paddy, and telling him in short words normally reserved for the most respected of fish wives, how he'd already ruined Christmas and her chance of getting very, very drunk.

South, across the river, the clouds started to darken with a grey-green blanket, shutting out the winter sun. The weathergirl had predicted snow, and now all bets were off.

I finished my tour of duty and drove home. I couldn't help but rewind the day, examining everything that had happened. I stopped at a hole in the wall and checked my balance, the overtime had gone into the account. I had more than enough. I diverted to a nearby local second-hand shop, where almost all of the stock wasn't dubious. I saw what I wanted, asked the owner to run a UV light over the case, and seeing no obvious post code marked on it I made a purchase, that for the first time in years wasn't for my wife – the vacant half of my ill-conceived marriage.

'You can confirm this is straight? Not nicked?'

'Do you really think I'd sell a dodgy telly to a local copper, come on mate, play the game?'

'Fair enough. Good job I'm local then. I had to ask.'

'Between you and me, and as you're off-duty this one came from an auction warehouse across town, I think they were insurance jobs, sold as seen, I bought six of 'em, this is the last. The case is cracked but it works well and is as straight as the proverbial die. Is it for you?'

'No, it's for an old army mate.'

'Well in that case you can have it for ninety.'

'Thank you. I appreciate that.'

'Anything for the wife? I have some lovely jewellery.'

'Nope, in that department I'm done.'

It was the first year we wouldn't exchange presents at all, it was a sign of things to come.

The next day I was back on duty, walking along London Road, head down into a developing blizzard – the hazard of being new to the job meant you went pretty much everywhere on foot. I loved it; it was how you really learned to police. Above the wind my radio hissed its presence. 'Go ahead, Al.' I shouted, theatrically into the handset.

'Mr Francis from twenty-seven Wilford Grove has just rung. He said to tell you his video had turned up on the doorstep. He said he'd like to see you tomorrow if you can find the time.'

'Received, Alistair, thank you.' The weather no longer mattered. I'd made it, no longer new, but now a part of the fabric of the community. I'd spend many years there, learning the ways of the world, who to trust and who not. The shift passed without incident. A day later I was back on duty, Christmas Day, early shift, the slap-up breakfast was abandoned due to a domestic and a drunk driver from the night before who lost his argument with a lamppost, but at least I didn't have to walk there; we travelled at speed in a patrol car on an empty snow-covered road.

The hours ticked away and it seemed that the locals were not going to revolt after all. That would come in the days that followed in the hedonistic journey towards New Year's Eve, where up until the stroke of midnight the pretty girls that the city is famed for would grab a kiss and a few minutes later would be trying to kill you for arresting their boyfriends.

'Merry Christmas, team. See you in four days.' We shook hands and I turned right out of the rear car park and headed south. I had nowhere to go and yet didn't feel at all lonely. I'd seen lonely people and I wasn't one of them. The snow was developing now, larger flakes dancing hypnotically in my head-lights as I drove along Wilford Grove, quietly by-passing Annie's place and parking outside number twenty-seven. I stepped into the fresh snow, hearing it crunch under my boots, then knocked on the imposing steel door.

David Francis turned each lock and opened the door, kicking some of the drifting snow from his doorway. 'Hello, lad. I didn't think you'd actually come. I've bought a chicken and thrown some spuds in the oven; I make my own gravy too. You're welcome to stay but only if you like sprouts. If it helps, I tipped the last of the scotch away last night, even walked up to St

Faith's and said a quiet one for my dear old mum at midnight mass.'

'I'm pleased to hear it, Mr Francis. And yes, if the offer is still on the table, I'd love to join you. Just hold the door, I've got something for you.' I walked to the car and lifted the TV out of the rear seats – a flat panel set that had until recently belonged somewhere else. It was the thought that counted.

Annie Adams stood in her lounge watching closely, licking the top of a Strongbow can in what she thought was a provocative manner. Bob was right, I knew it was her and made a mental note to always be busy when a job came in at her place. I had enough issues with my own relationship as it was.

I wrote the post code and surname on the TV with a UV pen – pessimistically, it would make it easier to find if it was stolen again. 'There you go. I can wire it up whilst you make sure those sprouts don't overcook, how does that sound?'

He stood in the front room and stared. I swear I saw a tear building. He looked at his mum, staring back from the photo frame. He scratched his head, made a noise as if he was trying to speak, then cleared his throat.

'I don't know what to say, constable, I really don't, I'm speechless. No one has ever done anything like this for me, ever.' He went quiet and a solitary tear broke through the defences and rolled down his cheek, he tried his best to disguise it. 'Thank you. If ever I can return the favour, you only have to ask.'

'Well, I've got a wife who is causing me a few issues, I may take you up on that offer one day, how are those sprouts looking?'

'Still green as God made 'em. Fancy a double lemonade?'

'It's Christmas, Mr Francis, let's go mad shall we and have a Coke?'

'Lets. Oh, and by the way, I had a visit from my sister and her lad this morning. Christmas Day, that's a first. You should have seen his face when he opened the trainers. Loved 'em.' He took a sip of the tame drink and turned up his nose. 'And it dawned on me last night, I haven't got a bloody clue what your name is. I can't keep calling you constable. I'm Dave, Dave Francis.' He held out his large hand. It was warm and felt strong and sincere. Like the man himself.

'I know.' I smiled back; he was emerging from the chrysalis of loneliness.

I held the hand and spoke. 'My name's Jack. Jack Cade.'

'Well, it's an honour to meet you, Jack. Frankly I hope to never have to meet you professionally again.' He laughed and clashed his glass against mine.

'How about a deal, I'll drop in for a tea when it's raining and you can tell me what's really happening around here. I can give you a codename, be like the old days in Belfast.'

'Hardly, I could shoot people then, I can't now. But you can call me…' He paused. 'You can call me Ebenezer; he was a man who had a visit from a well-meaning spirit. Let's see if I can get around this place without being seen and without the need for spirits. Sound good?'

'Sounds perfect. A toast, if I may, to Ebenezer, to his future good health and to my wife, wherever she might be today, and to her imminent departure from the marital home. Cheers, Merry Christmas, Dave.'

'Merry Christmas, Jack.' He downed the Coke. 'That's bloody awful. I need something stronger. Would you join me in a very small one to toast the season?' He showed the size of the measure with his thumb and forefinger. 'I promise I'll cut back, every time you visit, I'll have cut back more. From here on in, I'll no longer be called the miserable old drunk from number twenty-seven, but the slightly less miserable recovering alcoholic. Now there's a present I could never have hoped for, honesty. Thank you for being my guardian angel, Jack. Means a great deal.' He turned and walked into the kitchen whistling a festive tune.

It was good to see him upbeat. Calling his sister was the best thing I could have done.

He came back with another drink and two Christmas crackers.

'An old army mate of mine dropped a box of these off a week ago. Not seen him for years. Kev Stathern and I were on an EOD course together back in the day and we've stayed in touch – he's a keen Nottingham Forest fan as you can see by the colour of these things.' He handed me one end of a bright red cracker. I was about to pull it when I thought I'd ask a question.

'Did you say EOD course – as in Explosives Ordnance?'

'I did. He was a Royal Engineer. And?'

'And you're going to open a cracker sent by a mate you haven't seen for ages, who just happens to show up out of the blue? Do you trust him? Seeing as though he's a Forest fan?'

Francis smiled broadly. 'Now wouldn't that be funny, if after all these years he actually wanted revenge for what I did to him on that course?' He looked me in the eye. 'So, what's it to be, could go your way, could go mine, one of us might lose a hand...'

We pulled at the bloody thing, both with our eyes slightly squinted. It exploded with a resounding crack which echoed in the sparsely furnished room as a Nottingham Forest keyring dropped into Francis's lap.

He laughed. 'Jack, I've not had this much fun since I blew the leg of Kev's chair one Wednesday evening. I guess we're even.'

'I won't ask.'

'No don't, what goes on tour and all that.'

'Promise me you'll stay in touch and we can beat your demons together? And I suggest you check that lottery ticket...'

'I will! And you have my word. But why bother with someone like me?'

'Well, David, someone has to and I reckon I might need your skills one day – you can't put a price on experience.'

'And I'd rather it was you than her across the road, despite what she thinks, that is one present I will not be opening this or any Christmas.'

'I've got to ask by the way. Your back gate, a neighbour of yours told me to wait a minute the other day then open it. What was that all about?' He knew I knew.

He looked sheepish, scratched his head then looked up. 'My mate rigged it up. The engineer. He said it might keep the little buggers away from my back garden. It was working quite well until yesterday. When I came home, I found it open. I think the timer had failed. I knew straight away that something was wrong. And then I saw it.'

'What?'

'Half a glove and some skin on the handle? I think my mate might have got the voltage a bit wrong, I mean how would I know, I'm no engineer?'

I stared at him for a second or two. 'Sorry, just rewind a moment, Dave. This glove, tell me about it, we might have been able to lift some DNA from that. You should have said.'

'Oh, there was DNA on it alright Jack. No doubt. His skin was melted to the glove.'

It was beginning to dawn on me now.

'Let me just ask this once Dave, was your back gate actually wired up to something?' I asked incredulously, yet fascinated, slightly favouring my right hand.

'Well, it was, but it's not now. I guess I'm in trouble as I threw the glove away?'

'Only if I receive a complaint and that's hardly likely to happen, is it?'

'Well, I guess not. I told him to add a little shock, you know a zap like a cattle fence, but it turns out he wired it up differently as he wanted to teach them a lesson. No one ever used the back gate. And if they did, they knew to wait a minute. My old neighbour up the road reckons he heard the bang from his place and could smell something burning.'

'I take it it wasn't his sprouts? Honestly Dave what are we going to do with you?' I tried not to laugh.

'To be fair I was probably only committing a crime when it was turned on, and that only happened when you grabbed the handle and completed a circuit. I'll go round and apologise tomorrow.'

'You'll do no such thing. Just make sure when your mate comes back, he rigs it up so you only receive a shock when you've actually climbed over the bloody thing. Deal?'

I stood on his doorstep, clutching an unopened bottle of single malt – he was happier to give it away than pour it down the sink. I shook his hand and waited for him to lock the door behind me, then stood alone in the street. It was dark now. Christmas Day. I was stood, alone in a place that wasn't my home, caring not where my wife had ended up and importantly who with. As I walked to the car, I noticed that the only street light that was working was outside David's house, glistening like a star. It seemed appropriate, given the day and how it had drawn me to it and the person who lived there.

I turned back to his door, knocked quietly, part of me hoping he wouldn't hear me, because I knew that what I was about to propose was potentially asking a great deal.

'Lad, you're back soon!'

I handed him the bottle. 'Dave, I think we both know this needs to be handled carefully, admitting you have a problem is one thing, dealing with it is another. The way I look at it, up until today you've had no one to help, no one to set you a goal, to carry you until you're ready to be lowered to the ground. I'm going to leave this with you, let's see how strong-willed you really are eh soldier?'

He reached out for the bottle, pushed it away slightly, then gripped hold of it. 'You trust me?'

'One hundred percent.'

'Then you have a deal. No one has trusted me since I left the army. How about by Easter, I'm dry?'

'Next year?'

'Yes, you cheeky bugger, next year.' He had a smile that spoke many words.

'Good. Now lock your door and I'll see you for that tea soon, and don't forget what I said about the gate.'

We would meet again. In fact, sooner than either of us would know, he would save my life and my reputation, two things I valued enormously. Our paths would cross once more, and they would keep crossing. I just knew it. So did he.

He was home now, but no longer alone.

ONE OUT, ALL OUT

ADRIAN HOBART

BUCKTHORN POULTRY FARM, HOLKHAM, NORFOLK,
DECEMBER 1979

'Snow!'

Excitement pulses through the hutch. The more excitable
birds surge towards the door like giddy hatchlings, each jostling
for the best view of the yard outside. I hold back, watching the
spectacle with a wary eye. There's nothing quite so unedifying as
the battle to climb the pecking order, in my opinion. Besides,
I've witnessed many a poult lose an eye in the melee over the
past few months. I prefer to keep mine open and in their rightful
place, thank you.

'You know what that means?' squawks one particularly poultish bird as he cranes his neck above the throng. 'Christmas is
almost here!'

The mere mention of the C-word causes such a commotion
the hutch sways from side to side. Feathers fly, beaks clash and
spurs lock. The noise is unbearable, until our leader, Godfrey,
shakes his wattle and clears his throat.

'That's enough!' he bellows, his voice a deep baritone,

commanding and strong. He extends his wings, waiting for silence to fall. His sharp eyes sweep across the gathered birds and they stiffen as one, their heads lowered. 'That's better,' Godfrey says. 'You should be ashamed of yourselves. All that fuss for a few flakes of snow. If there's one thing I will not tolerate, it is a breach in discipline. Need I remind you, we are Hutch One. What does that mean?' He waits for a response. None comes. He shakes his head wearily, his snood swinging. 'Memories like a flock of tits,' he mutters. 'I can't believe I'm having to repeat myself. We are Hutch One. The best of the best.' There's anger in Godfrey's voice. 'We are Norfolk Blacks. The original breed. Our blood line stretches back over a hundred years. That means something. That means we act with decorum and good manners. None of this rabble-rousing or hysteria. Do I make myself clear?'

A murmur of acknowledgement mixed with the occasional apology. A lone voice from the back cuts through. It's one of the younger birds, his voice an adolescent croak hovering between maturity and a poultish squeak. 'But sir! I've never seen snow before. Aren't we allowed to be a little excited?'

Godfrey's wattle tightens, and he fixes the youngster with a frosty stare. 'Not in this hutch you're not. If you want to be all flighty, then join the pheasants in top field. See how long you last with them. We stand for more. Traditional values, handed down generations. I know it's exciting that Christmas is around the corner. We've all heard the stories. Of the sparkling tree, the presents piled high below, and how the humans applaud us and give us the honoured title, "star of the show". I know it's hard to not let it go to our heads, or to puff our breasts out in pride, but we must show a stiff upper beak in all things. Settle down, eat your feed, keep your beaks to yourselves and behave.'

'Don't listen to a word 'ee says!' a voice calls from outside. All heads swivel towards the door as a large brown turkey, with a proud red throat and wattle that matches the colour of his bald head, strides up the gangway and pushes his way through the crowd. My companions give way and the stranger takes centre-stage.

'Who are you?' demands Godfrey, his feathers puffed up in anger so he's now almost twice his size.

'Who I am i'nt important. Why I'm here, is.'

He has an accent I can't place; all flat vowels and self-regard. The newcomer turns a circle, fixing each of us in turn with a jet-black eye. The effect is chilling, as if he can see into our souls.

Godfrey steps down from his roost and squares up to the stranger, and hisses in a low voice, his beak ready to strike. 'I said, who are you? What's your business here?'

'Very well,' the stranger replies impatiently. 'My name is Arthur. Arthur Scarbill, and I'm here to offer my assistance, comrades.'

'Assistance?' Godfrey asks. 'Why would we need your assistance?'

'Because, you've all been labouring under a massive misapprehension. A lie, in fact.'

'And what lie is that?' Godfrey bristles, indignation evident.

'The lie that has been perpetuated for generations by birds like you to keep your fellow turkeys in line – that Christmas is this wonderful occasion, that we should all look forward to it and accept the working and living conditions offered to you. Well, I'm here to tell you, that all changes today. No more lies. No more cramped accommodation. No more single breed enclosures. Together, comrades, be we Harvey Speckleds like me, Norfolk Blacks like you, or the Cambridge Bronze boffins in Hutch Two, we can take a stand. We can live life as *we* wish, by our *own* rules, and for as long as *we* choose.'

A ripple of gobbles ricochets through the hutch, some feet stamping in support. Other birds look baffled, others worried by Scarbill's belligerence. Hutch One is not used to argument or debate.

Godfrey steps forward, his right foot scratching menacingly as his presses his beak against Scarbill's. 'That's enough. You're not welcome here. We don't need your breed of sedition and propaganda in this hutch.'

Scarbill stands stock still, apparently unintimidated. 'I'm just here to share the truth. Let the other birds here decide if they want to hear it.'

'They don't,' Godfrey counters.

'Actually, I do.' It's the young bird who spoke up earlier.

'So do I,' says another, triggering a chorus of agreement.

Godfrey takes two steps back, another resigned shake of his wattle. 'Very well. You have the floor Mr Scarbill.'

'Comrades,' Scarbill begins. It's not a term we're used to hearing in Hutch One. 'I stand here as the elected representative for the National Union of Poultry Species, and it falls upon me to appraise you of the gravity of your situation. For too long, turkeys, geese, ducks and even chickens have laboured under a grand misapprehension perpetrated by the management and abetted by the likes of Godfrey here.'

Godfrey scowls but remains silent. Scarbill's delivery is mesmerising.

'They tell you that Christmas is your destiny. Your birth right. That it's some wonderful occasion where you, the humble bird becomes the "star of the show". Well, I'm here to tell you that the reality is, and I want you to listen to me very carefully, very different. When the farm hands come for you in two weeks' time, gather you up and usher you into the transports, they're not taking you off to some paradise. No, my brothers, they're taking you off to a facility, and I'm not going to dress this up, where you will be stunned, killed, plucked and prepared for the dinner table of those same humans who have fed and nurtured you all this time.'

The hutch falls into silence for a few moments, before a cacophony of anxious gobbles rises and birds scurry in all directions, like the headless chicken I once had the misfortune to witness a few weeks ago.

Scarbill watches, his beak twitching in satisfaction that his speech has had the desired effect. He clears his throat once again.

'I know it's a shock, but you deserve to know the reality. I'm sure that Mr Godfrey here will tell you I'm telling you a pack of lies, but I'm afraid it's the truth.'

A head rises above the tumult. 'Tell us, Mr Scarbill. What can we do?'

'I'm glad you asked me that question, Mr?'

'Turvill,' the bird replies.

'Well, Mr Turvill. You can unite. You can fight back. You need only say the word and my national committee will send support to you here in Norfolk. Solidarity is the only way to fight back.'

'But what support can you offer?' asks Turvill. 'The humans are so powerful!'

'Our union is part of a wider movement. You can count on the backing of related trades who will come out on strike in support of your cause. The National Federation of Dairy Animals for one. The sheep, goats and pigs are sure to follow, and comrades, I have assurances that Corvus, the association representing the crows, rooks and ravens, will provide flying pickets to aid you. You need only say the word.'

I watch as my brother birds debate the merits of Scarbill's proposals.

Godfrey though, has heard enough.

'Silence!' he demands. This time the hutch does not comply. 'I said silence!' Gradually the birds come to order. 'That's better. Now, I've listened to Mr Scarbill with great interest and given him the benefit of the doubt, but I can categorically say I have rarely heard such a load of nonsense in my life. Where's the evidence to support his claims? If what he says is right, how is it that generations of our ancestors didn't warn us?'

Scarbill swivels round to face Godfrey. 'Because, comrade Godfrey, none of your ancestors ever lived to tell you the truth. The ones that remained here to breed never knew what happened to their brothers and sisters. They just *assumed* they'd been lucky to be chosen to celebrate Christmas. But I can tell you, I've seen what happens with my own beady eyes. I was one of the lucky ones. A crate of us fell off a lorry just yards from the abattoir and were able to escape. We watched as our friends were "processed" for Christmas. What I saw I cannot unsee.'

'We have only your word for this.' Godfrey counters. 'I would suggest that this is just a naked attempt to stir up trouble. We are an ordered hutch. We don't tolerate unrest and radical views here. Mr Scarbill, we have given you the courtesy of a hearing, but now I would appreciate it if you took your leave.' Godfrey signals to two of the stronger birds to close in on Scarbill.

'I'm not going anywhere until the comrades here have a chance to express their views. I propose we put this to a ballot. A vote to decide if you unite with your fellow Poultry Species and refuse to participate in Christmas, or if you support the status quo and decide, despite the warnings I have given you, allow yourselves to follow tradition and support Christmas.'

Godfrey mutters for a moment, then nods his head slowly. 'Very well, we'll put it to a ballot. Although I strongly object to Mr Scarbill's appraisal of the situation, I won't stand in the way of democracy. All those who wish to overturn years of tradition gather in the left corner, and all those in favour of Christmas gather in the right corner.'

The noise rises once more as the debate rages between the hutch-mates. Some birds head for one corner, only to be persuaded to return to the other. It takes several minutes before the two groups are formed and a hush returns. I've always been a traditionalist myself, so take my place in the right corner.

Fifteen of us stand in the right corner, in support of Christmas. Fourteen in the left. One of us remains undecided. Turvill.

His wattle twitches with indecision as his friends on both sides urge him to join them.

'I can't decide. I'm sorry, I just can't,' Turvill whimpers. 'If I go left I go against so many years of tradition, but if I go right, I might be voting for my death. All our deaths! It's too much responsibility.'

I step forward. I've known Turvill since he was a poult. He's always lacked confidence. 'Trust your feelings, old friend. Close your eyes and follow your heart.'

He nods gratefully and does as I suggest. His beak twitches as if in silent prayer.

The hutch holds its collective breath.

Turvill steps to the—

Left! The ballot is tied.

Scarbill scowls at our group. 'I can't say I'm not disappointed. I would urge you all to consider your decision and the impact it could have. You need to believe me, what I've told you is no fairy tale. I urge one of you, just one of you to change your minds and cross the floor. Vote for a better future. Show solidarity with your fellow birds across the country. Together we can stop this brutality, once and for all.'

He lets his words land. All around me turkeys exchange glances with each other, looking for answers. Eventually, Clarence, one of the smallest members of our hutch, breaks ranks and steps over to left corner.

Scarbill turns to Godfrey in triumph. 'We have a majority in favour of industrial action.'

'I wouldn't be so sure about that, Mr Scarbill. You see, Hutch One standing orders, Section 3 Composite 2B state that in the case of a close vote, the senior turkey, in this case me, will have a casting vote. And I intend to exercise that right.'

. . .

Scarbill stands stock still, his head high in defiance, watching as Godfrey struts purposefully towards the right corner.

The turkeys of Hutch One have voted for Christmas! A cheer rises from our side of the divide.

It's Scarbill's turn to shake his head wearily. 'While I respect the result of this democratic process, don't say I didn't warn you. Remember, your union is always there for you. I bid you good day.' With that he hustles out into the snow, leaving Hutch One divided in two, until we hear a familiar noise – the rattle of the feed bucket outside – and then as one we charge down the gangway. There is one thing, after all, that unifies us – the love of a good pre-Christmas dinner.

SEARCHING FOR SANTA

LINDA HUBER

George pulled the duvet right up to his chin and held on tight while he kicked his legs to stop himself falling asleep. The night was a long time when you were waiting for Santa, and Mummy and Dad hadn't gone to bed yet so it probably wasn't even midnight. Still clutching the duvet, George rolled onto his side and stared at the ski sock he'd borrowed from Dad. It was hanging all sad and empty over the back of the chair. What would Santa put in there? And would he bring the train set George wanted, or would it be the little brother he'd asked for too? Or both? Mummy'd only laughed when he said he was asking for a brother; she said Santa knew better than that and a lovely new computer to play long games on while she and Dad were busy doing other things would be the best present ever for George. Dad said George wanted a set of ski gear for the holiday they were going on soon, but George wasn't sure about that either. So it was definitely a good idea to wait up for Santa to explain that a train set was what he really wanted. Or a brother. But nobody ever seemed to get brothers or sisters from Santa, so maybe Mummy was right about that. And he was going to fall asleep here if he wasn't careful – he should get up and wait by the window.

It was chilly out of bed when you only had pyjamas on. George pulled on his Superman slippers and his lovely warm red dressing gown. He looked a bit like Santa, wearing this, didn't he? He flopped down on his knees at the window, but nothing was happening on the street below, and there weren't any stars out either, to guide Santa on his sleigh. Which direction would he come from? George stared up at the sky – ooh, look, it was snowing! He watched as big white flakes floated down, then more, and more. He'd never seen snow in Wakeborough before. He could build a snowman tomorrow, if they had a carrot. And Santa liked snow, didn't he, so that was good…

George stood up and tiptoed to the door. He would just go out for a moment and see the snow properly. He might find Santa too. Maybe he was on the roof already. George crept downstairs, shh, quietly now, along the hallway, past the kitchen, past the snug.

Mummy and Dad were in the sitting room with the door shut. George stopped for a moment, listening to the raised voices, then he sighed. They were arguing all over again about Great-Aunt Amanda's necklace. Great-Aunt Amanda was Mummy's great-aunt really so she was George's great-great-aunt and she was very, very old until she died, and then she gave Mummy a dirty old gold necklace with big glassy stones in it, all different colours. Mummy said it was an heirloom. George didn't know what that meant, but Dad called it a monstrosity so an heirloom couldn't be anything special – and Mummy had said it was priceless, too, which didn't sound like much either. Good things had prices, didn't they? And really good things like trips to Disneyland had such big prices they couldn't afford to buy them. George sighed again. The necklace obviously wasn't important, so why were they always arguing about what to do with it? Grown-ups were funny.

He stepped into his wellies, then stood on tiptoe to push the latch on the door up so he'd be able to get back in again, and slid outside. Ooh, the snow was lovely, all swirly and cold but not as cold as he'd thought it would be. George caught a few flakes on his tongue, and giggled. He stared up at the sky, but Santa was still nowhere to be seen, and there was no sign of a sleigh parked on any of the roofs round about, either. George pulled his dressing gown cord tight. He'd just go to the corner and look down Merton Avenue.

The street was deserted. George arrived at the corner and peered round. Nothing, just a man with a dog going into a house on the other side. And no Santa. Maybe at the next corner?

George skipped along. This was fun. He would play that game where you went one way at the first corner, then the other way at the second corner, and then one way, and the other way... On and on he skipped, right and left, but there was still no Santa, and on again, and one way, and the other way, and on and on – and here was a nice big road. George ducked into a shop doorway so the car that was coming didn't see him. The shop was shut; they all were, so it must be very late. When the car had swished past, he peeked out again.

Ah, this was better. He could see more shops further along, and oh! One building had lots of red lights in the windows. He'd never seen that before. Red was Santa's colour, so maybe that was Santa's shop. Did Santa have a shop? He had a workshop... somewhere. There were people along near the red lights too, but this end of the street was quiet. George looked round. He'd run down and have a quick look, in case it *was* Santa's workshop, and then he'd go home. It was getting cold now, and the snow had gone off again.

The pavement here was pretty dirty, so he walked close to the buildings. It was the kind of street where the houses were right on the pavement with no front gardens, and now and then there was a dark little lane going up between houses. They looked a bit scary. George was just scooting quick-quick past one when a man rushed out and they banged into each other and George fell down. The man nearly did too. He dropped the bag he was holding and three wallets and a shiny candlestick and two phones fell out.

'Jeez... Watch where you're going, kid.'

The man pulled George to his feet and swept his things back into the bag. He was wearing a black mask half over his mouth and a black hat like Dad had for skiing right down to his eyes, so you couldn't see his face very well.

George dusted off his hands. He was all dirty now.

The man bent towards him. 'You're a bit small to be out on your own. Where's your mum?'

George looked up and down the street. No one else was near enough to see them.

'She's at home. I'm out looking for Santa.' He stared at the man's bag. 'Why have you got three wallets?'

'Ha!' The man laughed, then changed the bag to his other hand so that George couldn't see into it. 'I collect wallets.'

'Oh. I collect shells when we go to the beach. But we don't go very often.'

The man was looking at him with a very odd face, and George rubbed his eyes. 'I think I'll go home now.'

'Sounds like a plan. Where do you live?'

'Middleton Avenue. It's that way and then you go down and then... and then I don't know.' George stared behind him, and big, hot tears filled up his eyes and rolled down his cheeks. He was lost, wasn't he?

'Oh, for fu–, goodness sake. What's your name, son?'

George sniffed. 'George.'

'Right, George. I'm Kev. Come on. I don't know where Middleton Avenue is, but my phone's in the van. We'll look on the map and I'll take you home. Your dad'll be sending out a search party soon.'

Kev grabbed George's hand and pulled him further along the road to a dirty black van. He opened the passenger seat door for George, then got into the driving seat and took another phone out of the glove compartment.

'Why do you keep your phone there? Do you collect phones, too?' George leaned back while Kev jabbed at his phone. It was smelly in here, but it was nice to be in out of the cold.

'It's there so it doesn't ring while I'm on a job. Forgot to switch it off once and they nearly caught me.'

Mummy and Dad had their phones switched off at work too. George stared as Kev scowled at his phone. Kev was a bit scary. And Mummy always said not to speak to strangers. George's lip began to tremble.

Kev Hardy shoved his phone into his inside pocket and blinked across at the kid in the passenger seat. Poor little sod looked like he was going to burst into tears any minute. A kid in tow was the last thing he needed, but he couldn't leave George here, heading straight towards Wakeborough's red light district on a cold and cheerless Christmas Eve. Kid must have walked for miles; Middleton Avenue was right out on the edge of town. In one of the posh suburbs, in fact, the kind of area that had plenty of pickings and too many security devices.

A glimmer of an idea fizzed through Kev as he looked at George's tousled little head. Mummy and Daddy would be rich. And presumably keen to get their little Georgie back. Keen enough to part with a nice wodge of cash... A reward, yes, for returning their son home safely.

Kev cleared his throat and stabbed the key into the ignition. 'What number are you on Middleton Avenue, Georgie-boy?'

George swallowed loudly. 'Mummy says I'm not to talk to strangers.'

'Fu–, dearie me, I'm not a stranger, am I? You know my name, and I know yours. We're mates, Georgie.'

But George was staring down at small hands clasped together on his dressing-gowned lap and blinking fast. Kev breathed out loudly. Stupid kid didn't know how to help himself, and he didn't have time for this right now. Frustration rose, then his phone blared out. This would be Jay.

It was. 'Where the shit are you, man? Did you get the stuff?'

'I did, but… I've got a kid in the van.'

'Ooh, naughty. What's her name? And this isn't the time, Kev, man.'

Kev closed his eyes. With Lil waiting for him at home, he had no need of girls in the van, as Jay well knew. And hell, he needed to get back to Lil. The baby was teething and Lil wasn't getting enough sleep and he wasn't bringing in enough money and Benny – who'd be about the same age as Georgie here – needed bigger shoes every five minutes. And he had no job, no prospects, thanks to the pandemic, and no way to support them all unless… unless he 'borrowed' bits and pieces from other people. He hadn't planned to go into business with Jay, who was a pro at it, but that was what had happened. Kev wiped a hand over his face. Problem was, he wasn't taking from the rich to give to the poor, i.e. him and Lil. He was taking from the poor to give to the… destitute. Or they would be soon. They'd be out on the streets, unless they went to Lil's mum in Ireland. And how would they afford the journey?

Jay barked down the phone. 'Kev – you gone to sleep on me? What kid?'

'Small one. Male. Lost. Rich.'

'No way – you get him right over here and we'll work out how to make the most of him.'

'Got it.' Kev ended the call and gaped at Georgie, who was wiping a runny nose on the sleeve of a dressing gown the like of which Kev's kids would never wear. With Jay's help, George's dad would be persuaded to make a considerable donation, wouldn't he? Kev started the engine, his lips pressed together. Georgie wouldn't enjoy it, but needs must. It was this kid's comfort versus his own little Ben's.

'Are we going home now?'

'Yup.'

Kev pulled out and drove east, the only car on the road now. He slowed down to go through traffic lights, and George jerked upright in the passenger seat.

'It's that way! I know this bit – you should have gone down there!' His little voice squeaked, then fell away.

Kev glanced across the car. Big, silent tears were rolling down Georgie's face and shit, he couldn't do this. He screeched left into Dock Street then turned up Wellington Road, where the best chippie in Wakesborough was – yes, thank God, it was still open.

'It's okay, Georgie-boy. I thought we could do with a snack, that's all. You hungry?'

George stared. Kev leaned over to grab his bag from where he'd thrown it onto the back seat. He yanked out a wallet and opened it, then dropped it back into the bag and tried another.

'Jeez... does nobody carry cash nowadays?'

The third wallet did. Kev pulled out a couple of tenners and waved them in the air. 'Bingo. Okay, Georgie, you wait right there. We'll have some chips and then I'll take you home. Right?'

Two minutes later he was back in the car with an aromatic parcel.

George's eyes were round as saucers. 'I've never had chips from a chip shop.'

Poor little rich kid, huh? 'Help yourself, son. Good, aren't they?'

Kev's phone rang again while they were still eating. He

handed the chips over to George and took the call – Jay, of course.

'You lost too now, Kevvo? Listen, I've got big Jim here and he reckons he has an idea for your kid. Bring him to Jim's place and we'll take it from there.' He disconnected.

Kev sighed. Poor little Georgie. But Jay wouldn't appreciate it if he didn't take the kid to big Jim's. He couldn't afford not to, now.

He turned to George. 'Right, sunshine. Time to go. Chuck the paper on the floor.'

Kev put the car in gear and they moved off again. George was brighter now, he even smiled at Kev when they slowed down to avoid a stray mutt on the road.

'Is that dog lost too?'

'Nah. He'll soon be home again.'

'Just like me.' Another little smile.

They stopped for the red light at the crossing. George was staring down Vine Street, the way they'd go if they were heading for Middleton Avenue. But they weren't.

George sniffed. 'I still didn't find Santa. Do you think he's been? I asked for a train set and a brother.'

The lights changed, and with them Kev's mind. No, no-no, he couldn't do this. Poor little sod had enough to deal with. He yanked the wheel round and they swerved into Vine Street. He would go it alone.

George sat up straight while they drove through dark streets. This was better, he knew where they were now, and Kev was more cheerful, too.

'Never fear, Santa hasn't been yet, Georgie-boy. We'll have you home in two ticks, and maybe your dad's put a reward up, eh?'

George looked out again. Santa was nowhere to be seen, and something was telling him Mummy and Dad were going to be cross. But at least he'd had chips.

Everything looked just the same as it had when George left. There was nobody on the street, and the sitting room lights were still on. Kev parked across the road from George's house and just for a moment he looked really sad.

'Not a neighbour out searching, never mind police vans with sirens. They haven't missed you, sunshine.'

That was good, wasn't it? But Kev still looked sad. He took George's hand as they went across and up the path, and George leaned back to see the sky. Still no Santa. Kev reached out to ring the bell, but George was quicker. The door swung open, and they went into the hall.

The sitting room door was only half shut now. George went in, but Mummy and Dad weren't there. Kev was right behind him, and he made a funny round 'o' with his mouth.

'Very nice, Georgie.'

Kev walked over to the coffee table and stared down at Great-Aunt Amanda's necklace in its flat black box. He leaned over to see it better.

'*Very* nice.'

George looked around. Where were Mummy and Dad? He went back to the hallway and stared at the door of the snug. It was shut, but there were some strange moany voices in there. They must be watching TV.

Kev was behind him, and he reached out and grabbed George before he could run into the snug.

'Might be better to wait a bit, Georgie.'

Kev was talking in an almost whisper, and the moany noises were getting louder. George frowned.

'Is it a film?'

Kev snorted, and George stared. What was funny? Grown-ups were all weird.

'Good idea – I mean, yes. Sounds like an, um, action romance, and we don't want to spoil the ending for them, do we? Maybe you should just scoot back to bed, Georgie. But first – is this your dad's jacket?' Kev pointed to the coatstand behind the door.

George nodded. There was something odd going on – but he was home where it was safe, so it must be all right really.

Kev patted Dad's jacket, then reached into the inside pocket. 'Bet your dad has a nice wallet.'

He pulled it out. Dad had an old black wallet and it was pretty ordinary.

George shrugged. 'Mummy's got him a nicer one for Christmas.'

'Has she, now? Think he'll mind if I take this one for my collection?'

George shook his head. The noises in the snug were scary now. It didn't sound like a very nice film.

Kev put Dad's wallet into his own pocket, then took George's hand again. 'Don't worry, son. Grown-up films are often like that.'

They went back into the sitting room, and Kev lifted Great-Aunt Amanda's necklace.

'D'you think I could have this, to pay for the petrol to bring you home?'

George considered. 'I don't think it would pay for much petrol. Mummy says it's priceless.'

Kev went a bit red at that, but he stuffed the necklace and its box into his jacket anyway.

'Doesn't matter at all, George. We're mates.'

A sort of scream came from the snug, and George swallowed.

Kev patted his shoulder. 'That's the film about over, son. Now here's what we're going to do. You go back up to bed before they notice you're not there, and I'll whizz off home too. And we'll keep all of this a secret, huh? You don't ever tell anyone I was here, and I won't ever tell anyone you went out when you shouldn't have. Deal?'

Kev was good at organising things so you understood exactly what to do. George nodded hard. 'Deal.'

'Good. Now you get right off to sleep, okay? Because Santa only comes when you're sleeping, see? That's why you didn't find him.'

George thought about that. It made sense, really. No one ever saw the real Santa on Christmas Eve.

Kev was wiping the sitting room door handle now, that was nice of him. Chips did give you greasy fingers. George took his wellies off, and put the latch on the door back down.

Kev winked at him. 'Remember – it's a secret!'

George held the front door open, because Kev had both hands in his pockets now. He waved as Kev drove off, then closed the door and tiptoed upstairs. Mummy was laughing in the snug now, so maybe it had been a good film after all.

George hurried across the landing into his bedroom and slid back under the duvet. Off to sleep now, just as fast as he could, so that Santa could come. Santa would know he wanted a train set, wouldn't he? Or a brother...

A CHRISTMAS SUSAN: PART II: THE GHOST OF CHRISTMAS PRESENTS

ANTONY DUNFORD AND WENDY TURBIN

DECEMBER 24TH, 2021

Detective Inspector Susan Brown remembered the Christmas Eve of 2021 for the rest of her life. It was more memorable than all her other Christmas Eves, with the possible exception of 2016. At least this year Richard Adams hadn't died again, but apart from that, 2021 was right up there.

It began with a knock at the door.[1] Susan was in the middle of reviewing her notes from an old case, just on the off chance she'd missed something. The case in question was a murder, and the case had been closed with a successful prosecution based on a full confession under no possible duress. For some reason, it made her uneasy. Then came the knock.

It was her partner, Detective Inspector Ian Feltpen, carrying a Christmas wreath in one hand and his three-year-old daughter, Felicity, though DI Feltpen insisted on calling her "Fuzzy", in the other.

DI Feltpen put his daughter down.

'There you go, Fuzzy. Go run your sticky fingers over whatever Auntie Susan polished most recently. My money is on the television she hasn't switched on since the last century.'

Felicity ran off into the living room giggling like a kookaburra on helium.

'Merry Christmas, Fifty, this is for you,' DI Feltpen said, handing over the wreath. 'I've given up on you ever getting any of your own decorations, so this year I have decided to provide them myself.'

Susan stared at the wreath without taking it.

'What am I supposed to do with that?' she said.

DI Feltpen stared, then laughed.

'Why, make soup, of course!' he said. 'Or, at a pinch, you could hang it on your front door, make people think you've a soul. Tell you what, let me do it.'

There was the sound of a crash from the living room, and Susan hurried off to find out what Felicity was knocking over, leaving DI Feltpen to fiddle with the front door knocker.

In the twenty seconds since Felicity had entered the living room, she had successfully reversed the effect of the twenty years of cleaning and tidying Susan had bestowed upon it. Every square inch of TV, table, teak, and glass in the place had tiny handprints all over it despite Felicity's hands appearing clean and grease-free. All Susan's case notes, loose sheets in date order with coloured labels sub-categorising them by crime type, conviction status, and geographical location, had been carefully dropped into a wind tunnel before being returned to the room in no particular order. The sound that had caused the crash had been a tray Susan didn't remember owning, that had contained a teapot she didn't remember filling and two fragile bone china cups she didn't remember being in quite so many pieces. Biscuits had landed chocolate side down, each and every one.

'Oh,' Susan said.

'Fuzzy, Fuzzy, Fuzzy!' DI Feltpen said, bursting into the room and making his daughter giggle by pretending to be a bear. 'We'd best not keep Auntie Susan too long, she's clearly in the middle of tidying up after an epic get together last night to which you and I were not invited.' DI Feltpen feigned wounded pride as Felicity giggled so much Susan feared the child might wet herself. And the cream carpet.

DI Feltpen swooped down and tucked Felicity upside down under one arm. The child giggled even more.

'We'll be out of your hair now, Fifty. The wreath is on the door. Don't forget about tonight. Six o'clock sharp or Fleur will have my testicles in a floury bap.'

A silence descended on the flat so complete it took Susan a few moments to realise it had been caused by DI Feltpen and Felicity leaving.

The silence was broken by something dripping onto the carpet. Something that wasn't tea. Susan sniffed. Fish oil? What on earth?

After barely four hours of tidying and cleaning Susan remem-bered something. Something she had to not forget. What was it?

DI Feltpen had said it himself. Don't forget about tonight. Six o'clock sharp. Or Fleur will "have my testicles in a floury bap".

Susan rapidly shoved the words relating to DI Feltpen's testi-cles as far from her mind as possible, speeding them across the floor, through the front door, and down the lift shaft without waiting for the lift.

Which left the rest of it. Something about tonight. Six o'clock sharp. She checked her work diary. There was nothing there.

She thought.

There was another diary in her phone, she was sure she'd

seen it. Called "Home" or something. She'd never opened it before but sensed it might be worth a go.

Sure enough. Six o'clock on the evening of Christmas Eve was an entry marked "Dinner at Bill's Restaurant". The invitation had come from DI Feltpen. Susan could see other people had been invited. Fleur Feltpen, the DI's wife who worked in pathology at the hospital. DCI Squared,[2] their boss, who "wasn't so bad in a social setting", according to DI Feltpen. Detective Superintendent David Sergeant, who seemed to hang around wherever DCI Squared was. And a name Susan didn't recognise. Inspector Brian White. She had never heard of him.

She googled Inspector Brian White.

Oh, dear.

Anyway, it was silly, she couldn't go. She had no idea what to wear. And even if she did, she wouldn't have anything suitable.

Then she noticed the attachment embedded in the diary entry. She opened it.

"Fifty!" it read, "Fleur has bought some things suitable for you to wear. I left them by the door to your bedroom when Fuzzy was running interference. Six o'clock! Don't be late!"

This branch of Bill's restaurants was in the Buttermarket, a grand, Georgian building on North Street. All of the downstairs tables were empty, but from the noise, Susan deduced the upstairs ones were not.

Carefully, because of the shoes, and self-consciously, because of everything else Fleur had thought might be suitable, Susan climbed the stairs.

'Good evening, madam. Do you have a booking?' said a waitress who was in the act of passing.

'Fifty! You remembered! Over here!' said DI Feltpen in a voice that carried from the other side of the restaurant.

The waitress smiled and picked up a menu, leading Susan to the table in the far corner.

DI Feltpen and Fleur sat with DCI Squared and DS Sergeant at a table for six. They all rose to greet her, shaking hands, hedgehog hugging.

'Sit next to me, Susan,' Fleur said, patting the seat beside her.

'Can I get you anything to drink, madam?' the waitress asked.

'Just another glass, thank you,' DI Feltpen said. He had lifted his own glass as an example. It was a champagne flute. Susan noticed there was a bottle in an ice bucket on a stand next to DI Feltpen.

The waitress brought another glass, filled it with champagne, and topped up the others.

DI Feltpen stood up, holding his full glass.

'I know Brian's not here yet, but he texted to say he's going to be a little late. Something to do with a macro. Or possibly Velcro. Anyway, I'm an impatient sod and I can't wait any longer.' DI Feltpen cleared his throat. 'As some of you, Fleur and Dawn particularly, will know, for the last three years I have been writing a novel. It's taken a while, because once you remove time at work and time guarding things from Fuzzy's curiosity, there's only been about three minutes a week in which to write. But I have made use of them. I sent my novel off three months ago, and last week I signed a contract. Yes, my novel, *The Murder of Sam Weller*, featuring intrepid DI John Huffam, will be published in May by Macmillan under the pseudonym C. Y. Comb!'

DCI Squared and DS Sergeant were on their feet, shaking hands with DI Feltpen and giving decidedly unhedgehog hugs.

'Congratulations, Ian!' DCI Squared said.

'Way to go, Sharpie!' DS Sergeant said. 'Am I in it?'

Susan didn't know what to say. She'd never really read fiction since an incident involving *Watership Down* when she was a child. There were too many facts to learn as it was. She had no time for things that had been made up. She raised her glass and clinked it against DI Feltpen's, taking a sip of the champagne as the others did. It was fizzy. She rather liked it. She'd forgotten DI Feltpen's first name was Ian. How very informal.

'Any similarity between characters in my work and peoples either living or dead is purely coincidental,' DI Feltpen said with a completely straight face. 'So if, for example, the protagonists, DIs John Huffam and Marjorie Weep appear to bear any resemblance to myself and my colleague Susan here, that is completely unintentional.' DI Feltpen laughed out loud and drained his glass. Susan took another mouthful from her own.

'Is your contract just for the one book?' DCI Squared – Dawn – asked.

'It's for three! The marketing says *"The Murder of Sam Weller: Chichester Chronicles Book One. A Huffam and Weep Mystery."* It's all series these days. Huffam is like Roy Grace, but takes a large instead of a medium.'

'Have you written the others?'

'I have some ideas,' DI Feltpen said, tapping his nose.

'Why C. Y. Comb?'

'Ah, it's a Christmas joke,' DI Feltpen said, but would be drawn no further.

A waitress brought another bottle of champagne, as well as Inspector Brian White.

Susan hadn't seen anyone with a parting that straight, well, ever. Inspector White's entire appearance was geometric. His trousers had creases as true as steel rulers. His shirt collar ended in two perfect triangles. His glasses were round. His mouth, a line, like a one-dimensional letterbox.

'Where would you like me to sit?' Inspector White said to DI Feltpen – Ian.

Ian stared at Inspector White for a moment, looked at the

only empty chair at the table, then burst out laughing, much to Inspector White's discomfort.

'Please, Brian, here, next to me,' Ian said. Inspector White – Brian – gathered up his dignity and sat, facing Susan.

'I must apologise for my tardiness,' Brian said. 'My household accounts spreadsheet wouldn't balance, and I had to go back over the last twelve months. It turns out the window cleaner gave me fifteen pence too much change, but it was a worry for a while.'

'I am sure it was,' Ian said. 'But you can relax now. Would you like some champagne?'

'Oh, no. That would be far too extravagant. I shall have a small lager, thank you,' Brian said, studying the menu.

'You are here as my guest! Order whatever you like. Life is too short to worry about extravagance!' Ian had refilled his, and everybody else's, glasses and was punctuating each sentence with a swing of the bottle, almost, but never quite, slopping champagne onto the table.

'That's most generous, Ian, but even so, it is extravagant,' Brian said.

Susan noticed Fleur was looking at her. Everyone else was watching Brian who waved to the waitress.

'Rump steak, medium, no sauce, with boiled potatoes and without peas,' Brian said, ignoring the menu.

'Oh, goodness me, I haven't even looked yet,' said Dawn.

There was a general bustling and the intense silence of five people trying to concentrate on menus descended for all of one and a half seconds.

Susan looked all over the menu, skipping her usual steak order.

'The pheasant looks good,' Ian said.

Susan couldn't spot any pheasant.

'And the squirrel casserole,' agreed DS Sergeant – David.

'Will you two stop it,' said Dawn. 'What are you having, Fleur?'

Susan took another mouthful of champagne. It really was rather nice.

DECEMBER 25TH, 2021

Susan awoke. Something was wrong. No, everything was wrong. She couldn't smell her lavender bedlinen. She wasn't wearing her pyjamas. Someone was repeatedly hitting her over the head with a lump hammer.

She sat up. This turned out to be the single stupidest thing she'd ever done in her entire life. It caused her head to explode.

After a few minutes she realised her head was actually still there. She also realised the reason she couldn't smell her sheets was because she was lying on her sofa. The reason she wasn't wearing her pyjamas was because she was still dressed. The reason someone was repeatedly hitting her over the head with a lump hammer was not yet clear.

Her coat was on the floor next to the sofa. She had a flash of memory, of someone placing her coat over her like a blanket. Oh, no. The flash of memory was followed by a flash of insight. The lump hammer. She'd read about this. It wasn't a hammer, it was the effects of dehydration and alcohol poisoning. It was her first ever hangover.

It was Christmas Day and it had all started wrong. She had to fix it.

She struggled off the sofa with the grace of a faun on a frozen pond. She hung up her coat, drank some water, stripped off, showered, put her pyjamas on, threw her clothes in the laundry basket, and got into bed. Everything was now right.

She checked her clock.

Everything was now right, but three hours later than it should be.

She climbed out of bed and went into the living room. She took her little bundle of cards from where she kept them in a drawer. She put them up, one by one. The last one her mother had ever sent her. "To Susan. From Mum." And then the one from DI Feltpen – then DS Feltpen – five years ago. And the four from DS, then DI Feltpen, and Fleur, each year since. "Merry Christmas, Fifty, Seasons Greetings, Bestest Wishes, Hope Santa brings everything you dream of, love Ian and Fleur. XXXXX"

She lined them all up in a row on the coffee table, smiling at them, trying to ignore the pounding behind her eyes.

There was a knocking on her front door. Not, unusually, DI Feltpen's enthusiastic staccato. More gentle, more formal.

It was DCI Squared. Dawn.

'Susan, I – can I come in?'

Susan nodded, which turned out to be the second biggest mistake she'd ever made after the earlier sitting up episode. Dawn walked past her into the living room. Susan followed.

'Oh, Susan,' Dawn said. Susan realised Dawn was trying not to cry. 'It's Ian and Fleur. Their taxi. It was hit by a lorry. They were both killed instantly.'

With those words, Susan realised that every good thing in her life was gone.

A week later Susan was at work, but she could have been anywhere, as everywhere was the same now. Her feet had concrete blocks around them, and the world was filled with water. Every time she thought there were no more tears, she learned that she was wrong.

A young constable told her that DCI Squared wanted to see her in her office.

'DCI Icarus to you,' Susan admonished, feeling surprisingly averse to the use of Dawn's nickname by the junior officer.

She made her way to the office, swimming through the corridors and up the stairs, her chest crushed, unable to breathe.

'This is Alfie Clarke,' Dawn said as Susan walked into the room. 'He's a solicitor acting on behalf of Ian and Fleur.'

Susan shook his hand. It was cold and clammy, like a fish.

'I was instructed by my client to read you this letter in the event that anything happened to him and his wife,' Alfie Clarke said, taking two sheets of paper from a leather attaché case. They were covered in Ian's handwriting, which looked like a spider having convulsions had fallen into an inkwell. Alfie Clarke started to read.

My Dearest Fifty

Whilst researching The Murder of Sam Weller *I chanced to consult a fortune teller. I was considering whether or not John Huffam should journey outside the corporeal for his crime-solving methods, as others have. I was shocked when the woman cheerfully predicted my imminent death.*

Whilst I suspect she was trying to be dramatic, and my death is no more imminent than a win on the Premium Bonds, the event put the thought of it in my mind, and Fleur and I discussed all scenarios. Better to be prepared. Her maxim, not mine. Mine is less about preparedness and more about ice cream, as I am sure you can imagine.

This letter, which obviously I hope you will never know about, covers the circumstance of Fleur and I dying before Felicity is eighteen. We leave our estates to our daughter, naturally. But until she is eighteen, we trust her to your care. I challenge you to call her Fuzzy, and to keep doing so for as long as she lets you.

The only exception to this are the Huffam and Weep novels. All royalties for The Murder of Sam Weller *are yours to contribute to Felicity's upbringing, and to keep you in trouser suits. I hereby charge you, Susan Brown, with the continuation of the Huffam and Weep series. Get writing. Find your inner you and become C. Y. Comb. Don't become a Brian White.*

Your friend

Sharpie

P.S. I chose the pen name C. Y. Comb – Christmas Yetto Comb. A nod to the day you don't need to open your mother's last Christmas card anymore.

Susan arrived at Fleur and Ian's house with her suitcases. Fleur's elderly parents were there to let her in. They had been looking after Felicity since the accident.

'Auntie Susan,' Felicity said. She was standing at the top of the stairs, her face a mixture of wariness and playfulness.

Susan had thought about this a lot.

'Hello, Fuzzy,' she said. 'Do you want to come and help me tidy up the living room?'

Felicity's face crinkled in confusion.

'But it's not messy,' she said.

'My goodness, so it isn't. Do you want to help me mess it up first, THEN we can tidy it up?'

Felicity grinned like a kitten spying a Christmas tree.

Later that day, after Felicity had finally gone to sleep in the middle of the fifth story Susan had read her, Susan sat in front of Sharpie's computer. She read the plot ideas for the second Huffam and Weep story.

She stared at the keyboard. She had no idea how to do this.

[1]*Of course it didn't. The 24th December 2021 started several hours before the knock on the door, but as Susan was asleep for most of the time between then and when something interesting happened there seemed little point in mentioning it.*

[2]*Detective Chief Inspector Dawn Icarus had previously been known as "DI Squared" when she was a Detective Inspector. On promotion to DI, it looked as though her nickname would have to be rethought, until someone saw her HR file and learned her middle name was "Charlotte".*

CHRISTMAS EVE CALL OUT

LIN LE VERSHA

At least his phone hadn't gone off while they were in the concert hall, piercing the Bach Christmas Oratorio with its discordant ring. No, it waited until they were sliding through the muddy field to their car.

'Yes?' Hale answered, his hand on Steph's arm, signalling that she should plant her feet firmly on the slippery slope. An elderly couple grunted and tutted as they were forced to change direction to get round them up the mud hill. Hale pulled her to the side, out of the way of the departing audience, eager to be home, in the warm before the snow set in.

'Really? Yes, that's right, only a few miles away. I'll see you there.'

Switching off his phone, he threaded his arm through hers so she could lean on it as they struggled up the slope, now treacherous with the sleet that had turned to snow in the few minutes they'd been stationary.

'Don't tell me, we need to phone *The Red Fox* to cancel?'

'Afraid so.' He squeezed her arm. 'There will be other Christmas Eves.'

They continued to squelch their way along the row of cars

until they found theirs. Steph's actually. She felt disappointed that once again, their plans had been hijacked. The booking had been made months ago, and they were looking forward to the late afternoon Christmas concert at Snape, followed by the tasting menu at the best restaurant in Oakwood. It was their first Christmas together and for once they wanted time to themselves, without the police force demanding the attention of Chief Inspector Hale.

As a police officer for almost thirty years, Steph understood the tensions only too well. After a moment's mixture of acceptance, resentment, regret and sadness all muddled up, she sighed and sat beside him as the car slithered on the mud behind the slow-moving queue of cars desperate to get out of Snape Concert Hall.

'What is it?'

'A death up the road, in Woodly Grove, just outside Oakwood. Domestic, by all accounts. *Cherry Orchard*, Marlborough Road, do you know it?'

A picture of the collection of posh Edwardian houses in the village on the other side of the common pushed its way into Steph's head. 'Yes, head for the common, the other side of the pond on the Norwich side of Oakwood. Know where I mean?'

'Got it.'

They drove in silence through the white attack of snowflakes smashing into the windscreen and making it difficult to see the kerb. It felt as if they were the only car out in the silent world that slowly transformed into a clichéd Christmas card. As they drove across the common, the trees above trapped the snow as it fluttered past their branches, making white tree ghosts emerge from the blackness.

At last they reached *Cherry Orchard* and pulled up behind a police car, an ambulance and a white van – the CSI team. This looked grim and on Christmas Eve, too.

'Should I wait here?' Steph realised that whatever was going on was serious and, as a civilian, she would probably not be welcome and get in the way. Hale had recruited her as a Civilian Detective to help with a couple of his cases, but this wasn't to do with the sixth form college, where she worked, so she sat back. A rush of freezing air made her jump as her door opened and Hale leaned in to help her step over the ice on the puddle beneath the door.

'Come on, if you're coming. It's freezing out here. They all know you and you might even be of some help!'

She trod on the ice carefully and welcomed the firmer footing of the gravel that led to the front door. The three-storey solid red house was a beacon of light, all windows lit up and throwing shadows across the whitening garden. Stamping the snow off her boots, she shed tiny ice worms that lost their shape as soon as they landed on the mat. Hale signed them in.

'Evening, Sir, Steph.'

Stepping further into the enormous red tiled porch, she stood up straight and smiled into the face of Marriot. Was it John? A constable she'd worked with about two years earlier before she left the police.

'John! How are you?'

Hale stood back to allow the reunion.

'Fine, thanks. Got married last summer—'

'To Melanie?'

'Great memory. We're expecting our first child.'

Hale stamped his feet to free the ice from his boots, and Steph sensed his irritation.

'Why don't we go in? And Marriot, go indoors and sign in from there. You'll catch your death if you stay out here much longer.'

Once again, Steph was impressed by the way in which Hale took calm control of any situation. People appeared to relax when he was around, not taking their mind off the job but getting it done more efficiently and without the stress of wondering if they were doing the right thing.

They followed Marriot and walked through the chilly hall; the walls crammed with stags' heads and African masks, undercut with an ankle-slicing draught from somewhere. This house might look grand, but it would be no joke living here in the winter with the east wind.

They walked to the sitting room, from where they could hear a low mumble. The massive room was stage-set bright. An enormous overhead chandelier, wall lights in the shape of stags' antlers and about eight table lamps threw out light onto the surreal scene. In front of the huge white stone hearth, the logs now glowing embers, a man in a white forensic suit was drawing up a sheet to cover a body. He stopped when he spotted Hale.

'Evening, Hale.' He drew back the sheet so Hale could view the body. From the doorway Steph could see it was a woman of about eighty dressed in what she would call 'county clothes': brown tweed skirt, sensible brown brogues, pale beige twinset with a yellow and brown silk scarf around her neck. At first, she couldn't see why the woman was on the floor. She looked as if she was asleep, her face framed by an iron-grey rigid helmet of permed curls remained perfect despite whatever had happened to her. On the far side, the pathologist pulled her cardigan aside and revealed a small entry wound of a bullet or a knife about the height of her heart. The blood had been soaked up by the red Persian rug.

Although it was Christmas Eve, it wasn't obvious this house had noticed. No tree, no lights, not a single greetings card on the mantlepiece. Only when searching the room for signs of celebration did Steph notice the small man sitting to the right of the hearth – the word dapper came to mind. The wings of the leather armchair hid half his head and his feet just touched the ground.

From the part of him she could see, Steph estimated his age

as about eighty. He sat to attention, his spine rigid against the back of the brown leather chair, which had a well-worn patina on the tips of the arms and the edge of the cushion. A tartan rug covered his legs and above that he was dressed formally, a brown tweed sports jacket, beige Viella shirt and a deep maroon tie. She assumed the body at his feet was his wife as, if they were to stand side-by-side for a photo, they would make the perfect couple. But how come she was dead?

Standing on the threshold, Steph didn't feel she had the right to enter the room. Hale was whispering to the pathologist, his back to the man in the chair so he wouldn't be able to hear their conversation. He nodded, giving the pathologist the signal to leave and he in turn gestured to the technicians standing by the large bay window, the red velvet curtains drawn behind them, reinforcing the image of a play.

All at once the stillness was ruptured by everyone moving, except the man in the chair; the still point of the room. As carefully as possible, the body was loaded onto a stretcher and carried out of the sitting room. Hale walked across the room with the group, down the hall to the front door, where the pathologist held out a plastic bag to him, which Steph could see contained a gun. He opened the front door for the stretcher bearers with the body to leave and an icy blast hit her. Hale was deep in discussion with the pathologist. She could hear them talking, but not the words.

'Are you planning to stand there much longer?' Surprised, she turned round as a loud voice came from the chair. 'It's jolly cold over here. Please come in at once and shut that door.' She was reminded of radio newsreaders from the mid-twentieth century, who had perfect intonation and wore evening suits to broadcast the news.

Unsure what she should do, she moved a step into the room then felt a hand on her back guiding her towards a leather button-back Chesterfield in front of the fire, now a pile of grey ash with a few splattering embers in the dog basket. She sat down and Hale took the matching chair on the other side of the fireplace.

'Now that's better, m'dear. Warm yourself by the fire.'

Responding to orders, the fire found a new piece of wood and a flame spluttered for a moment before retreating again.

'May I add some more wood?' Hale asked as he was halfway out of his seat and moving towards the pile of logs, neatly stacked to the left of the hearth.

'Certainly, old man. Good idea.'

Hale didn't flinch at the description but stacked more wood on the fire, and they all stared as the flames started to consume the dry wood with a crackling sound. Soon the sharp smell of burning wood hit her and made her feel Christmassy. Then she returned to reality as Hale spoke.

'You are Sir James Whitaker?'

'Present and correct, sir.' The man straightened his back further, held up his head and gave Hale a sharp salute. Was he sending him up? No, there was nothing in his face to suggest he was behaving out of character. This was him.

'And that lady was your wife?' He glanced at his notebook, now open on his knee. 'Betty?'

'Correct again, sir.'

There seemed to be a standoff between the two men as both waited for the other to speak. Hale went first.

'Would you like to tell us what happened here this evening, Sir James?'

'James will do, old chap. No need for formality. Not now anyway.'

'Sir James, will you tell us what happened here tonight?' Clearly Hale had decided formality was exactly what was needed.

'Do I need to phone my lawyer? They do it on the box all the time. And I don't want you to force a confession out of me or make something up, do I?' As if to emphasise his point, he fished out a monocle from a little pocket in his waistcoat, fitted it to his eye and peered at Hale as if he was a specimen. Steph could hardly believe what she was seeing. This man appeared to have come from a past age or a 1940s film.

One of Hale's strengths was his patience, but she knew the signs, as he ran his fingers through his dark hair, he was starting to lose it.

'You are, of course, free to call your lawyer whenever you like, but at the moment you've not been arrested or charged with anything. We're simply collecting information on the events here this evening that led you to phone 999 and inform us that your wife had been shot.'

'And as the only person present, I assume I am your principal witness or, inevitably, your prime suspect.'

Hale looked him straight in his monocle. 'Indeed, Sir James, your assumptions are correct.'

Sir James lowered his head and became transfixed by the space on the rug where his wife had been. Now the only trace of her was a large bloodstain and even that didn't really stand out on the red, filigree pattern on the rug. A flaming log at the top of the pile shifted and threatened to roll out of the hearth. Hale leaned forward, picked up the poker to prod it back. Sir James didn't stir and appeared to be hypnotised by the stain on the rug. Hale darted a puzzled glance at Steph and frowned, moved his eyes towards Sir James and nodded. She got his message.

'How old was your wife?'

Sir James jumped as if he'd been stung and turned to her, a confused look on his face.

'Sorry, m'dear, didn't quite catch that.'

'Your wife, how old was she?'

'Be eighty three on Boxing Day. We shared the same birthday, you know. I'll be eighty-four. Damn difficult having our birthdays so close to Christmas. Damn nuisance, it was. Never got the same amount of presents as other children, you know. Our parents would say, "This is for your Christmas and birthday." But my brother and sister's presents were always the same as mine.' He paused and returned to the stain. 'Hard luck that was, our birthdays... We had that in common.'

He appeared to drift off for a moment and shifted his attention to the flames. Steph gave him space. The ticking of a tall grandfather clock on the wall behind his chair and the settling of the logs as they burnt down magnified the silence.

'How long were you married?'

He turned back, jumping out of his thoughts.

'Would've been sixty-three years on the twenty-seventh.' His face came up at last and gave a half smile to Steph. 'You wouldn't understand those days, m'dear. In my time, if you were under twenty-one, your parents had to give their permission for you to marry. Mine refused. Didn't approve, you know. So I married Betty on the day after my twenty-first and her twentieth birthday. Cocked a snook, you might say.'

Once again, he switched off and turned away.

The look he gave her was full of memories and his eyes filled with tears. Sixty-three years was two generations, and they would have shared world changing events: computers, the internet, space flight – they'd have seen it all. How many Prime Ministers?

He'd returned to staring at the stain, which was now drying to a deep red and disappearing in the rug's geometry. She scanned the traditional sitting room, which reminded her of an Agatha Christie film, full of dark brown furniture, most of it antique and well-polished, gold framed landscapes with a few portraits and faded wallpaper. Faded, yes, exactly the word to describe this room that belonged firmly in the twentieth century. She could feel Hale's impatience with her, but she sensed Sir James was not a man to be rushed. She frowned at Hale, indicating he should leave her alone to get on with it. Sir James would give more if she let him do so in his own time.

An enormous sigh from his chair suggested he was ready to continue, or was he nodding off in the warmth of the fire? Apparently desperate for action, Hale poked the fire, forcing the flames to erupt and the side of her face closest to the hearth felt the blast of heat for a moment.

'If you don't mind me asking, why didn't your parents approve of Betty?'

'Wrong stable, m'dear.' He obviously thought that was sufficient explanation as he stopped and returned to the stain.

'Sorry, I'm not sure what you mean.' Looking across at her, he frowned. She felt like a stupid child under his incredulous gaze. 'Really, I don't. I think it must be different now.'

'You think so? Perhaps it's not so much on the surface but it's there all right.'

He sighed but continued. 'I came from a traditional army family, a line of generals or Oxford men who went into the universities or the church and we even had a couple of MPs. See what I mean, m'dear? The backbone of English society. Boring crowd really – no gambling, no divorces, no skeletons, I'm afraid.'

Nodding and smiling, she encouraged him to carry on. They'd get there, eventually.

'Betty came from what our American friends call the wrong side of the tracks – a waitress in *The Talbot*, you know the hotel just off the High Street?'

'Yes, I know it, the seventeenth-century coaching inn.'

'That's the fella! She was beautiful... a proper lady, whatever those catty women thought. Intelligent in an unassuming way. Left school at thirteen but always on top of the news and well read... well, you only have to go into my study to see her section of books to know that. They never understood her. Never tried.'

'Who?'

He sighed. 'The whole lot of them. My family, the army... even our fellow church-goers, would you believe it? Spouting all that stuff about having a plank in your eye and who will throw the first stone, pity they don't live it. Vile women and their men just as bad. Should be ashamed to go before the Lord on a Sunday. Despicable, the lot of them.'

He leaned forward, grabbing the poker from its hook behind a miniature knight in armour, and stabbed the burning logs to make his aggression physical. In the firelight, shadows highlighted the wrinkles on his face and his grey hair. It was a well-worn face with smile lines etched deep. Steph could imagine the excited young bride with this young and handsome man.

'What was your job when you got married?'

'Major in the army, m'dear, destined for the top. Didn't happen, of course.'

'Oh?'

He shook his head, his lips tight, then sighed. 'Sling a few more logs on that fire, there's good chap.'

Hale looked a little put-out at being ordered about by a man who could well be a murderer, but did as he was told, hiding a yawn when he thought Sir James couldn't see him.

'Want your bunk, old chap? Long day, I bet. Then you have me to contend with. Reckon you were furious when they called you. Christmas Eve too.'

Hale looked a little shame-faced. 'Of course not. It's been a long day but we need to hear everything you can tell us.'

'Before you order me to the guardhouse, eh?'

He reached to the wine table on his left, where a tray held a cut-glass decanter and several glasses.

'May I offer you both a drink? It is Christmas Eve after all, or it is the blessed morn yet?' He pulled out a gold watch on a chain from his waistcoat pocket, flicked open the cover and smiled. 'No, a few minutes to go 'til we welcome in our Lord. Join me?'

'Thank you. Just a small one.'

Hale must be convinced they would be here for the long haul

if he was ready to accept a drink. Steph took the glass that was held out to her and passed it to Hale. She wondered if she was included in this male bonding over whisky and saw she was. The deep amber liquid warmed her throat, and she felt it running down into her empty stomach. Relaxing, as the warmth spread inside her and staring into the flames, she was reminded of the coal fires of her childhood, where her face was roasted red while her back froze.

'Now, what were you asking, m'dear? Oh yes. Our marriage. It was good, or as good as most. No offspring. Tried, but wasn't to be. We rubbed along well enough. I, posted around the world for Queen and country and Betty happy enough to trot along beside me and make the best. Yes, that's what we did, made the best... always made the best.'

He stopped, gulped the last mouthful from his glass, and poured himself another. He didn't offer a re-fill to them, but anyway, they'd hardly started theirs. Hale raised his eyebrow at Steph and looked across at the decanter. She got his message but thought this man was more likely to give up all he knew slightly oiled. Life would be sober for him soon enough and it was Christmas, after all. She pretended she hadn't understood, suspecting Hale wouldn't confiscate the decanter quite yet.

'Always made the best. Should have been better.' Now he was becoming enervated and a little cross. 'What a snobbish nation we are. Class, m'dear, class did for us in the end. They got their own back. Oh, not in an obvious way, oh no, but with slights so subtle, you might think we were paranoid. Then there were the omissions. We weren't invited to that dinner or his wedding or to meet the top brass when they visited. Always just on the edge of the circle. Just outside the in-crowd, is that what you'd call 'em?'

Another splash from the decanter to the glass and Steph felt Hale become tense and edgy.

'That must have been hurtful.'

'Hurtful? Damned disgrace, I call it. Not worthy of Her Majesty's Army that behaviour. More like a school playground.'

Hale prodded an escaped log into the core of the fire. They both watched as he tried to re-arrange the wood so it would burn evenly, and she could hear the soft whisper of snow as it blew against the windowpanes. The tall clock struck the hour, its chimes tinny. Midnight.

Steph recalled midnight services she'd attended with back row drunks yelling out carols like football songs and staggering up to the altar. She and Hale had planned an early night after the concert. After this, he'd have to go to the station and with any luck be back in time for lunch, which she'd better time for supper, but then at least he'd be there and she would see him later.

'But then you retired here?'

'Inherited grandfather's house and we've been here... let me see... must be going on thirty years. Sweet little village you'd think, but had to protect my Betty more than ever.'

Hale frowned across at her and made a *what the hell is he going on about?* expression. 'Protect?' He prompted Sir James.

'Damn strange word to use, dear boy, eh? But that's what she's needed, protection. Yes, protection from the bitches and gossips hereabouts. The English village is not the gentle place it pretends. No, I decided when we got here, we'd live on our own terms, away from their poison.'

He poured another large glass and shoved the decanter to Steph, indicating she should take it to Hale. Not used to playing the waitress, she placed it on the table beside him, then sat down again. Hale helped himself, then held it out to her, his eyebrow raised. She shook her head and mouthed, 'Driving.' So that was decided then. She would be the chauffeur to the station and then home. The decanter remained on Hale's side of the fireplace, out of Sir James' reach.

'Sorry, you were saying, you kept yourselves away from the social life here?' said Steph.

'Yes. I made all the necessary arrangements while Betty looked after the house. She had a good life, no decisions, no stress, a domestic haven. Betty was happy to stay here, all the time at home, with me, just me.'

'Did she never go out?'

'Didn't need to, did she? I got her everything she needed.' His voice was louder and its tone defensive.

Steph could feel Hale squirming around in his armchair and when she turned to him, his eyes moved to the clock. It was well into Christmas Day.

Hale leaned forward. 'Will you tell us what happened here this evening?'

'Oh, the shooting, you mean? Of course, you'll need to know about that, won't you?' He waved his hand over the table where the decanter had been and, not finding it, looked perplexed, but failing to locate it, he shrugged his shoulders and continued.

'This evening was like any other, you know. Betty cooked supper, a rather fine partridge delivered by Gary, our butcher... decent chap, Gary. Vegetables from the garden – she grows all our own vegetables, you know, then for pudding... now what was pudding? Got it! Lemon posset... "Very tasty, m'dear," I told her. I'm sure I told her. Always did.' He paused as if trying to recall the conversation, or at least his side of it.

'Excellent cook, Betty. Years of practice. She washed up while I came in here, mended the fire, read the paper. Found an interesting article about brain tumours. Fascinating how one's perception changes when things happen in life, isn't it? Ironic, is that the right word? Don't talk about it much. Knew it would be a rough time ahead for the old girl.'

They all stared at the flames as a log settled, spat out sparks and crackled, cutting through the respectful silence as they absorbed this information.

Steph was saddened by the inevitable tragedy the woman had been facing and wondered if assisted dying would ever be legal. 'I'm sorry. It must have been a difficult time for her... and for you too, of course.'

Sir James looked across at Steph as if at last she had said something worth listening to. 'Absolutely right! She couldn't carry on without me.'

'Without you? But... I thought you said she had a brain tumour?'

'Oh no, m'dear, wrong end of the stick. I'm the one with the brain tumour. Not her. No, Betty's as fit as a flea!'

Glancing across at Hale, who looked as confused as she was, Steph couldn't take in what Sir James had just said.

'You see, she'd never survive without me... not with me gone. I do everything. Always have. Totally lost without me. Only got a few weeks.... so I had to act.' His piercing stare moved from Steph to Hale. 'You do see that, don't you?'

She could feel Hale's silent amazement as they both began to unravel the story. Despite the blazing fire, Steph felt chilled. 'Did she... I mean... did you both discuss this?'

'Good heavens, no, m'dear. She never knew what was best, so I had no choice, did I? You do see that?'

Horrified at this apparent execution, Steph stared at Sir James, unable to find any words. He leaned towards her as if to re-assure her and pat her knee, but couldn't quite reach, so patted the edge of the cushion instead.

'Wouldn't have felt a thing, m'dear.'

At last Steph spoke. 'So, what actually happened?'

'After supper, every evening for the last thirty-odd years, Betty would wash the dishes, then bring me a cup of coffee with one of those little chocolates, you know, with mint inside them. Can't think what they're called, but very tasty. Anyway, as usual, she stood in front of me, holding out the cup. She said, "Your coffee, dear". He paused. Was it for effect, or was he recalling the scene? Steph wasn't sure.

'I lowered my newspaper and shot her once, that was all. Just once.'

Intrigued, Steph couldn't help herself. 'Why did you choose that moment?'

'Quite simple, m'dear. I've never liked coffee.'

SANTAS SLAY PART I: THE DESERVING CLAUSE

A B MORGAN

CHRIS BLAND HAD BEEN THRILLED WHEN HE SHOOK his Christmas cracker to free a tiny golden Santa which dropped silently into his lap. He puffed out his chest and couldn't help the broad grin that filled his face as he gazed around the dinner table at the annual gathering of the Secret Santas.

'Take your time, Chris,' Mike Waldeck, president of the guild, had advised. 'In the knowledge that we will choose wisely and choose carefully, all you have to do is come up with a suitable gift for the chosen recipient, and you have one whole year in which to arrange secret delivery.'

Mike took to his feet, glass in hand and smiled benignly down at Chris. 'Everyone, envelopes please.' In silent accord, each member of the Secret Santa Guild passed their envelopes to Mike, including Chris. 'And remember our motto,' Mike added, raising the glass of mulled wine to the gathered members. '"Because they deserve it!"'

The words were repeated in unison.

The loudest voice was that of a very proud Christopher Bland. Next December, he would be the one sitting on the lorry in tinsel and snow-clad grotto, trundling around the streets of

Great Yule, dressed as Santa. He would be the one who would bring presents to the children on Super Santa Saturday, and he stroked his chin in anticipation of treating himself to a new beard.

After the envelopes had been opened and the nominations complied, Mike cleared his throat and banged a spoon on the table. 'Now it is my pleasurable duty to announce the recipient of next year's Secret Santa Guild surprise. As you all know, it will be Chris's job to devise the nature of the surprise, but without further ado I can tell you that the winner, by a substantial margin, is...' He looked down at Chris and nodded sagely. 'Enid Speight.'

Chris swallowed down the rising nausea, as Mike continued. 'Enid was once a teacher at the school here in Great Yule and, having retired from her last teaching post elsewhere, she has returned. Taking on the post office from Frank, she has also stepped into his shoes as church warden. We know she's not a fan of Super Santa Saturday, but the guild is fully inclusive, and we will not judge her any more harshly for her traditional views about the festive season. Chris... make it memorable.'

A nervous grin made its way onto Chris's face. 'Mem... mem... memorable... yes. I will indeed. Th... th... thanks, Mike.'

The enormity of the task ahead began to dawn on Chris and he excused himself from the table, needing space to think. In fact, thinking about his obligation to the guild was all he did throughout spring and into the summer months. When autumn approached, strange and alarming notions began to disturb his sleep – and his dreams were doom-laden visions of failure. He must come up with a surprise suitable for Enid Speight, it was his duty. He couldn't back out. He couldn't be seen to fall flat... but try as he might, he couldn't bring himself to make a decision and on top of this there were tough acts to follow. Not least that of his friend Tim Philpot, the local builder.

When the scout leader disappeared two years ago, the guild

had pulled out all the stops to secretly refurbish the scout hut, Tim's building company really showed their worth and had contributed several loads of concrete. Could Chris conjure up something of that magnitude? He doubted it somehow.

The year before, the surprise present had gone to Phoebe Freshwater although it was a shame that her llamas needed rehoming so soon after the new fencing had been installed.

Comparisons were not necessarily helpful in this case, but what on earth would be a suitable present for the likes of Enid Speight? Chris was stumped.

In all it took him nearly the whole twelve months to come up with an idea which would mean a last-minute delivery on Christmas Eve; the very final day of his tenure as Super Santa. Super Santa Saturday was going to be his one and only opportunity and the plan was to be audacious.

The idea had finally formed with a mere fortnight to go before the real Santa was due to put in an appearance. Christopher Bland stood in line in the post office wondering how he was going to deliver a new washing machine to Enid Speight's cottage without her catching the Secret Santas in the act.

It had reached the ears of fellow Secret Santa, Sally Crompton, that Enid Speight's ancient washing machine had broken down. The vicar had mentioned it to her in the library only the week before. Apparently, he was toying with the idea of buying one for Enid out of his own pocket rather than allow her to continue making free use of the machine in the vicarage, which she did while complaining bitterly to him about how useless it was. The gift of a new one would therefore be practical and useful, something Enid would find acceptable.

Chris stared through the thick Perspex at the woman serving at the post office counter and shuddered. There she was, Mrs Enid Speight. She wore black from head to toe; a sure sign that Mr Speight had finally escaped his wife's wrath by dying. *A blessed relief for the poor bloke. He probably wanted to die...* Chris thought, ruefully. *How old would she be now?,* he wondered. *Late sixties, maybe.* It was hard to guess because, even when he was a child, she had appeared to be middle-aged and frumpy, frowning, and formidable.

For the first time in decades, he was about to speak to his old schoolteacher, and it was not something done willingly.

He looked down at the carefully wrapped parcels in his arms and deeply regretted that he hadn't made time to send them the previous week when he was in Lancaster. Today was the last day to send them to his nieces for Christmas and, because the gifts had sat in his van for a week, it was too late to go elsewhere.

Behind him in the queue was Tim, his oldest friend, and in front of him was the fragrant Jane Cooper who approached the counter making a request for first class stamps. The reply from the fearsome Enid Speight was as sharp as her pointy nose. 'Book of four or twelve?'

'Actually, I need nearer twenty,' Jane replied meekly.

'And I suppose you'll be wanting the Christmas ones…'

Valiantly ignoring the impatient huff from Enid, Jane said, 'Yes, please. The Christmas stamps are always so cheerful.' Averting her gaze, she looked up at the poster on the wall advertising the forthcoming festivities in the town, fixing a polite smile in place. 'I'm so looking forward to this year's Super Santa Saturday, aren't you?

Chris swivelled his head to read the words on the poster which advertised the annual events, ones which would reach a crescendo with Super Santa Saturday. "Have yourselves a Great Christmas!", the poster declared; a sentiment so apt for a place like Great Yule, a market town that nestled between Little Yule, Upper Yule and Lower Yule. Quintessentially British, the market square of Great Yule was cobbled, with a cast iron water pump at its centre. Surrounding the square were winding lanes filled with higgledy-piggledy cottages which oozed historical charm. Chris was proud to have been born and raised in such a peaceful place.

Enid Speight tutted loudly, shattering his reverie. 'There is more than a sense of creeping paganism hereabouts,' she said, looking past Jane Cooper and directly at Chris. 'People have forgotten that Christmas is a religious festival. As church warden, I shall be reminding them. What with Saturday falling on Christmas Eve this year, the vicar will no doubt insist on the market closing early. I'll make sure to give him my full support.'

Chris held his breath, praying that Jane wouldn't rise to the bait set so blatantly. He watched in trepidation as she slid the stamps into her bag and paid by debit card.

Behind him in the queue, he felt Tim step closer. 'The vicar needs to grow a decent pair of baubles,' Tim whispered into the back of Chris's head, making him jump in panic in case Enid Speight overheard the comment.

Jane seemed to brush off the attempt to lure her into a debate about the rights and wrongs of Super Santa Saturday, and she carried on chatting nervously. 'Everyone loves the Christmas market. So colourful and joyful.' She glanced very briefly at Enid, who was sneering at her and shaking her head in disgust.

'Too much commercialism,' Enid said, curling a top lip.

'Well, it does bring much needed business into the town,' Jane replied. 'Anyway, must dash.' Flustered, she smiled weakly at the two men as she rushed out of the door, with pity for them showing in her eyes.

It would be his turn next, Chris realised, and his stomach lurched at the prospect. He turned round to look at Tim for reassurance and it was given in the form of a hefty steadying hand placed on his shoulder. Tim leaned in to whisper once more. 'Good luck with old Iron Breeches,' he muttered, giving Chris's shoulder a squeeze. 'No doubt Father Christmas will be giving her place a swerve again this year... Mind you, she deserves a visit from Old Nick, not Saint Nick. I bet the old hag doesn't even own a stocking...'

Chris gulped at what Tim was inferring and he gulped again as he stepped forward.

Being in the same room as Enid Speight was something to be avoided, and in general Chris had managed this very well since her return to live in Great Yule. However, today he would have to face her, look into the beady eyes in the sure knowledge that she would delight in belittling him just as she had all those years ago.

'Bland. Chr... Chr... Chr... Christopher,' she mimicked cruelly in her scratchy voice. As she did so, Chris was transported back to her classroom where the shame about his stammer had been made so public and became much worse because of it. There she was, the Wicked Witch of the West, Elmira Gulch incarnate. Heart pounding fearfully fast, he could hardly bring himself to acknowledge her, knowing that if he tried to speak, he would falter, and she would win. Again.

Inhaling through his nose, he composed himself before making a humming noise on the outbreath. Without the evil tongue of Mrs Speight to paralyse him, in the main he had lived stammer free as an adult. But being so near that dreadful woman now resulted in its instant return and with it the crippling embarrassment. Trying to control his breathing was the only way to manage the anxiety she instilled, and he willed himself not to stumble over his words.

'These two, airmail p... please Mrs Sp... Sp... Sp... eight.' He placed the parcels one at a time on the scales unable to look at her, anger and humiliation welling up inside him in equal measure. He curled his fingers making fists, feeling his fingernails digging deep into the flesh of his palms.

'I said you'd never amount to anything much,' Enid Speight commented as she printed off labels. 'I hear you're a locksmith these days. And I suppose you think you are Mr Important since the silly guild voted you on as a member. Well, let me tell you a thing or two about the so-called charity fundraising exploits of your precious guild: They were mean with their contribution to the church roof. Doling out money to a hospice may seem worthy, but these days I think it's called virtue signalling.' She groaned, forcefully. 'That will be £26.70. Cash or card?'

Chris checked the notes in his wallet and fumbled for change in his pocket, taking his time to count it out. If he rushed he would become more anxious, and if nerves got the better of him, he would stammer once more, and he didn't want her to have the satisfaction. 'Hmmm,' he muttered. 'I seem to be ten p... p... pence short.'

'Well, pay by card. Or is that too difficult for you? F... f... forgotten your p... p... p... PIN?'

The movement behind him was swift and he stepped to one side as Tim pushed a ten pence piece onto the counter. He then took hold of Chris's elbow and directed him to the door, aiming a comment over his shoulder at Enid Speight. 'That's no way to speak to anyone and this is the last business you'll get from us or the guild. You might want to signal a few virtues yourself instead of being so spiteful. Your attitude is appalling. Expect a formal complaint.'

'There's no need to be threatening,' Enid squawked. 'I'm a god-fearing church goer and I won't be spoken to in that way. And who are you going to complain to this time? Eh? Eh?'

Chris launched himself out onto the pavement to wait for Tim who fired the parting shot before leaving without completing his business. 'You may fool some people, but you are a hypocrite, Mrs Speight. A holier than thou, sanctimonious, hypocrite. Merry bloody Christmas.' The door was slammed with such force that the glass rattled in the windowpane next to it.

Back resting against the wall outside the quaint post office, Chris took long slow breaths and Tim waited with him. When he had composed himself, Chris shook his old friend by the hand. 'Thanks. I'm glad it was you in there with me. For a moment I thought I was going to vomit all over the floor like I did when I was ten.' Despairingly, he put his hands in the air. 'Why? At thirty-seven years old, why do I still put up with her shit?'

'Stop beating yourself up. You're tougher than you think. You and I didn't let her ruin our lives completely. We did something about it. Not like poor Joe Wilson.'

The two men had been at school together, and Tim had witnessed and experienced, first-hand, the ritual bullying Enid Speight meted out to whoever was in her sights. For five years it had been Chris she had targeted most frequently. The children in her class kept a terrified silence about her cruelty until it was revealed by Tim to Chris's mother and the bullying stopped because the whip marks on Chris's back could not be denied. Enid Speight was removed from her position at the school without explanation from the board of governors.

'She has to go permanently this time, old mate,' said Tim pushing hands into his jacket pockets. 'I know she's like Teflon; nothing sticks to that woman, but we can't keep pretending she's not an evil old witch, because she is.' He sighed as the two marched in step down the pavement towards Chris's van, the name C.J. Bland Locksmith emblazoned on the rear doors.

Stopping suddenly Tim pushed his face towards Chris. 'I mean… look at you. You run your own business, you have a family, friends… a decent life. And then she reappears, and you crumble because you know she is out to make your world a misery again. It's not right.'

He pointed up to a small billboard where another poster advertised the week-long Christmas market. 'Only two weeks to go,' he said with a broad smile. 'I hope you're ready.'

'As I'll ever be,' Chris replied with a nervous laugh. 'A washing machine isn't much in the great scheme of things, but I'm adding a handmade box of chocolates for good measure and something festive from Santa just to piss her off.'

Tim nodded along. 'Tell me again how this plan of yours is going to work.'

'Well, the good news is that she keeps a spare key hidden under a flowerpot outside…'

In the market square on that particular Christmas Eve, the sights and sounds were poetically Dickensian. Stall holders shouted their wares, carol singers raised the spirits, a fairground merry-go-round tootled a happy tune, children chattered with unbridled joy, and a roast chestnut waggon produced magical long-forgotten aromas.

On the far side of the square stood a flatbed lorry with Santa's Grotto on board and there, sitting on a straw bale, giving a jovial 'Ho-Ho-Ho' every now and then, was Christopher Bland. His beard was beginning to itch a little, but the padding of his Santa suit was keeping him nice and warm. He had no complaints despite having to endure the twentieth rendition of Bruce Springsteen's Christmas tune blaring out from inadequate speakers at either hand. *You'd better be good, for goodness' sake…*

From his elevated vantage point, in one brief moment of respite from patting children on the head, Chris counted a grand total of thirty-two people dressed as Father Christmas. Or should that be Santa? Or perhaps St Nicholas… Red and white had never been so predominant, he decided. Dressing up had always given him a confidence he didn't possess as the ordinary Chris but being the most important Santa of the day was the pinnacle of his Santa career to date. And he had never felt so delighted to perform this civic duty. What a step up from being an elf.

The afternoon darkness had arrived and with it the temperature plummeted, but where was Enid Speight? The spikey old woman would surely make it her business to pour scorn on proceedings by harassing stall holders to close and to pack up by five o'clock, just as she had threatened to do on behalf of the spineless vicar.

Just when he thought she wasn't going to show, she appeared bustling through the crowds of Christmas jumpers and woolly hats, and he sighed with relief. His plan was underway. 'Here she c... c... comes,' Chris muttered under his beard. 'Full of good cheer and p... p... peace and love and understanding...'

'Turn the music off,' she screeched, waving a gloved hand in the air. As always, Enid Speight wore black: a full-length black wool coat, one with a fur collar, topped off with a black hat with fur trim to match and on her chest was an amethyst brooch, her one concession to colour.

She forced leaflets into the hands of passers-by. 'Midnight mass is at nine-thirty,' she reminded them with a snap. 'But don't bring the children. They should be in bed.'

Nobody challenged why the service was held early. It was known that the Reverend Toby Potter couldn't stay awake past eleven o'clock at night on account of the medicinal brandy he took to calm his nerves. Just like Chris, his anxiety state worsened whenever he was in the company of Enid Speight.

The small post office in Great Yule was sited next to the vicarage and since Enid had made it her business to become church warden, the vicar had resorted to daytime drinking as a coping strategy. He exuded alcohol fumes wherever he went, which he blamed on 'the communion wine being uncommonly strong these days'. Unable to cope with confrontation, he had easily been persuaded by Enid to abandon the usual Nativity play in favour of a more sombre service on Christmas Eve. The fun was being sucked out of Christmas by Enid Speight.

Something would need to change. That change was now in the hands of Christopher Bland.

In a private dining room at the Fox Inn later that same

evening, Chris took to his feet and spoke without a moment's hesitation. 'Ladies and gentlemen of the Secret Santa Guild, I would like to thank you all for your assistance in delivering a brand-new washing machine, for plumbing it in, and for removing the old broken machine. You were magnificent. I watched in admiration. I'm sorry I left it right to the last day, but I think you'll agree that the gift was a suitable one and befitting Mrs Speight's principles – cleanliness being close to godliness, and all that.'

There was a titter and a few chuckles at this quip. 'Above all, the timing was perfect.'

From Santa's Grotto, Chris had seen the transit van draw up to the side of the post office. Driver Santa and his mate had entered the gate while Look-Out Santa had kept his eye on the recipient as she walked through the crowded market. It had taken them over forty minutes to complete the task. 'I had the devil's own job with the waste pipe,' George Miller said, shaking his head apologetically. 'Sorry if I made you sweat a bit, sunshine.'

The Lady Santa next to him, patted his hand. 'Not to worry George. We did it. And what's more I think she'll use it before the night is out.' She gave a delighted chuckle and hugged herself. 'I may have accidentally looked through her window on my way home from the market and I saw her fiddling with the settings and diving into the box of chocolates. Stuffing her face, she was.'

Chris looked at his fellow guild members and smiled. 'Thanks once again for your help, encouragement, and wise words. I couldn't have done it without you.' The applause was affectionate and, as he took his seat, they all reached for the Christmas crackers in front of them. 'Here's to next year's worthy Super Santa,' Chris said and at that moment there was a frantic knocking before Julia, the landlady of the Fox Inn, popped her head around the edge of the door.

'The vicar is on the phone for you, Chris. He says it's an urgent job.'

Chris checked his watch. Nine o'clock was fast approaching. 'What's he done, locked himself out of the church? The service starts in half an hour...' He waved at Julia. 'On my way, although I'd best dash off to the gents for a Super Santa Superman manoeuvre,' he declared. 'Can't go out looking like this... Won't be long. Most likely a simple job.'

As Chris stood up, Tim cursed. His pager was beeping, and he fumbled beneath the folds of his baggy Santa suit to retrieve it. Tim was a retained fireman. Something was up. 'Too much of a coincidence, wouldn't you say?' he asked Chris with a wink as he too rushed for the door to make a dash for the local fire station. 'Although I thought we'd be doing this tomorrow!'

Unusually, the vicar sounded relatively coherent as he tried to explain to Chris over the phone, what the dilemma was. 'Enid didn't show up with the order of service leaflets, so I popped round to see if there was a problem. She's normally early and she lets the bell ringers in.'

'Right...'

'I phoned the fire service because they're only up the road but then I thought of you. I can see her lying on the floor and I think she's had a fall. Her door is locked.' The door to the post office itself was at the front of the building and would be bolted firmly and alarmed. The entrance used by Enid to access her home, was at the side of the house approached through a gate leading off from a shared driveway.

'Does anyone hold another key?' Chris asked, even though he knew the answer to that question.

Panting loudly, the vicar said, 'No, but the spare key was in its normal hiding place. For some reason it won't turn in the keyhole.'

'You get off to the church. I'll see what I can do.' Chris kept his voice calm but inside he was bubbling with nervous anticipation. The sight of the Fire and Rescue Service arriving at the post office would attract considerable attention. Exactly what he had hoped for.

He was staring through the leaded-light window at the side of the house when Tim and three of his colleagues arrived on scene in a four-wheel-drive appliance, rather than a large pump engine. 'What have we here?' Tim asked as he approached, barely able to keep the excited tension from his voice.

'The keys are on the inside of the door, in the lock. She's legs akimbo on the kitchen floor.' Chris dare not look at his friend for more than an instant. The reality of what he had done was about to be exposed and the expectation of what that would bring with it had become unbearable.

'And right on cue, here comes George with his camera. He can't resist an emergency service story for the local paper. He'll be looking for his best ever Super Santa Saturday exclusive,' Tim said. 'Do your thing and get us inside. Then we shall have a much better idea what we are dealing with and whether or not to call an ambulance.'

Under the watchful eye of members of the Fire and Rescue Service, Chris manipulated the lock and soon had the door swinging on its hinges. He stepped back. 'I'll stay out here in case you need me for anything else.'

The scene that greeted the fire officers was one they would never forget. Slumped against a sparkling new washing machine, Enid Speight was dressed in a red-and-white Santa tunic, a Santa hat askew on her head, her chocolate-smeared chin on her chest. Flickering coloured lights danced on her pale cheeks as the fairy lights around her neck flashed in random patterns. With her legs splayed out on the ceramic tiles, in her upturned flaccid right hand there rested a large carrot.

'It seems like our Enid has been partying,' said one burly officer pointing to sooty boot marks leading to and from the open fire. 'And she wasn't alone. By the looks of things, Santa came down her chimney a little earlier than expected. And that's NOT a euphemism.' He shot a disbelieving look at a lifeless Enid Speight who was being attended to by a female officer called Linda.

'Mrs Speight, can you hear me?' Linda said firmly. With a vinyl-gloved hand, she probed for a carotid pulse, tried at the wrist, and checked for beathing before declaring that Enid Speight was dead. 'We had best call the boys in blue,' she said. 'It could be a simple heart attack, but... in some weird way, this does look suspicious.' Flicking a concerned look at Tim she waited for his decision.

On the stone hearth of the fireplace was a dinner plate on which rested a glass tumbler, the dregs of something alcoholic lurking at the bottom. Next to that was a sheet of paper written upon with curling cursive script in large letters.

'Well, the door was locked from the inside, and there's no sign of a struggle or a break in,' Tim said, shrugging at his bewildered colleague while nodding in admiration to his friend Chris who remained in the doorway, grinning silently to himself. 'Hang on though, what does the note say?' Tim enquired. It was handed to him just as George Miller forced his way past Chris and into the kitchen. Believing it prudent to make a half-hearted protest about privacy and the incident being a police matter, Chris muttered something along those lines just in case the gathering crowd of onlookers were listening.

As Linda stood to prevent George from taking a sneaky shot of Enid with his ever-present camera, Tim read the words of the note aloud. 'Bloody hell, listen to this!' he announced. 'Better not put this in the local rag, George.' He coughed gently and straightened. 'This says: "Thanks for the sherry and the mince pie. Tis the season to be jolly. Merry Christmas." And it's signed with a great big letter S.'

Tim shot a warning look at George Miller. 'And before you start snapping away at fireplaces and sooty prints like some crime scene investigator, think again. Fair enough, the police will take a good while to get here from HQ but that's what you get for cutting rural services… and they already have their hands full, trying to work out how Phoebe Freshwater's drug-mule llamas transported so much cocaine across the county before she misunderstood the electrics of her new stock fencing last year… but we are not qualified to do their job for them and have already messed up a crime scene.'

'Quite right, Tim,' George replied, turning on his heels. 'Far be it from me to stand in the way of justice… I mean, how hard will it be to find a jolly fat man in a Santa suit sporting a white beard who may have been seen in the vicinity this evening…?' He began to laugh and clamped a hand to Chris Bland's shoulder on the way back out of the door. Well out of earshot, he said, 'Nice one, Chris. Bloody brilliant in fact. And what's more,' he whispered, 'she deserved it! Ho, ho, ho.'

DOUBLE FIRST

R.D. NIXON

UNIVERSITY OF PLYMOUTH. DECEMBER 23RD, 8.15 PM

THE STAIRWELL REMAINED DARK; THE AUTOMATIC light hadn't flickered to life as it should, and the concrete steps sent the hollow bang of the upstairs door echoing down through the floors. Then silence. The door had slammed twice, but there was no way of knowing whether Jodie's pursuer had followed her, risking life and limb on these dark steps, or whether they had changed their mind and sprung to the adjacent lift instead. There was no sound. Nothing but a shifting, whispering chill that stroked the back of her neck and set her nerves quivering.

Jodie twisted her head to peer pointlessly upwards, her neck aching with the strain, and her hands flat against the roughly rendered stonework as she pressed herself back against the wall. She kept deadly still for what felt like forever until, eventually, desperation pushed her and she levered herself off the wall and edged forward, one shoeless foot feeling blindly for the top of the next flight of steps.

Which was when she heard slow, measured footsteps on the

concrete. Two sets: one below, and one above, and both were moving towards her.

PART I

SOUTHSIDE CAFÉ, ROLAND LEVINSKY BUILDING. FOUR HOURS EARLIER

Jodie sat at the table after the meeting had broken up, ostensibly writing notes, in reality staring out of the first-floor window, pondering how different Christmas would be this year. Goodbye, Darren, Happy Christmas, don't let the door hit you in... etc.

It had already turned dark out there in manic shopping-land, the dazzling lights of the Drake Circus mall reflecting only in a mass of confused colour on the rain-slicked pavements; people hurrying to and from that glass-fronted building, most of them laden with bags and umbrellas. Heads down against the blustery evening. No enjoyment left in it now; this was last-minute stuff.

Damn, forgot Margaret. Again.

You know *your gran can't wear wool!*

Why did the neighbours have to stick a "little pressie" in the porch? Now we have to reciprocate, or be forever "the tight-arses at #73."

Then there would be that eternal dilemma: only half an hour left on the car park ticket, and a massive queue in Waterstones. Was it worth the risk? *Didn't you download the RingGo app? Why not?*

Endless bloody stress. Where was the fun in that?

It was also the day of the faculty Christmas party, and everyone else on the admin team was looking forward to the chance to let off some steam. Jodie clicked her pen shut and shoved it inside the coils of her wire-bound notebook, before wandering back to the admin office, where people were already starting to shut down their computers. Pretty soon they would all be heading out for their meal, complete with crackers, hats, and spilled drinks. More frenetic merry-making. But first, drinkies with the dean, of course.

Every year, before the various office meals, the dean laid on nibbles and wine in his rooms. Academics and admin were invited in to mingle and chat, though they always ended up standing around in their usual little groups, talking about the same stuff they talked about in the office. But still, the wine was free, so no-one really cared.

People buzzed about the office now, washing cups and setting out-of-office messages on their emails, chatter about who had which days off over the break flowing around and between them all:

I'm in on Christmas eve, but only until lunchtime.

This is my last day, see you next year! (dutiful laughs in response.)

The whole uni's shut for the in-between days, isn't it?

Every year the same.

Jodie cheerfully kept up her end of this unofficial Christmas verbal bingo, but amidst all the tinsel, the tiny decorated Christmas trees and the glittery earrings, her mind kept returning to her undecorated home, her own tree still in its plastic box in the shed, and, of course, the calendar on the wall, totally devoid of any of the usual cheerful scribbles.

No *Darren's parents pm*, or *Darren out with boys*, on there this year. Darren was off making Sarah's Christmas a sparkly, M&S joy, and defacing *her* calendar with the various dates and channels *Die Hard* was showing. Right out of nowhere, just a few weeks ago, after nearly ten years. It didn't help Jodie's fractured self-esteem that he'd recently transferred into her faculty, and had spoken to her with distant but pointed friendliness, as if they'd never shared a bed or a drunken game of Monopoly in their PJs. At least he'd taken his Christmas leave early and wouldn't be on today's meal; it would have been even tougher on the emotions once the Sauvy was flowing.

On the plus side, of all the verbal Christmas bingo phrases, her own metaphorical stamp went on, *this is my last day,* but without the always "hilarious" *see you next year!* She was moving offices in January, to the faculty of Science and Engineering. Away from Arts. Away from Darren. She looked at the pile of crap she had to take home with her as a result; there was no way she was carting it all down to the Slug and Lettuce now, she'd call back for it before she caught the bus home. Some of the team had scuttled off to change and apply make-up, and Jodie went as far as brushing her hair and slipping into low heels instead of her comfy flats, but beyond that she really couldn't care less. Not this year.

They trooped into the dean's office, where the smell of pastries, tangy snacks, and garlic dips hung in the air, and several academics were already standing around chatting. The dean, who was a couple of weeks newer to the university than Darren – *stop thinking about him!* – made a short but rousing speech, thanking everyone for their hard work during the always-difficult first semester, and said how much he hoped to foster a dynamic and co-operative atmosphere between departments, and between professional services and the student body. Everyone clapped and smiled, and privately knew damned well that everything would be as it ever had been. Which wasn't to say *bad,* just... the same. It didn't matter which new broom was head of the faculty.

Not long afterwards, Jodie somehow fell into a conversation she actually found interesting, and learned that the dean was apparently a very clever bloke. Not just good at climbing the ladder, but it seemed that, in his own discipline, he'd been exploring the idea that an illuminated manuscript, discovered in Somerset and dated from around 900 CE, was in fact an elaborate and skilful forgery.

The owners of the manuscript were particularly keen that this not be the case, of course, but it was looking increasingly as if their lucrative livelihoods were about to blow away in a stiff

December wind. Likewise, those who supported this theory were equally keen that this new information *should* come out, being scholars, and therefore seekers after truth. According to the Art History tutor Jodie was listening to, there was a lot of noise being made about the dean's research, in both academic and business circles, and he'd been coming under some pressure to discuss it openly. Until now though, he'd been a little backward in coming forward, claiming he had yet to get all his ducks in a row.

The dean's PA—into whose conversation Jodie had accidentally been absorbed, by virtue of taking a side-step when she'd meant to take a backwards one—announced with some pride that he'd had to book last-minute train and hotel tickets for the dean and the head of Art History. London, apparently, and leaving tonight. There was a live podcast event first thing, and it seemed that the dean's research, finally compiled and, apparently, irrefutable, was going public for the first time. The tutor grinned from ear to ear at this news. Cats and pigeons were mentioned, along with the horizontal arrangement of those potentially damaging, and very quacky, ducks. Quite the menagerie, in all.

People were starting to drift off, and Jodie left the group to its ongoing discussion while she went to find those who were heading off to lunch. The room had that sad, end-of-party look now: the Pringles bowls had been picked dry, apart from a few gum-stabbing shards best left alone, and glasses were emptying and not being re-filled. The sandwich tray only displayed a curly tuna, and a ham which had fallen into two halves, revealing dry corners and a scrap of meat in the centre.

Appetites duly sharpened, people were pulling on coats and looking around for stragglers before they began trickling out of the first-floor office and down the wide staircase to the ground floor. Jodie talked cheerily enough with whoever she found herself walking next to, but once again, in her mind, she was already on the bus home, having done her festive duty and said her goodbyes. A closed front door, a tub of Quality Street, and the festive TV guide and black marker pen awaited, but this year there was no need to put a circle around *Die Hard*.

As she'd feared, there were hugs at the meal. Drinks too, which helped, but that meant she was becoming dangerously emotional, and it was something of a relief to leave all those loved-up, happy-familied, slightly drunk people to argue about where they were going on to next. Cocktails seemed to have the majority vote, and Jodie couldn't think of anything worse.

She remembered, halfway to the bus stop, that she was supposed to be picking up those two bags of accumulated tea bags, note pads, folders, pens and goodness knows what else, and taking them home. It was tempting to leave it all and collect it in January instead, but the thought of coming back to the office after all those goodbyes, and possibly running into Darren as well... No, thanks. It was only a short walk back to the uni anyway.

The Roland Levinsky building always feels weird after hours. It goes from being the buzzing centre of uni life, to a cold, open-plan network of multi-level walkways, dance studios, and glass-fronted art spaces. The university's flagship building, it stands at the edge of the city centre like a stern parent, gazing out over the shops with its vast walls of tinted windows. When it's empty, the sounds echo strangely throughout, especially in the cross-point at the centre; a four-storey open space that forms the foot-print of the major part of the building.

It was empty now. The students had gone home, and no

academics or cleaners remained. Security would patrol at various points, no doubt, but they were based further up the campus and Jodie hoped her swipe card would get her access this late in the day, or those bags were staying put; not a chance she was going up to find someone to let her in now.

The door gave a muted clunk and slid open, and Jodie hurried across the echoing concrete floor of the crosspoint, looking forward to getting back into her flat shoes, before remembering they were lurking at the bottom of one of the bags of desk-crap, and she didn't know which one.

Her cleared desk looked strangely lonely in the empty room. Already the decorations that the team had put up, with such happy anticipation, seemed old and tired, and it took her a moment to remember that Christmas hadn't even happened yet. In previous years that would have been a nice thought.

She dropped her handbag into the top of one of the carriers, and made her way back to the stairs, but after a few steps the bag in her right hand gave a dull jerk and swung away, gaping open and with half the torn plastic handle still clutched pointlessly in her hand. She gave a grunt of annoyance, twisted the broken plastic around her fingers, and made for the lift instead.

Tiredness was creeping over her now, and she broke into a yawn just as the lift gave its familiar muffled ping, and the politely robotic female voice announced that the doors were opening. The yawn widened, and Jodie allowed herself the luxury of it; it'd be good to sit down with a cup of tea and catch up with some telly. Good? It'd be utter bliss. The brushed steel door sprang back, and Jodie took a fresh grip of her broken bag and stepped into the lift. Abruptly, the pleasant anticipation of comfort vanished, and the remainder of the yawn locked the back of her throat up hard and tight, stealing the breath she needed to scream.

PART II

Jodie stared at the horrific tableau that met her stunned eyes, but it wasn't until one of the two crouched figures moved that she understood the danger she had walked into. She dropped her bags, as the doors began to slide shut, her eyes still fixed on the slumped body in the corner and belatedly recognising the new dean. He was "fostering a dynamic and co-operative atmosphere" with a plastic bag, which had been snugged down over his head and was even now being tied tightly at the neck.

With a presence of mind she'd never imagined she possessed, she leaned in and hit the button for the second floor, the highest point this particular lift would go, and flung herself back out onto the solid floor.

Doors... Closing...

The hooded figure, still in the process of pulling the cable tie with one hand, lurched forward to grab her, but tripped over the dean's outstretched, feebly flailing arm, and Jodie felt a moment's wild relief as the doors began to move across the ghastly spectacle, blocking it out.

The stairs were only a few feet away. She turned to run, but had taken only a few stumbling steps when, to her horror, she heard the lift doors spring back again. A glance over her shoulder showed her the bags she'd dropped, right in the door-way, and the blurred figure of the dean's attacker scrambling over them.

She had time to register that it was a female form before it was out of the lift. Rather than head straight for her, the woman broke to her left and cut off Jodie's route to the stairs, leaving the only escape down past a row of tables, towards the café at the far end of the building. Halfway down the open passage, which overlooked the spacious ground floor, one of Jodie's party shoes slid on the carpet and her heart leapt into the back of her throat. She could hear her pursuer's footsteps behind, and she grabbed a chair and pulled it across the narrow walkway, buying just enough time to slip out of her shoes and leave them behind.

As she ran, she patted her coat pocket for her phone, but it was in the bag she'd dumped into one of the carriers that was still keeping the lift doorway from closing. The entire building was like one of those optical illusions; staircases that only went so far, lifts that might or might not deliver you to the floor you thought they should; some of them only went between lower ground, and second or third. You could spend all day going up ladders and down snakes, and never really know where you'd end up; bemused students often came to reception to ask, and never had Jodie felt more empathetic.

On the far side of the café there was another lift, but to corner herself in it, in the hopes that the maddeningly slow door would close before the dean's murderer reached her, would be insane. It had to be the stairs.

8.15 PM

So now she stood, breathless, halfway down one of those snakes, in the hollow echo chamber that was the back staircase. The sound of footsteps rising from the ground floor gave her a leap of hope, but she didn't want to shout, to make whoever it was aware of her presence, in case it alerted the dean's attacker above. She had no way of knowing that whoever was coming up the stairs was any less of a threat than the woman coming down.

She heard a faint click, and then a beam of light swept up through the railings and directly into her face, and she buried her eyes briefly in the crook of her elbow. The harshness of the light faded, and a familiar voice drifted up to her: her name, spoken with incredulity and almost disbelief, but no more than she herself felt at the sound of it. Darren...

Just for a heartbeat, the question flashed across her mind:

what were the chances? and then she was sobbing under her breath and using his torchlight to guide her down the steps.

They collided mid-flight, and he pulled her into a close embrace, muffling her frantic words against the wool of his coat as he tried to soothe her. She pulled back, and grabbed his hand, dragging him back down towards the ground floor. She tried to get the words out past a blockage in her throat, that might have been either fear or relief, but wasn't sure he understood her babbling; he'd have shown a lot more urgency if he did. The footsteps from above moved faster, and Darren finally got the message and allowed Jodie to lead him out into the crosspoint, where the exit signs over the doors were beacons of freedom.

She let go of his hand and ran, the floor ice-cold and slippery underfoot through her tights, but even as she reached the nearest exit she heard her pursuer crash through the door from the stairwell and her heart staggered in her chest. She punched the rectangular door button with the edge of her fist, once, twice, but nothing happened, and she let out a despairing cry. She shouldn't need her swipe card to get out – it was a fire hazard – so someone had clearly disabled the locks since she'd arrived, and a pound to a penny it wasn't campus security.

Then Darren was at her side and they turned to face the woman who'd attacked the dean. She had stopped a few feet away and was looking at them as if assessing her chances against two, and Jodie felt a flash of triumph as she simply nodded briefly, turned away, and ran for the staircase.

Jodie's hope took another leap; the woman clearly had no weapon, or she'd have made a more effective job of doing away with the dean... who might actually still be alive. It was obvious the assassin was more interested in finishing the job, satisfied that the hood was protecting her identity. Jodie murmured as much to Darren, adding that, together they should be able to overpower the woman and possibly save the dean's life. Darren nodded gravely and placed a finger to his lips. She understood;

sound in the Roland Levinsky building was a live thing, with an unpredictable mind of its own.

In the stairwell he flicked his torch on again and they both started up at a run, but instead of exiting onto the first floor, he continued towards the second. For a moment she was puzzled, then realised it was the sensible thing; the assassin might easily be waiting by the door, and they'd stand no chance. She followed without question, relieved she was no longer alone, and when he kept climbing she remained fairly close behind, although now having slowed to a faintly puffed walk. Thoughts of pyjamas, tea, and telly were so far distant as to be laughable, but now Darren was here, freedom was a step closer, and who knew; perhaps she'd be circling *Die Hard* on the TV guide after all.

Jodie could feel the cold of the stairwell air on her skin, but she herself was sweating and out of breath. The rich Christmas lunch sat heavy and lumpen, and her head was starting to pound from exertion and stress; she was pulling herself up by the iron railing now, rather than just holding it. As she climbed, her thoughts began to turn away from what had happened to the dean, and onto the sheer madness of not only being a witness, for the sake of a few notebooks and tea bags, but then finding Darren, of all people, coming to her aid.

She stopped, mid-step, remembering that tiny nod the killer had given them downstairs... Given them? Or only Darren? Her breathing, already short from the climb, caught in her throat and became thin and shallow. Darren turned, and in the light of the torch his face looked...wild. She told herself the torchlight was creating the eeriness, but he seemed swathed in living shadows; the darkness around both of them threw everything into a hideously detailed relief, and the persistent questions grew louder.

Who had disabled the touchpads for the doors?

Why did he have a torch?

Why was he here?

If the questions were now thundering in her mind, the answers were screaming. It all made some fantastical kind of sense now: the suddenness of Sarah; Darren's unexpected move to this faculty so soon after the dean had taken the job; his absence from the meal... Sarah might have been the one to carry out the murder, but it didn't make Darren any less dangerous. He was clearly being used, but he was in it to the eyebrows.

Jodie's hand on the rail became slick with sweat. She somehow found a smile that also conveyed temporary exhaustion, and waved him on... She'd catch him up once she had her breath back. He didn't believe her, she saw that at once.

A whirl, a blur, two steps down to where Jodie stood petrified, and he grabbed her wrist and yanked her forwards. A shriek broke loose, and the sound it made as it bounced off the bare walls and up and down the stairwell terrified her. Terrified her that it was so loud, so helpless-sounding, and, even more so, that there was no-one else around to hear it.

Darren didn't speak, just hauled her up after him, and she had no choice but to follow as her feet slipped on the steps; to lose her balance would be to crack her head on the concrete, and that would be the end of everything. His fingers were like iron and she could feel the small bones grinding together, but a flash of anger lit her from inside, and she was determined she wouldn't show another sign of weakness. She'd die first.

PART III

They rounded another bend; the next break would bring them into line with the door onto whichever floor they'd reached. She felt herself tightening up as she considered her only chance, and she knew she had to be ready at exactly the right moment, and, somehow, with exactly the right move.

Halfway up the set of steps she began to hang back again, and to make small whimpering sounds. Darren whipped around to glare at her, and she held back for just a moment longer, until she sensed he was about to lose his temper. For a second she thought she'd misjudged, and panic trailed icy fingers down her spine, but although she realised now that she hardly knew him at all, it turned out she was still an expert when it came to his moods.

He pulled hard on her wrist, and she put every bit of strength she could summon into her legs, and bounded up three steps at once. Darren, caught off-balance, stumbled and relinquished his hold on her, and she shoved as hard as she could, sending him crashing into the wall. The torch clattered to the ground and went out, and she wished again that she were wearing shoes; a good kick between the legs while he was sprawled would have earned her a little more time, but as it was she'd put herself out of action in the process, achieving nothing.

Instead she grabbed at where she thought the door handle should be, but had to slap around in the dark for a precious extra second or two before she found it, then she was through. The meagre light from the crosspoint reached up to what she discovered was the sixth floor, and into another of those maddeningly ambiguous areas where a potential exit could as easily be a locked studio.

She took a chance on where she thought the lift should be, and nearly wept with relief to see she'd made the right choice. At the opposite end of the building from where the dean had been struck down, there was still a chance this lift might take too long to reach her, particularly if it was on the ground floor, but she was too shattered, and short on time, to weigh it all up.

She punched the button, hardly breathing as she listened out for the banging of the stairwell door. It never came, and she slowly unclenched her fists as she allowed herself to think that perhaps he'd hit the wall harder than she'd thought, and was lying stunned in the dark.

The lift arrived, with its incongruously well-articulated,

Floor… Six, and Jodie nearly melted as she waited for the doors to part. Half of her expected to see either one of her enemies inside, but it was empty and she lurched in and hit the *0*, and *close doors* buttons in quick succession.

The lift started on its way down, and she had time to wonder how the hell she was going to get out of the building, before it picked up pace and she was just grateful to be flashing her way down through the floors. With a quick snatch of breath she hit the *2* button, realising she could be walking straight into danger if she took the predictable route.

But the lift slowed at 3. It stopped. *Floor… three. Doors… opening.*

Oh, Christ… Jodie hammered at the close doors button again, frantic to over-ride the inevitable, but the doors swished smoothly back and Darren's tall form blocked out the light. Now he no longer held the torch in one hand, and her arm in the other, he had taken the time to pull out what looked alarmingly like a flick knife.

The blade was still shut, but this time Jodie didn't think twice. She swept her leg up in a straight line, not caring which bit of it struck him, just hoping to create a path and follow it with a connection of some kind. Her aim was off; there was no room to manoeuvre properly, and her toe struck the lift door with a sickening crunch, while Darren merely twisted away.

It gave her the sliver of a chance though, before he turned back to face her, and she was out of the lift and limping away before he could grab her again. Fear and pain propelled her towards the same stairwell she had just escaped from. she didn't care now that it would be pitch dark; she'd slide down the rail if she had to…

She didn't make it. Darren pulled her away from the door, flinging her back onto the narrow walkway that looked straight down three floors, to the crosspoint. The protective railing was anchored firmly, and heavy duty glass covered the gap, but it still felt as if she were about to go flying over. The blade was out now, and Darren was ready to use it. On *her*. As if he hadn't hurt her enough already…

The fury bit hard and deep, and it cleared her mind of all the fuzzy terror that was hampering her thoughts. It was the age-old no-brainer: kill or be killed. Before she had realised exactly what she was going to do, she had twisted against the rail, bringing him and his deadly blade closer, then she stooped and locked her arms about his knees. All it took then, was the strength to straighten up, and her anger gave her that. She heard something pop in her back as she did so, but that was a pain to worry over later.

As his hips came up level with the metal rail Darren came to life and, belatedly realising what she was doing, he struck out. A thin line of heat flared down her upper arm, and a clumsy blow with his other hand sent bright lights spinning across her eyes. Then he was gone.

His shriek filled the building, from crosspoint to apex, and his flailing hands found nothing to cling onto as he plummeted three floors to land on the concrete. Jodie's savage triumph overflowed as she staggered back to the rail and looked down at his sprawled form, at the blood spilling from the back of his shockingly mis-shapen head, and at the incriminating blade that now lay near his prone form. Thank god.

Or, in words he would have understood better, *Yippie-ki-yay, motherfucker…*

She slid down the barrier, dazed, one hand clapped to her bleeding arm, and trying to muster up the strength to move. Her first – definitely – dead body, and it was the man she'd loved from the age of seventeen.

From up here she could hear her phone playing its jolly little tune in the other lift, its only audience unable to show any appreciation. Sarah must have gone while the going was good, making her escape just before campus security rolled up for their regular patrol and all hell broke loose. The police arrived too, in due course, and, following the path of Darren's fall they found her leaning motionless against the blood-smeared glass.

Being informed of her rights was another surreal first, and as Jodie was led along the walkway to the lift, she looked down at the now taped-off crime scene on the first floor. Her bags were still there, and she considered asking if she could have them back, but closed her mouth on the query. That desk-crap had nearly killed her, it could damn well stay there until January.

PAYBACK

BRIAN PRICE

SALLY

SALLY NEVER FAILED AT ANYTHING SHE SET HER MIND to. But she did this time and it was Pete's fault. If he hadn't come home early from the pub and found her, she would have succeeded at suicide as well. Life wasn't perfect but she had a home, a partner, and was looking forward to starting a family. Until recently, she enjoyed her career, doing a job she was proud of. But a new manager, with the humanity of a chainsaw, had undermined her so much that she felt a failure at everything.

Lying in a hospital bed, a drip in her arm and her stomach sore from the gastric lavage, which washed out the paracetamol before it could wreck her liver, she thought back over the previous six months. The sleepless nights, the exhaustion, the drinking, the rows with her partner – all these she blamed on one person. Kelly Thornbury. The woman who had wrecked her life by making her workplace intolerable.

Nothing she could do was good enough for Kelly. Her work-load had increased enormously and her supervision meetings with Kelly consisted of a barrage of criticisms and unreasonable demands. She had to work at home during weekends, just to keep up. Sally was a professional person, capable of making her own judgements and managing her commitments. But, since Kelly had arrived, she had been belittled, undermined and insulted. Kelly's bullying wasn't confined to Sally. Her colleagues had suffered in the same way and several had left their jobs as a result. It was the organisation's culture, of which Kelly was a part, which drove them away.

Sally deeply regretted giving in to her despair and the pain it had caused Pete and her parents. She realised that the prompt actions of the paramedics and doctors had given her a second chance, one she would not waste. The only thing to do was to fight back. And she bloody well would.

The days off while she recovered gave her time to plan. For the first time in months, she was away from work and had time to think. She was determined to pay Kelly back for the misery which she had caused her and her colleagues. Sally wasn't a violent person but she was clever. Maybe there were better ways of getting revenge than through physical confrontation?

Sally spent hours devising ways of humiliating, or otherwise harming, Kelly, from letting down her tyres to poisoning her coffee. The more fanciful and illegal ideas she quickly discounted, as well as those which could throw suspicion on herself. Eventually, she settled on a couple of projects which carried a slight risk but which would be highly satisfying to carry out. She waited until she was about to return to work before starting her campaign. She wanted to see the results of her efforts.

Sally knew where Kelly lived and what her regular movements between the office and home were. She also knew the registration number of Kelly's black Ford Focus. It was easy to hire an identical model for the day, from a firm a couple of dozen miles away. Using painted cardboard and black insulating tape, cut to the appropriate sizes, she made copies of Kelly's number plates. Pulling into a side road not far from the office, and checking that no-one was watching, she fixed the copied plates to the hired car, her hands shaking. They wouldn't fool a police officer but, from a distance, they could pass for genuine. Shortly before Kelly was due to leave the office for home, Sally pulled out of the side road and headed along the route Kelly would take.

As she approached the only functioning speed camera in town her heart went into overdrive and her hands on the wheel became slippery with sweat. Looking around for parked police cars – or possible unmarked ones – she was relieved to see that there were no suspicious vehicles in sight. Just before she reached the camera, she put her foot down, reaching 42 mph as she passed the yellow box, which flashed obligingly.

Sweat pouring from her, and her heart thumping almost loud enough to hear above the engine, she pulled into the next available side road. She removed the false plates and sat in the car, trembling, for ten minutes. Gradually, her terror gave way to a feeling of exultation. Kelly would get a speeding ticket and points on her licence, while she had got away with it. For the first time ever, she felt she had exerted some power over her nemesis and it felt good. So good that she couldn't wait to launch the next phase.

Returning to work, with Kelly's speeding ticket no doubt in the post, Sally underwent an intrusive back-to-work interview. She had to convince Lorna Brake, Kelly's boss and the chief executive of the organisation, that she was fit to return. She didn't dare say why she had overdosed but made up a story about having a blinding headache and accidentally taking too many tablets, because of the confusion it had caused. She knew that, if she blamed Kelly's management style for her suicide attempt, she would be accused of gross misconduct and sacked. Lorna's manner was as sympathetic as a rat trap and all she said was 'Don't make that mistake again.' She countersigned the form on which Sally stated that she felt fit to return and dismissed her without so much as a 'Welcome back.'

Sally's organisation was set up to help vulnerable people in the community, be they homeless, substance abusers, gamblers, victims of domestic violence or in chronic debt. Originally part of the local authority, the organisation had been privatised as a community interest company. Sally, and most of her colleagues, cared deeply about their clients, often putting in hours of unpaid overtime to support them. The managers had different attitudes, however, being driven by targets and statistics rather than the human needs of the people they were supposed to support. They had no training in the fields relevant to the clients yet criticised the way in which those actually doing the work performed. Since privatisation, Lorna had replaced a service ethos with a bullying culture. The four managers followed her lead in squeezing every last drop of productivity out of the staff and anyone complaining was threatened with disciplinary action. Salaries had been cut and working hours extended. Most of the staff were desperate to leave but opportunities for people with their skills, in that part of the East Midlands, were rare.

Many of the organisation's clients had problems with alcohol and were put on various treatment regimes. During a training day, Sally had found out about Antabuse, a drug given to alcoholics which produces an adverse reaction should they drink anything with alcohol in it. She remembered this when she was lying, nauseous, in the hospital bed. Sally discovered that Antabuse can be purchased from overseas sites, via the Internet, and she determined to acquire some.

Two days after returning to work, Sally had her first supervision meeting. Kelly had always treated Sally with an air of superiority but this time she was downright aggressive, making it clear that Sally would be given no special treatment following her illness. She would be expected to clear her backlog of work without delay. Sally didn't dare to point out the unreasonableness of Kelly's attitude but secretly rejoiced. The ticket's arrived! she thought.

Three weeks later, Christmas gatherings were taking place and the Antabuse Sally ordered had arrived. Staff were allowed an extra half hour for lunch to celebrate and most of them went to a local restaurant for a hurried Christmas meal – with no alcohol permitted if they were returning to work. The managers had an evening meal planned and this gave Sally her opportunity. Kelly was an avid coffee drinker, taking it black, sweet and strong. While she was in the toilet, and everyone else was absorbed in completing paperwork before the Christmas break, Sally struck. On the pretext of dropping some expenses sheets on her desk, she stirred two ground-up Antabuse tablets into Kelly's coffee. She wouldn't be around when they took effect, but she could imagine the results at the managers' dinner that evening.

KELLY

The Swanley Hotel was famous for its food, but was not so expensive that the cost of the managers' meals couldn't be massaged through the company's expenses system. The group took their places at the table, anticipating a fine meal and plenty to drink, all on the company's account. Presiding over her minions, Lorna was every inch the Queen Bee, with her Gucci handbag prominently displayed on the table and an expensive dress straining to contain her chest. Once the waiter had poured champagne, she raised her glass 'To another profitable year,' she toasted. Her colleagues joined in the salute, drained their glasses and settled down to consider the menu.

A few minutes later, Kelly began to feel ill. She broke out in a sweat, started to tremble and lurched to her feet in a frantic attempt to reach the toilets. Unfortunately for her, and for her colleagues, she didn't make it. The full effects of the wine, combined with the Antabuse, kicked in and a torrent of vomit poured from Kelly's mouth, filling Lorna's cleavage and soaking her precious bag. Kelly dashed for the Ladies, trailing vomit behind her, while waiters flapped ineffectually at the pool of sick on the table. Lorna was incandescent and stormed off to confront Kelly, who was hunched over a toilet bowl as her body tried to clear the last of the alcohol from her system.

'You stupid cow,' snarled Lorna, no trace of sympathy in her manner. 'You'll pay for cleaning this dress and replacing my handbag. I'll discuss your behaviour in the office on Monday.'

Reeking with the smell of sick, Lorna stalked out of the restaurant, grabbing a full bottle of wine on the way. Her three remaining colleagues, whose appetites had vanished, also left, promising that the company would cover the restaurant's cleaning costs. Kelly eventually emerged from the toilets, weak and wobbly, and slunk to her car without looking at the staff or the horrified customers. She didn't notice Sally in the corner of the hotel car park, making a call on her mobile.

As Kelly's car pulled out of the car park, somewhat errati-cally, the blue and red lights of a police car ordering her to stop appeared in her mirror. She knew she wouldn't fail a breath test but the indignity of being stopped and tested, while reeking of vomit, made a ghastly evening even worse. She had never felt so miserable in her life.

SALLY

The next line of attack landed in Sally's lap without her looking for it. She didn't have much of a spam filter on her emails, although she never opened anything suspicious, so it was inevitable that a kindly Nigerian prince would offer to share his wealth with her, in exchange for her bank account details. This gave her an idea. Signing in to her emails at an Internet cafe, just in case her own laptop picked up a virus, she opened the email and copied down the address where the details should be sent, filing them carefully away before deleting the message.

Sally's opportunity presented itself after the Christmas break. She needed to talk to Kelly about rearranging a meeting, but Kelly wasn't at her desk. Reaching for a pen and Post-it note, she spotted Kelly's open chequebook. Swiftly, and with her back to the rest of the office, she slipped out her phone and took a snapshot of the open book. At home she printed off the image of the chequebook and immediately deleted it from the phone's memory. Two things interested her, apart from the account number and sort code: Kelly had been in the process of writing a cheque to Lorna for twelve hundred pounds and there was a four-digit number, written faintly inside the chequebook cover, which, Sally surmised, could be Kelly's PIN. Details of the Christmas dinner debacle had filtered down to the rest of the staff and Sally guessed that the cheque was to cover cleaning Lorna's dress and replacing her bag. The size of the sum gave her a warm glow.

Sally held off launching her attack, in case Kelly remembered leaving her chequebook on the desk and suspected someone in the office of copying her account details. So, two months later, she visited an Internet cafe in a neighbouring town and logged on to a specially created email account using Kelly's name. She made contact with the 'Nigerian prince', provided Kelly's details and wished him well.

While waiting for her opportunity to introduce Kelly to her African friend, Sally had not been idle. Using an image copied from the Internet, and text of her own devising, she prepared some rather special business cards which she printed off at home. Taking advantage of the dark evenings, and wearing glasses and a scarf over her distinctive red hair, she stuck the cards up in telephone booths, on community noticeboards, lamp-posts, supermarket customer ads boards and anywhere else she could find.

KELLY

The results of Sally's business cards were prolonged rather than instant. Numerous naughty punters who dialled Kelly's work mobile number were disappointed to find that 'Kelly the Spank Engine' would not be prepared to 'take them in hand'. Kelly was pestered day and night by would-be 'clients' and was frequently interrupted in meetings. It didn't help when an anonymous tip off to the local paper claimed that a manager in a local community support company was supplementing her salary by providing salacious services. Called up before Lorna, Kelly swore that she was the victim of a practical joke, or a misprinted phone number, and asked for her number to be changed. Lorna agreed, grumbling that it was a nuisance and would cost the company money.

Two days after Sally passed on Kelly's bank details, the bomb-shell landed. Although company policy forbade the use of personal phones during work time, Kelly used her smartphone to check that her salary had cleared into her bank account. When the balance came up on the display she shrieked, dropped the phone and nearly fainted.

'What's the matter with you – and why are you using a personal phone?' snapped Lorna, who had just entered the room.

'I... I... I've been scammed.' Kelly could barely get the words out. 'My account's empty – someone's cleaned it out.'

There were a few murmurs of sympathy around the office and no small amount of disguised satisfaction. Sally proffered a glass of water to Kelly, the concerned expression on her face contrasting with the bubbling glee she felt inside.

'You'd better get on to your bank to find out how it happened. Perhaps they can get the money back,' she said, knowing full well that the funds were gone forever.

Kelly carried on sobbing at her desk until Lorna could stand the noise no longer.

'Take a day's leave and go home,' she instructed Kelly. 'Sort this out and be back in the office tomorrow morning. You need to be at the staff meeting.'

Kelly stumbled out the office, a look of utter despair on her face. And Sally didn't feel the slightest bit guilty.

Kelly slunk into the office with a hangover, as Lorna began the staff meeting with a warning.

'What I am about to say, and the actions which will follow, must remain confidential. Do you all understand?'

She glared around the room, eliciting nods from all present.

'Because of a communication problem at the middle management level,' her eyes briefly flicked towards Kelly, 'we've missed the deadline for completing service user plans for several hundred individuals. We're being audited at the end of the month and our future funding, which means your jobs, depends on these plans having been completed by the deadline. So, from now on, there will be no leave granted, there will be a rota for Saturday working and you will backdate the plans, when you complete them, to a date before the deadline.'

Several people groaned when Lorna mentioned Saturday working and she continued.

'If you look at your contracts in detail you will see that I can require you to work outside normal office hours, if I deem it necessary. And I do.'

'I'm a Christian,' said Katy Maguire, 'and I don't believe in lying.'

'You'll backdate those plans or find another job' retorted Lorna, leaving the room before anyone else could raise objections.

Lorna's accusatory glance was not lost on Kelly. She never told us about the deadline and now she's trying to blame me, in spite of everything I've gone through, she thought.

Kelly had been harbouring a burning resentment of Lorna for some time. She was used to bullying those below her in the hierarchy and didn't appreciate the same treatment from above. She had never dared to challenge Lorna before. But perhaps now was the time to take action? With Lorna gone there could even be a chance for promotion. Despite the recent glitches, her record was better than those of her three colleagues at the same level, so she would be in with a good chance. Yes, getting rid of Lorna would be an excellent idea. She knew that an official complaint to the board of directors would be pointless, and would just get her sacked, but she was determined to find a way to bring her down. And that meant gathering information.

Over three successive Saturdays, staff worked their way through the backlog of service user plans and it wasn't difficult for Kelly to compile a list of those fraudulently backdated. She wasn't IT-savvy enough to hack into parts of the system dealing with Lorna's salary but she did discover, from leafing through a heap of paper expenses claims on the admin clerk's desk, that Lorna was claiming travelling expenses between her home and the office. That may be OK with the company, she thought, but I'm damn sure she's not declaring these to the tax people. Smartphone shots of a selection of these claims joined the list of plans on her flash drive.

Kelly racked her brains to think of other ways in which she could get a hold over Lorna. She continued to poke around piles of papers, look at unlocked computer screens when no-one was around and listen to unguarded phone calls. Her spying paid off when Lorna's son, Justin, turned up at the office one day, driving a sporty VW Golf. The list price of the car was over £27,000 and she wondered how a student could afford a vehicle that expensive. The answer came to her when she spotted tax and insurance renewal notices in the admin clerk's in-tray. The car was registered to the company and Justin was listed on the insurance as an employee, despite the fact that he had only worked for the company, at an inflated salary, for just four weeks one summer. More evidence went on her flash drive, together with notes explaining its significance.

The next piece of ammunition in Kelly's armoury came about purely by chance. Furious with a staff member who hadn't met his targets, she knocked on Lorna's door and was about to open it when she heard a breathless 'Wait!' from inside. Kelly obeyed and a minute later Dave, the company maintenance hand, left Lorna's office in a hurry, pushing past Kelly without a word. Lorna called Kelly in, her face flushed.

'What do you want?' she snapped, 'What's the idea of interrupting our meeting … about the damp in the male toilet.'

'Sorry, Lorna. It's just that Martin has missed his targets three months running and I want to start disciplinary action against him. He claims it's because their new baby is keeping him awake all night but that's no excuse for skiving.'

'OK. Do what you want. Give him a warning or something. Now get out and send Dave back in.'

Kelly's suspicions as to what she had interrupted were reinforced as she dropped her eyes from Lorna's and spotted a pair of silk knickers on the floor, in front of Lorna's, unusually clear, desk. She managed to record a subsequent 'maintenance meeting' on her phone by leaving it on the floor outside Lorna's office. Words were barely spoken but panting and heavy breathing predominated. Another item for her flash drive.

It was well known in the office that Lorna enjoyed a comfortable lifestyle. She took holidays in exotic locations, drove a flashy car and, as Kelly knew to her cost, bought expensive clothes and accessories. Her salary was not public knowledge and Kelly had often wondered how she could afford such luxuries. The company accounts, however, were published and, on examining them, Kelly noted a series of payments to design firms, business consultancies and equipment suppliers – a total of £230,000 over three years. It was a matter of minutes to look these outfits up on the Companies House website. Not entirely to Kelly's surprise, the directors of five of the six firms were Lorna and her partner. Kelly downloaded the details onto her flash drive and closed her laptop with quiet satisfaction.

❄

The cumulative impact of Sally's efforts had taken its toll. Kelly was jumpy, more aggressive than usual, and prone to making irrational decisions without thinking through the consequences. She was beginning to feel that someone was targeting her. But who? She knew that everyone she supervised, apart from mousy Sally, hated her, but she had them under control. They were too spineless to plot against her. Perhaps she'd ask Sally to keep her ears open, just in case. But could it be Lorna? Kelly knew she was still furious about the incident at the Christmas dinner. Perhaps she hated her personally as well as picking on her professionally.

Kelly was barely sleeping. Her clothes didn't fit properly, because of her overconsumption of wine and chocolate, and were frequently creased and stained. Her mouth often ran away with her and she was heard to refer to the staff she supervised as 'a load of workshy snowflakes'. Unfortunately for her, this outburst happened at a multi-agency meeting, so the damage couldn't be contained within the company. Belatedly realising what she had done, Kelly rushed out of the room. She went home and stayed there for three days without formally requesting leave, unable to face the atmosphere at work. Misconduct, in the eyes of Lorna, for which she would have to pay.

When Kelly returned to work, she had come prepared. Lorna summoned Kelly into her office as soon as she entered the building, her face ablaze, and Kelly was delighted to see how upset Lorna was. She smiled to herself.

'Have you any idea what you've done, you crazy bitch?' Lorna shouted. 'You've brought the company into disrepute with your stupid remark and the staff are threatening to make a formal complaint. I've told them that managers are not to be criticised, but they've got the union involved and they won't be so easy to scare off. There's now a question mark over our funding next year and you've put all our jobs at risk. Your performance over the past few months has been erratic, to say the least. You frequently look scruffy and I've smelt alcohol on your breath on occasions. The sex scandal has been an embarrassment, you've taken leave without permission and your behaviour at the Christmas meal was appalling. Do you seriously think you can continue working here?'

'Do you?' replied Kelly, a malicious smile on her face.

Lorna started.

'What the hell do you mean?'

'I mean I have information on you which could get you dismissed, prosecuted for fraud and maybe even charged with tax evasion.'

'Rubbish,' said Lorna, a faint note of uncertainty creeping into her voice.

'I know about the company car you provided for your son – and the inflated salary you paid him. You've been feathering your own nest by sending work to your own companies, I suspect at inflated prices. I have copies of your expenses claims which I'm sure the tax people would be interested in seeing. I also know you've been shagging Dave – on the company time – and I'm sure your partner would be interested in the recording I made. Also, I've listed those plans with the phoney deadlines and that would make interesting reading for someone. It's all on a flash drive and I'm hanging onto it as insurance. Perhaps we can talk about a salary increase when you've calmed down?'

'You blackmailing bitch. Get out of my office!' raved Lorna, unable to think of a suitable response.

Kelly left quietly, leaving Lorna to reflect on her uncertain future with the company and the threat to her family. The other staff in the office were agog. Although they couldn't hear what was said, they formed the distinct impression that Kelly was on the way out. Raised voices in Lorna's office usually meant only one thing. A firing. Surreptitious glee permeated the office for the rest of the day.

LORNA

For the first time in her career, Lorna felt threatened. She was used to getting her own way, either by bullying or by turning on an oily charm which, along with her blonde hair and short skirts, proved irresistible to a certain type of man. She knew she could avoid trouble with the tax office, by declaring her travel expenses from home to work and paying the tax due. But the business of the car, her companies and Justin's salary would not go away so easily. At best, she would lose her job. At worst, she could face prosecution. If her dalliance with Dave came out it would wreck her family and she had no doubt that Kelly would find a way of publicising it over the Internet or in the press.

Firstly, she would consult her solicitor. Then she would devise a way of dealing with the upstart Kelly, who had the temerity to threaten her. She had worked and schemed so hard to get where she was and the idea of losing it all was completely unacceptable. A desperate situation called for desperate measures and Lorna's judgement flew out of the window. Increasingly, she felt as though she was stumbling down a corridor with only one way out. And the walls were closing in.

Just before midnight, Lorna parked her car a couple of hundred metres from her target and walked briskly along the street, with a cap and scarf hiding her features and a can of petrol in her hand. A splash of liquid through the letter box, a petrol-soaked rag and a lighter was all it took. Shadowed by the growing flames behind her, the expression of triumph on her face was invisible. Her heart lifted, but something inside her whispered that she had been appallingly stupid.

KELLY

Kelly shuffled out of the bathroom heading for bed, the combined effects of antidepressants and a half-bottle of wine tangling her feet beneath her. She thought she heard a clattering at the front door but couldn't be bothered to drag herself downstairs to investigate. Anyway, she knew it was locked. A few minutes later, she smelled smoke and lurched towards the bedroom door. She managed to get it open and a thick cloud of hot smoke poured into the room. Coughing and disorientated, she staggered to the window and opened it in a desperate attempt to call for help. Acting like a chimney, the open window only made the fire worse, drawing flames and more smoke up the stairs. But Kelly never felt the flames. Toxic gases from burning carpets and furniture stopped her heart long before flames started licking around her body.

SALLY

When Sally came into work the following morning, she was surprised to find that Kelly wasn't at her desk. She was normally in before anyone else. Instead, someone had taped a sheet of paper across her computer screen bearing the message 'GAL 6:7'. This meant nothing to most people – apart from the person who had put it there.

By lunchtime, Kelly had still not appeared. Lorna had come in late and locked herself in her office, looking unusually haggard. With the two tyrants effectively absent, the atmosphere in the office was lighter than usual. One or two people even made jokes over lunch, in the cramped staff room. A few drank coffee at their desks, something Lorna had banned because she said it looked untidy. This all changed mid-afternoon when a police car pulled up outside and three plain clothes officers got out. After talking briefly with Lorna, one of them came into the open-plan area and asked for everyone's attention.

'Good afternoon, ladies and gentlemen. I'm Detective Sergeant Mike Fellowes and I'm afraid I have some bad news for you. Your colleague, Kelly Thornbury, was involved in a house fire last night. Sadly, she didn't survive. I'm sorry to say that the fire service suspects that the blaze was started deliberately. We are awaiting confirmation from the fire investigator, but we have to treat her death as suspicious.'

When the murmurs of shock and incredulity had subsided, he continued.

'We would like to talk to all of you about Kelly. Ms Brake has made the staff room and the meeting areas upstairs available to us. We'll call you up when we are ready and we'll be as quick as we can. Please don't talk to anyone else about this. Thank you.'

After briefly examining Kelly's desk, and removing the note from her screen, Mike conferred with his colleagues and the interviews began. Mike took Lorna and the other managers initially, while his two Detective Constables started on the rest of the staff.

Sally felt a sinking feeling in her stomach, fearful that her actions against Kelly would come to light. She had been very careful to cover her tracks but realised that at least some of them could be discovered, under the spotlight of a murder investigation. Giving Kelly the Antabuse was tantamount to poisoning her, although it did no permanent damage to her health. Perhaps her purchase could be traced? She was confident that the speeding ticket and Nigerian prince ploys wouldn't be discovered but was she on CCTV somewhere, putting up the business cards? She wouldn't be able to conceal her feelings about her tormentor. She may even be suspected of killing Kelly. Could she be in some way responsible, as a result of her actions? No, that was preposterous. She knew her colleagues would approach the interviews with either nervousness or indifference, unsure as to how much they should say about Kelly and her management style. But unlike Sally, they had no guilty secrets to conceal.

POLICE

Interviews completed, the police officers returned to the station to compare notes. Mike kicked off, with an air of puzzlement.

'I'm getting two completely different pictures of the company,' he said. 'According to Lorna Brake they are all a happy family and staff welfare is a primary concern. The other managers said something similar, although not so enthusiastically. But the rest of the staff I spoke to complained of bullying by management, petty rules and impossible workloads. No-one had a good word to say about Kelly, or Lorna for that matter.'

'That's what I found,' reported DC Mellors. 'This was one unhappy ship. Several people had left in recent months, because of management attitudes, and a couple I spoke to were on anti-depressants. I also had accounts of a row between Kelly and Lorna recently. No-one heard what was said, but they got the impression that Kelly was being fired.'

DC Porter nodded her agreement.

'That's odd,' mused Mike. 'Lorna didn't mention that. She said that Kelly was a valued member of the company but she was becoming concerned about her mental health. She advised Kelly to take some sick leave until she felt more able to cope. Did either of you come across anyone who could hate Kelly enough to kill her?'

'Not from what anyone said,' replied DC Porter, 'But Sally Dawson was clearly hiding something, judging by her body language. She fidgeted a lot during the interview and couldn't conceal her dislike of Kelly.'

'Did anyone explain this note on Kelly's computer? What the hell does GAL 6:7 mean?'

'Katy Maguire admitted putting it there. It's a reference to the Bible. Galatians Chapter 6, verse 7.'

'Meaning what?'

'The relevant part of it runs "whatever a man soweth, that shall he also reap".'

'Lou Reed put it better in *Perfect Day*,' muttered DC Mellors, but the others ignored him.

'Did Katy explain why? Could it mean that she knew Kelly was going to die? Did she have something to do with her murder?'

'I don't think so. She was mortified. She thought Kelly was going to be fired and couldn't resist a reference to divine justice. She's a devout Christian. Lorna forced her to lie over some deadline or other, but I don't see her as a killer.'

'Right. I think we need another chat with Sally Dawson and also with Lorna. Both of them are misleading us and I want to know why. I'll speak to them tomorrow.'

KATY

While the detectives were comparing notes, Katy was clearing Kelly's desk and packing up her personal effects. She noticed that the drawer had been forced open and the filing tray was in disarray. Assuming that the police were responsible, she continued with her task.

There was very little on the top of the desk – company policy forbade clutter – but there were a few items in the drawer. A box of tea bags, a packet of tissues and a personalised coffee mug all went into a cardboard box. When Katy picked up a pair of thin gloves, she noticed a lump inside one of them. Intrigued, she turned the glove inside out and a small silvery object fell on to the desk. It was Kelly's flash drive.

'Give me that,' a voice behind her snarled.

Katy turned round to see Lorna, white-faced and clutching a pair of scissors.

'What?'

'I said give me that.'

'But it was Kelly's.'

'No, it's company property. Give it to me or you'll regret it.'

'It not the sort we use. It was Kelly's. Why do you want it?'

Lorna gripped the scissors tightly, her knuckles whitening.

'Never you mind. I need it now or...'

'What are you doing Lorna?' interrupted Sally, who had heard the argument from the main office.

'Just reclaiming company property.'

'No, you're not. It was Kelly's. I heard what Katy said. What's on it that's so important to you?'

'Confidential company information. None of your business.'

'But we never put confidential information on a flash drive unless it's an encrypted Ironkey. You're lying.'

'How dare you. You're sacked, the pair of you.'

LORNA

Realising that she wouldn't be able to snatch the flash drive, Lorna fled the office, ran to her car and screeched out of the car park. She had to get away and think. For the first time in her adult life, she didn't know what to do and the thought made her sick. She had failed to find the flash drive, after she forced Kelly's desk drawer and, when she saw Katy holding it, her world collapsed around her.

Sitting in her kitchen, a large glass of gin in front of her, she reviewed her options. That bloody Katy would certainly have passed the flash drive on to the police by now and told them how she had been threatened. The evidence it contained could be damning but was Kelly bluffing? She didn't think so. She knew, from the way Kelly had handled the people she supervised, that she was both efficient and ruthless.

Maybe she could stay and brazen it out. She had no problem with lying to the police. She was skilled at dishonesty. Perhaps a short skirt and low neckline would distract DS Fellowes? No, that was nonsense. He was clearly a professional. If he had his suspicions, she was sure he would investigate.

Lorna was confident she wouldn't be suspected of Kelly's murder. She hadn't woken her family when she slipped out in the night and no-one had seen her when she poured the petrol through the letterbox. She had dumped the petrol can and her gloves in a skip on the way home. Again, her thoughts returned to the evidence Kelly had collected.

There was no denying she could be facing ruin and, possibly, prison. She knew they were bound to catch up with her sooner or later. If she was going to jail she would damn well make the most of her freedom before they arrested her. One last taste of the lifestyle she had enjoyed for the past few years. Paris? Rome? Rio? Wherever she could fly to from the local airport. After a frantic search for flights, she bought a ticket to Corfu, thinking she could lose herself among the Greek Islands for a few weeks.

She packed a few items of clothing, grabbed her passport and cash, and set off, telling her family that she was travelling on business. She realised that it would all be waiting for her when she got back, but at least they wouldn't be after her for murder. She would make her peace with her family later.

SALLY

Mike Fellowes had left his business cards with all the staff in case they thought of anything relevant. After they had calmed down a little, Sally and Katy agreed that they should call him.

'But it's our word against Lorna's,' protested Katy. 'And she's got more authority.'

'Not entirely,' replied Sally. 'I set my phone to record as soon as I heard her shouting. I thought something odd was going on. I didn't get everything but the recording starts with her apparently threatening you.'

They caught Mike in his office, as he finished writing up his notes on the interviews. As soon as they played the recording down the phone, he dispatched a couple of uniformed officers to pick up Lorna for questioning.

'That's very interesting,' he said, 'But it doesn't prove anything. Please don't plug the flash drive in, or tamper with it in any way, or you'll devalue it as evidence. I'm very keen to find out why it was so important. I know it's getting late but can you wait there until one of our forensic IT people collects it? And I'd like to speak to you both tomorrow morning.'

Katy and Sally agreed to wait and arranged to call in to the police station the following day, with some trepidation on Sally's part as she still feared that her campaign of revenge had been discovered.

Mike shook hands with them when they arrived at the station's front desk.

'Katy, could you give DC Porter a statement about what happened, please? I think you met her yesterday. Sally, come with me if you would. I need to take your phone. You'll get it back once we've copied the audio file.'

Sally followed Mike, dreading an interrogation, but the interview was painless with no mention of anything she had done. Once she had signed her statement, Mike spoke to her.

'You and Katy may need to give evidence in court about this. Will that worry you?'

'Court?' said Sally, astonished.

'Yes. Please don't mention this to anyone, until we have issued a press statement, but Lorna has been charged with arson and Kelly's manslaughter. It may even end up as a murder charge. I can't give you any more details I'm afraid, but we'll let you know if you are needed. Oh, before you go, can you clear up something for me?'

Sally's blood froze.

'Of course. If I can. What is it?'

'DC Porter had the strong impression that you were hiding something. It was also clear that you hated Kelly, more than the other people she spoke to. Care to explain?'

Sally wondered what she could hold back. She had to give him something. But how much? She decided to tell part of the truth.

'I did hate Kelly. The way she treated me was awful. In fact, I tried to commit suicide last year because of her. If it wasn't for my partner and the NHS, I wouldn't be here. I didn't say anything to DC Porter, in case she thought I was involved in Kelly's death.'

Mike seemed satisfied. He murmured a few words of sympathy and showed Sally to the door. She kept her fingers crossed, dreading a Columbo moment, until she joined Katy in the foyer.

POLICE

As the two women left the station, Mike gave a verbal report to his boss, Detective Inspector Harris.

'Lorna had left home by the time the PCs arrived to collect her. A neighbour told them that he'd seen her driving off in a hurry, with a suitcase in her car. Her partner said she had to make a business trip, but her briefcase was still in the hall. We put out an alert, and the car was spotted driving into the car park at East Midlands Airport. The airport police picked Lorna up in the departure lounge, on her way to Corfu. Her car boot smelled of petrol, even though it was a diesel vehicle. The tech guys interrogated the satnav and she was in Kelly's street the previous night. This was enough to hold her and, when the IT team looked at the flash drive, they found a load of stuff indicating that Lorna had been defrauding the company, dodging tax and behaving unprofessionally.'

'So, Kelly was blackmailing her?'

'It seems so. We've got motive for murder, means and opportunity, but no confession so far.'

'It's all circumstantial, though.'

'Yes, but once we show her what the flash drive contains, and the satnav data, she'll crack.'

'A nice collar, Mike. Well done!'

Mike grinned as he left the DI's office and then turned his attention to a problem handed to him by the neighbourhood policing team. Someone had been posting a sex worker's business cards around the town and people were complaining. The name on the cards was common enough, but he couldn't help thinking there was something familiar about the phone number.

PEPPERMINT CREAMS ON CHRISTMAS EVE

S.E. SHEPHERD

1891

I LOVE BEING IN THE PARLOUR WITH MY MOTHER. WE play card games.

'Just the ladies,' my mother says.

Of course, I wish Father was here with us. But I know that is not possible, and so does she, that is why she says it.

My father is in The Marlborough Arms. He is always in a public house these days. I heard someone in our street remark that he is lost. But I think he has every right to be. Lost is not dead. Lost is lost. He can be found. None of us are how we should be, or how we were.

This is our first Christmas without Albie. Always a delicate boy, my little brother succumbed to pneumonia last January, and he is never far from my thoughts. I know that my mother is trying her hardest to put joy into our card games. She does so to make me as happy as is possible right now. I am doing the same for her. We sit by the fire. It is so warm I can feel my face glowing. But step away from the flames and the draft of the room hits you. So here we sit, either too hot or too cold, and just occasionally we are about right.

When we have played several rounds of Hearts, winning and losing in equal measure, and I have gone on to be stuck with the old maid as a conclusion to all four rounds we have played of that game, my mother suggests it is my bedtime. I plead for just one more game. Searching the card drawer, I find a few hand-drawn cards at the back. Pulling them out, I ask my mother to explain the origin of these cards, and she says that she drew them herself when she was a young woman, not much older than I am now.

The backs of the cards are entirely black. I have never seen these cards before. Turning them over, my mother shows me their fronts. They boast beautiful, intricate black-and-white illustrations. She is a talented artist. I compliment her, and she thanks me.

I ask if we can play with them. Mother explains that there is no game to be played, they are simply art.

'That is a shame. I would love us to play a game with them,' I say.

'They are just for looking at,' my mother replies.

'Perhaps we could tell a story with them,' I suggest.

My mother considers my proposal carefully, then she says, 'That is a nice idea, Emily. I have not done that before. What kind of story shall we tell?'

I know the answer. 'A scary story,' I say.

Dropping her voice to a theatrical whisper, my mother says, 'All right. You are twelve now. I think you are old enough to tell such a story.'

I am scared, but excited. My heart fluttering in my chest, I move closer to the table.

'I think you will enjoy telling this story more than getting stuck with the Old Maid.' My mother smiles, warmly. 'Even if it will be a little frightening.'

I silently nod. Admitting only to myself that the reason I want to be frightened is because I want to feel something, anything other than the grief and loss I have felt for months.

My mother says, 'Right, I think first, we must choose a place.'

'A place?'

'Yes, Emily. Let us make it a place where a murder will occur.'

I shiver.

Picking up the pack, my mother selects three cards, and sets them face up on the table. There is an illustration on each. My choices are, one – a large gothic house, it is grand, about the size of our whole street, and it is almost certainly haunted, two – a small, terraced house, not dissimilar to our own humble home, there is a light on inside, this house is friendly, and three – a tall thin building with many windows, this building appears to reach for the sky. I choose the third. I have never before seen such a building. I point to one of the windows at the very top. I say, 'That is the place I choose.' I wonder to myself how a person could ever climb that many stairs.

My mother puts her finger on the card and slides it slowly and dramatically across the table towards me. She tells me to put it at the top of the table.

Next, she places three more cards with equally intricate drawings on the table. This time the illustrations are of people. Still using her theatrical whisper, my mother says, 'Who shall we choose to be murdered?'

I survey the cards laid out before me. There is a small boy, I believe he is a chimney sweep. I immediately disregard him. How could I choose a boy to be my victim so soon after losing Albie? My mother follows my gaze, she sees my eyes glide straight over the picture of the chimney sweep. Clearly under-standing and agreeing with my thought process, she nods. Her nod says – no, not the little boy. She indicates my two remaining choices. A distinguished older man in formal dress, his white hair escaping in places from beneath a top hat. He is facing to the left, looking off into the distance. I consider him for a moment, and then, on a whim, I choose the third option, a young woman, her dark hair is not tied neatly as mine and my mother's is, instead hers flows freely around her head. She wears a mournful expression.

My mother asks, 'What will you call her?'

I choose her name, 'She is Sarah.'

2021

Jack would describe himself as a career thief. If questioned, he would not be able to remember a time when he had made an 'honest' living. At the ripe old age of 66, he is unlikely to start now. Tonight, he decided to begin his burglaries by breaking into the flats on the top floor. He will work his way down, get those bloody stairs out of the way first. His knees are not good.

The first thing Jack notices is that this flat is not in the least bit Christmassy. Most places he breaks into on Christmas Eve at least have a crappy little artificial tree in the corner of the lounge. Jack is looking for cash, jewellery, or electronic items. In the old days he would steal TVs and video players, his back is still bad from all the lifting, not to mention too many nights spent sleeping on thin, hard mattresses. In the kitchen, Jack finds an iPad and some money; they go in his bag. Then he finds a small, cubed present, wrapped in gold paper with a red velvet bow. The present has a label saying, 'To mum, love from Sarah.' The only other Christmassy item in the room is a red envelope with the word 'Mum' written on the front, and a sprig of holly clumsily drawn in the corner in black biro, it lays next to the present. Jack isn't to know that this is the first Christmas that the words 'and Dad' are missing from the envelope. Just one of so many victims of COVID the previous January.

Ideally, Jack is searching for a phone. Phones are the best source of money these days. The easiest thing to sell. Everyone has an iPhone or a Samsung, some sort of smart phone. Jack knows that you just have to find them. But people will insist on sleeping with them next to their bed. He decides to leave the bedroom until last. He doesn't want to wake the occupant, who is, judging by the flat, clearly female. Just in case he does wake her, he always carries a weapon to warn people off. He checks in his pocket and feels the small hard object – a flick knife.

All of a sudden, Jack smells peppermint, a strong burst of it. He looks around, expecting to see a plug-in air freshener, one of those ones that spurts out an artificial smell every few minutes. Jack is not a fan of those bloody things.

1891

Mother has made peppermint creams. So sweet and pepperminty. They are really for tomorrow, but she says seeing as we are telling a story, we can have some tonight. As I help myself to the first one, my mouth is filled with a gooey sweetness, my nose flooded with the smell.

Mother asks me to choose a weapon. She places before me three more cards. I choose the dagger. Drawn with such precision, it has a beautiful decorative handle.

'That was quick. You are sure?' Mother asks.

'Yes.' I nod.

With her delicate index finger, she pushes the card towards me, and it joins the tall building and the young woman at the top of the table.

I place another peppermint cream into my mouth and feel the sugar begin to melt.

2021

Jack smells another burst of peppermint. He thinks to himself that if he could locate the damn plug-in, he would switch it off. He finds the smell slightly nauseating. He places the Christmas present in his bag. He'll open it later. 'It will be like Christmas Day,' he chuckles. Jack has not had a gift at Christmas for many years. His early Christmastimes were spent in care, and most of the latter ones were spent at her Majesty's pleasure. The few he did celebrate as a free man were lonely and unceremonious.

Jack takes a small bottle of hair oil out of his bag and oils the hinges on the bedroom door. This is a trick he learnt many years ago. Jack knows that there is every possibility that there could be someone asleep in there. He knows it is never a good idea to give the occupant the heads up that he is coming in. He opens the door without a sound and creeps into the room. Once his eyes adjust, Jack sees a young woman asleep in the bed, her thick, dark hair is splayed out across the pillow.

1891

Mother says that now we must choose a time for the murder. She translates the pictures on the cards for me; midmorning on an autumn day, such a beautiful illustration of an oak tree losing its leaves, or lunchtime in summer, a drawing of a picnic basket laid on the grass. I look at the third card. It's an obvious choice. The card shows a clockface displaying one minute after twelve, the moon shining in through the window behind tells me it is midnight and not mid-day. Judging by the holly and ivy around the clock it clearly depicts Christmas Eve. I choose it. My mother pushes it up the table, towards my other choices.

I reach for another peppermint cream, and my mother tells me to take it slowly with the sweets.

2021

Another thing that Jack doesn't know is that Sarah's dad always woke her at midnight on Christmas Eve to tell her it was finally Christmas. When she was little, he would tell her that Father Christmas had been and that there were presents downstairs. Sarah loved that moment. For her it meant that Christmas Day had finally begun. In later years, no matter where she was, out in a pub, with a boyfriend, clubbing with friends, her dad would ring her at midnight on Christmas Eve and tell her that Christmas had begun. It was a standing joke between them, a ritual.

This year, knowing it was her first without her beloved dad, Sarah set an alarm on her phone. She didn't want to miss midnight. Having spent a solitary evening in front of the television, Sarah had gone to bed at about 10.30pm. Tomorrow she plans to get together with her mum for a modest celebration. But both have agreed it will not be the same, one present only, a small special meal and a glass raised to Sarah's dad. Sarah allowed herself to fall asleep, safe in the knowledge that her phone would tell her when it was Christmas Day, as her dad no longer could.

As Jack reaches for the phone, the alarm begins to sound and Sarah's eyes open. Also reaching for it, Sarah gets there first and hits the stop button. Only then does she realise that she is not alone in the room. An elderly man stands no more than a foot from her bed. He is dressed from head to toe in black. Sarah thinks she must be dreaming. Dreaming of Christmases past, perhaps. But this man is far from Santa.

Jack says in a gruff voice, 'Don't make a sound or I'll stab ya.'

Sarah's mouth is wide open. She is about to scream, when, by the light of her phone, she sees the glint of Jack's knife.

The bedroom is suddenly filled with the smell of peppermint, and Jack wonders why anyone would have those awful air fresheners in more than one room.

1891

As I place yet another peppermint cream into my mouth, I know that I have eaten too many, and eating them so close together was not only greedy, but reckless. A wave of sickness forces me away from the fire and sends me flying toward the back door. Once out in the backyard, the coolness helps. It feels like there is snow in the air, waiting to fall, my nausea passes a little and I realise that I am now, in fact, freezing. I decide to return to the comfort of the fire.

Back inside, I see that the draft I created when I opened the back door has blown the cards around the table and onto the floor.

Three of my choices remain on the table. I push those cards back up to the top. But I cannot find the dagger. Mother and I search. I wonder if it has been blown into the fire. Such a shame – it was a beautiful drawing. Mother tells me not to worry and to choose a different weapon. This time I go for the brass candlestick and push it to the top of the table.

Together my mother and I examine my choices. Both in our most eery voices, we talk about the strange tall building with many floors, the sad young woman named Sarah, who has flowing hair, the beautiful brass candlestick, and, lastly, the time – a minute past midnight on Christmas Eve.

'I suppose we have our story,' my mother says.

'What happens now?' I ask.

'I expect the murder will take place,' she replies with an amused smile.

We laugh, because we know it is only a story.

My mother says I really must go to bed now. I agree, because I am still feeling a little queasy from all the peppermint creams.

As I rise to leave the table, I glance back, and have one last thought. 'Can I save her?' I ask. 'The young woman. Do you think I can I save Sarah?'

Playing along, my mother says 'Yes, I think you are just in time, but I imagine you will have to put someone else in her place.'

Not the boy, never the boy. I push the card displaying the distinguished gentleman to the top of the table. I swap him with Sarah. Now I look at him again, he is not as distinguished as I first thought.

'What will you call our new victim?' My mother asks.

'Jack.' I reply.

2021

Sarah dials 999. She says, 'Please send the police there is an intruder in my bedroom.' She gives her address and explains that the lift is not working, they will have to use the stairs. She says that the intruder has a knife.

'Is he still there?' asks the 999 operator.

'Yes.'

'Are you still in danger?'

'I don't think so.' From her position in the bed, Sarah looks down at the man lying on her bedroom floor. A large pool of blood is appearing on the beige carpet. The intruder has a gaping wound on his right temple. Sarah has never seen so much blood. Next to the intruder, on the floor, lies her bedside lamp. Pulled from its socket. It's a long, thin, brass monstrosity that used to live in her dad's office, and which he always said must go to Sarah after his death. The base of the lamp is square, also made of brass, and, as it turns out, extremely heavy. It was simply the first thing she saw, and thus what she reached for when she let out her scream as the intruder took a step towards her, his knife leading the way. It had been purely instinct to hit him. She had only meant to get him away from her. But at the moment one of the corners of the heavy brass base had made contact with his skull, he had dropped like a stone.

He now lay still. His eyes open. Sarah watched as they slowly clouded over. A moment later he gazed sightlessly up at her.

'Do you need an ambulance as well as the police?' The 999 operator asks.

'For me? No.' Sarah shakes her head. She whispers, 'I hit him – he's on the floor.'

'Does *he* need an ambulance then?'

'I don't think it will help.' With a rising sickness, Sarah realises the awful truth, 'I think he's dead.'

The time on Sarah's phone changes to 12.02am.

1891

I sneak downstairs just after midnight. My father has clearly returned from his drinking. He and my mother have retired to bed. The cards are still out. They lay jumbled on the table. Perhaps my father looked at them whilst intoxicated. I examine the white-haired man. He appears even more dishevelled than before. His face, that had at first been turned to the left, now looks forward, and his eyes have a dead stare. The young woman in the picture has changed as well. She seems a little less sad, and behind her I can make out the faintest shadow of a kind older gentleman. I'm pleased for the unknown woman who lives in the tall thin building. Pleased that she has a protector.

Before I leave, I pick up the chimney sweep card. I kiss the little boy's sweet face. 'It's Christmas Day, Albie.' I say. I carry the card of the small boy back up to bed with me.

THE LONG WAIT

KERENA SWAN

LAUREN STOOD BEHIND THE BEDROOM DOOR, EVERY muscle tensed to remain perfectly still, taking silent, shallow breaths. Not easy when her heart clattered in her ribcage like an over-filled washing machine. She heard a light footfall on the stairs and stopped breathing altogether. He was getting closer. Would the light she'd left on in the bathroom, with the door an inch ajar and the tap running, be enough to fool him?

The footsteps carried on along the landing towards the bedroom. A floorboard creaked under his weight and Lauren's stomach lurched. Any second now...

'Raah!'

Nick threw his arms in the air and backed away in shock as Lauren collapsed in a heap of giggles at his feet.

'You absolute knob,' Nick said, shaking his head. 'I'll get you for this.'

'What do you mean? You started it.'

Nick raised his eyebrows.

'You did! Watching that creepy film the other night, remember?'

'I only grabbed your arm,' he protested.

'Still scared the shit out of me.'

Nick grinned and walked to the bathroom. 'I will get you back for this,' he called over his shoulder.

That night, as they cuddled up in Nick's large and luxurious bed, Lauren closed her eyes and let her mind meander into snatches of dreams.

'I'm definitely going to get you back,' Nick hissed in her ear, jolting her awake. His breath was warm and damp on her cheek.

'Promise me you won't come to my cottage late at night and frighten me,' she muttered. 'It's bad enough living next door to Creepy Pete.'

'Creepy Pete?' Nick laughed. 'Why do you call him that?'

'I don't know. He just freaks me out.' Laura thought about it. He was always scrupulously polite and helpful but perhaps his eye contact lasted a little too long. 'Maybe he stands too close and invades my personal space,' she said.

'Maybe you're paranoid. Besides, I'm not promising anything.'

That was it then. Lauren would have to make sure the door to her thatched cottage was always locked from now on. People in her quiet village rarely locked their doors but she couldn't cope with not knowing whether Nick was in the house, ready to leap out at her to get his revenge.

A week later, with her feet curled underneath her and soft cushions at her back, Lauren sat transfixed by a scary psychological drama on the television. She was clutching a cushion to her chest ready to hide behind it when she heard scratching on the window. Startled, she looked up to see a white face looming out of the shadows and pressing against the glass.

'Jesus Christ!' Lauren's whole body jumped and she shot off the sofa.

Nick's delighted laughter could be heard clearly through the thick old glass and poorly fitting frames. Lauren ran to the kitchen, undid the bolt, and pulled open the back door. 'I told you not to frighten me here, you rotten bastard.' She punched him lightly on the shoulder. 'Are we quits now?'

'Hmmm. Maybe. Maybe not. Will a bottle of wine help you overcome your trauma?' He waved a bottle of Sauvignon Blanc in the air then squeezed past her into the kitchen. He took two large wine glasses from the cupboard and poured them both a generous measure.

'Only if you've got some olives to go with it,' she said, sulkily.

'Ta da!' Nick reached into his jacket pocket and pulled out a foil pack of nocellara olives.

'You know me too well,' she grinned, kissing his cheek. 'I still don't forgive you though.'

'Can we get the Christmas tree up?' she asked, a few days later. 'It's so dark and dingy this time of year.'

'Isn't it a bit early? All the needles will fall off before Christmas Day.'

Lauren loved that they had been out together the week before to choose a tree for their first Christmas together. They'd agreed to celebrate it at Lauren's thatched and beamed cottage because she had the cosy log-burner, a bigger oven for the turkey and a box of decorations in the shed.

'It's a non-drop one, remember?' Lauren said. 'You bring the tree in and fetch the decs from the shed while I pop round to Sue's. She bought some new lights for me today while she was in town.'

Nick reluctantly went outside while Lauren hurried down the path, keeping a watchful eye on the neighbouring garden to avoid talking to creepy Pete. As Nick hauled the netted tree into the cottage, she quickly ran back to the shed. This was going to be a good one. She stood behind the door, brushing a cobweb from her shoulder and glad that spiders held no fear for her. She had to bite her lip to suppress the giggle that threatened to erupt. As he opened the door she leapt out with a yell.

'You stupid woman!' Nick was white-faced in the gloom. 'I thought we were quits now?' He shook his head. 'You've just made a big mistake. A very big mistake,' he muttered as he stomped back down the path.

Back at Nick's house the following Tuesday evening, Lauren left him sitting on the sofa and went upstairs to the bathroom but when she returned he wasn't there. She poked her head into the kitchen but it was empty. As she crossed the lounge to take her seat he leapt up from behind the end of the sofa.

'Boo!' he said.

'Is that it? You didn't make me jump at all.' She laughed and threw herself onto the sofa. 'You need to try harder than that.' As soon as the words left her mouth she regretted it. What a stupid thing to say. She'd need to be extra vigilant now. Nick always wanted to be one step ahead.

It was dark when he crept around the cottage to Lauren's back door on Thursday. He lifted large flowerpots on the ledge near the door and ran his hand underneath each one. Brushing aside soil and crunchy old leaves his fingers soon found the hard metal loop of a key fob. He knew she left a key here for the cleaner once a week so she could let herself in. He unlocked the door, replaced the key under the pot then slipped inside. Lauren would be home from the gym soon so he needed to get everything prepared. Two minutes later he lay stretched out under her bed, a drink and sandwich next to him to keep him going until she came upstairs to bed and his phone on silent but ready to play the recording he'd made earlier.

For three hours he lay listening to the muffled sounds of the television through the floor, smelt the delicious aroma of hot butter and onions drifting up the stairs as she cooked her evening meal and finally heard her clean her teeth in the bathroom. The floor was hard and his back ached but he could barely contain his excitement as he thought of her reaction when she realised he was there.

The bed springs squeaked as she sat on the edge to nudge off her sheepskin mules and he couldn't help admiring her slim ankles. As she lay down and shifted into a comfortable position, the mattress bulged inches from his face.

He waited.

Eventually he heard the click of the light and the room went black. He'd just give her a few minutes to drift off to sleep before switching on his phone.

The voice on the recording was perfect. Low and gravelly. It started quietly at first, a murmur, a hiss, a growl.

'Who's there?' Lauren's voice was high-pitched and laced with fear. 'Nick, this is too much. You've gone too far now. I told you I needed an early night.' A click then light filled the room.

The voice grew louder. 'I'm going to cut off all your pretty hair and keep it.'

'Nick. Nick? Come out. I know you're under the bed.'

Lauren lowered her feet to the floor. He reached out and grasped her ankle. She screamed.

'You bastard! Get off. I'm never speaking to you again.' She tried to pull her foot away then her phone rang.

'Hi sweetheart, I can't sleep. I know it's late and you've got a big meeting tomorrow but can I come over?'

Pete slid out from under the bed, a handful of tie-wraps and a cloth gag in his hand. He snatched the phone and cut the call from her boyfriend.

He'd waited a long time for this.

THE DISAPPEARANCE OF KRISHNA'S EYE

MARK WIGHTMAN

TRANSLATOR'S NOTES

FOR MANY YEARS I HAVE BEEN AN AVID READER OF THE adventures of the great French detective Auguste Robillard, and I have always felt it to be the British public's loss that he was far better appreciated in his own country than in this. Perhaps that is partly because the published version of his casebook ended both suddenly and without any natural conclusion. For Robillard, there was no Reichenbach Falls, no return to Styles. He simply disappeared off the face of the literary map, and this may well have affected his popularity on this side of the channel.

Another factor may have been that Robillard's casebook was recorded and published anonymously and to this day we only know of his chronicler as '*un observateur*'. To draw an obvious parallel, this observer was to Robillard as Watson was to Holmes, or Hastings was to Poirot, but there are few clues to his real identity. There have been numerous theories, of course. Prior to the acclaimed detective's untimely disappearance, it became popular to credit the writings to His Excellency, the Comte de Pueyreddon. It is true that Robillard and the Comte were friends, even, some have suggested, intimates, but their supposed literary association owes more, I believe, to gossip than to fact. For one thing, the Comte's own diaries show that he spent most of his time in Deauville, travelling to Paris only during the season. It is therefore unlikely that he could have observed at first hand the full gamut of Robillard's case history.

Later, it became fashionable to claim the observer was Pierre-Louis Tasse, the fêted Parisian novelist and playwright. Again, there was ample evidence the two men spent time together and attended all manner of social occasions in each other's company. Indeed, one of Tasse's biographers suggested they may have shared lodgings for a time in a house on the Place de l'Odéon, owned by one of Tasse's patrons, Lady Forthright, though the evidence for that is suspect at best. Most tellingly, the style in which Robillard's adventures were documented is so obviously different from Tasse's opaque and abstruse prose that it is highly unlikely that he can have been Robillard's annalist, delicious though the idea might be.

Over the years, it has even been suggested, albeit in whispered tones, that the observer was none other than Robillard himself. I hope you will join me in giving that idea the short shrift it deserves.

From the extant published works, collectively known as *Les Écrits*, we can follow the meteoric career of the man who defied the impoverished circumstances of his upbringing to become the finest, most brilliant detective of his or any other time. It is probably true that Robillard's star reached its zenith about the time of the *Affair of Catherine the Great's Music Box*, for which he received the profound thanks of a certain noble St Petersburg family which cannot, for reasons that should remain obvious, be named here. We know also that following that success, Robillard's career waned. The practice of employing private detectives, always frowned upon by the official form of the species, seemed to become simply less fashionable, and we know from

Les Écrits that he was forced to turn his talents to increasingly mundane matters until eventually, in the autumn of 1925, when Robillard must have been in his sixties, his companion stopped writing the stories which had captivated so many, and no more was heard of about the man whom Sherlock Holmes himself described as "the detective's detective".

Until now.

As well as being a keen reader of the mysteries, I have assembled a modest collection of Robillardalia, and I am always on the lookout for possible additions. To that end, I recently attended a used book fair in Edinburgh, half-looking, as always, for unusual or rare artefacts. This is nothing but an amusement to me – I never expect anything serious to come onto the market in this way, but I have managed over the years to acquire among other things a copy of a 1950s anthology which, while common enough in itself, contained a rare, misprinted flyleaf, spelling Robillard's name as *Robellarde*, as well as several original pamphlets dating from the time when *Les Écrits* was serialised in *Paris Soir*.

I happened to stop at the stall of a bookseller from whom I have purchased previously. After rummaging around beneath his oilcloth-covered table, he presented me with an old shoebox, the contents of which, he assured me, I'd find most interesting. On inspection, the box contained a paperback novel, several pieces of large, glossy paper folded over, and a few other miscellaneous documents which looked older. The novel was a 1954 reprint of the first volume of *Les Écrits*, missing its cover and water stained, and of no interest to me. I knew what the glossies were before I unfolded them: copies of advertising posters from when a cheaply produced film based on a mishmash of Robillard's cases graced the cinemas of towns up and down the country. Posters such as this are of interest to collectors and if they'd been in mint condition, and rolled instead of folded, they might have fetched ten pounds each. But these were in poor condition, and in any case, I already own framed copies of the originals. I leafed through the remaining artefacts until I arrived at the last one. It consisted of a sheaf of papers, folded into thirds to hide the contents, tied with a now-faded pink ribbon, and sealed with a circle of red wax. Below the seal, scrawled in a hand I'd seen many times over the years, and which I feel I know almost as well as I know my own, were the words *La Derniere Affaire*.

Convinced that the manuscript was authentic, I made no more than a token effort at haggling with the man before parting with the most money I have ever paid for a Robillard piece. Once home, I carefully slit open the wax seal – now brittle after all these years, smoothed out the papers, and read.

It has taken me some time to transcribe what I read that day, partly due to the faded nature of the handwritten text, and partly to the stiff and somewhat antiquated French of the author. Since completing the translation I have spent several sleepless nights mulling over what I should do with it. What the reading public will make of the contents of the manuscript, I have no idea, but I do know it's a story that must be told and I tell it here with no further commentary, nor with any attempt at modernising its antiquated tone.

This, then, in its original entirety, is the story of Auguste Charles Robillard's final case.

MW, Dec '21

THE DISAPPEARANCE OF KRISHNA'S EYE (THE FINAL INSTALMENT OF *LES ÉCRITS D'UN OBSERVATEUR*)

This morning (*the manuscript read*) I sat in my usual chair in the little reading room (the one beyond the Stranger's room) at my club on the Rue D'Artois, where it is my habit to peruse the news of the day. Tucked away in a corner of *Le Figaro* I found the *Nouvelles des Colonies*. Normally, I enjoy greatly hearing the news from those exotic-sounding places: *Cochin China, Chandernagor, Île des Pins*… But today it was with a heavy heart that I read a small notice giving the news I realised I had been long expecting.

I am acutely aware that followers of my scribblings have long wished that I would tell the tale of Auguste Robillard's final case, but I had vowed that it would not be possible for me to write or say a word on the subject so long as I believed him to be alive. It is now ten years since I last heard from him, and I feel that with today's news my self-imposed burden is lifted. It is time to reveal what happened all those years ago and I rather think that now he is gone, and there is no one to question him, he would look kindly on the account. It is, after all, probably his finest moment.

It was the afternoon of 25 December 19—, a Sunday, if I remember correctly, and as cold a Christmas Day as I could recall when Robillard and I mounted the steps of the grand townhouse on the Place des Petits-Pères that was the home of M. François Boisseau, the famous financier and statesman, and his family.

Robillard had received an urgent summons not twenty

minutes before and had sent a message immediately, requesting that I meet him in the Place. As my own apartments were just around the corner, it was a small matter to don my overcoat and scarf and march round to where my friend already stood, impatient to be getting on with the matter at hand.

'What is it that brings you out on this of all days?' I asked.

He shook his head, and I was startled by his countenance; I could not recall him looking so grave. 'It is a bad job, my friend. Krishna's Eye: it is gone. Stolen.'

Krishna's Eye. *Stolen!* The existence of the Comtois stone was legendary. It had (so the rumours ran) been won in a duel by an ancestor of Mme Boisseau and had been handed down through the generations to the present day, with Mme Boisseau as its current custodian. I had not seen the jewel myself and relied only on accounts in the society papers as to its form: a round-cut diamond of no less than ninety carats of the clearest, purest blue, pulled, so legend had it, from the same mines as the Tavernier Blue, the Dresden Green, and the Koh-i-Noor, and now mounted in a platinum setting simulating that of a bird in flight.

When we were admitted to the front drawing room, it was a sombre scene that greeted us. On a sofa sat Mme Adeline Boisseau, weeping gently and occasionally dabbing at tears with a lace handkerchief. Beside her, to her right, sat her daughter, Élodie, an arm around her mother's shoulder, offering such solace as she was able. To Mme Boisseau's left stood her husband, still shaking his head in bitter disbelief.

A company of seven guests had assembled in the drawing room that day to exchange seasonal cheer and in anticipation of a feast which would not now be enjoyed. I had met all the guests before and they were instantly recognisable to me.

Travelling clockwise around the room, my eyes rested first on M. Alfred Comtois, the brother of Mme Adeline, a firebrand socialist who was known to be no admirer of his brother-in-law's profession.

Next, perched on the edge of a small occasional chair was Mme Vadeboncoeur, a cousin of Mme Adeline, and her constant companion.

Fr. Gaudin, the family priest, stood before a mahogany dresser, passing a set of rosary beads through his fingers with the speed and dexterity that comes from years of practice.

In the far corner, opposite to the door through which we had entered, huddled a group consisting of M. Ozanne, the family's physician, and Mme Ozanne, and M. Cartier, a merchant of some repute, and Mme Cartier.

Robillard addressed M. Boisseau. 'Is this everyone? There are no children?'

There were indeed children, Boisseau replied, six in total: three belonging to the Cartiers and three to the Ozannes. They were currently in the rear sitting room, playing with their new toys under the supervision of Mme Schaeffer, the housekeeper.

'And the other servants?'

Only two others, it seemed: The first was Savoure, the chef, who was in the kitchen, awaiting further instructions. After all, M. Boisseau reasoned, robbery or not, people still had to eat. The other was the maid, Clémence, whom we had already met as she had collected our coats when we arrived, and who now flitted in and out of the room dispensing glasses of sherry wine when they were required.

'Has anyone left the house since the theft was noticed?'

'No one,' assured the master of the house.

'Good! And have you called the police?'

'Not yet. I awaited your presence first.'

'Then let it remain between us for now. If you would make a room available to me, I will begin my questioning.' Robillard turned and addressed Mme Adeline with a look designed to inspire confidence. 'Fear not, Madame. I am Robillard, and Robillard does not fail.'

I will not tax you by recording here a verbatim account of the interrogations, even though I made such an account at the time. Instead, I shall lay out the salient facts, as we learned them.

The guests had all arrived on time at noon. Mme Adeline had secured the services of a *Père Noël* from a theatrical agency and that good fellow, resplendent in red tunic and white whiskers had entertained the children for nearly an hour, handing out gifts and telling stories of Christmases past. After his hour was up, he had changed back into his street clothes, collected his fee, and left by the rear of the house, so as not to be spotted by any young eyes.

After that, the children had been left in the care of Mme Schaeffer and M. Boisseau had escorted the remainder of the company into the front drawing room where the maid, Clémence, waited with a tray of aperitifs. It was then that Mlle Élodie noticed that her mother was not wearing the diamond that she had so looked forward to showing off. Mme Adeline clasped a hand to her bosom, uttered some words chiding herself for her forgetfulness, and went to don the jewel.

Glasses had been handed out and the company were awaiting the reappearance of the hostess when a cry rang out from the floor above. Krishna's Eye, which Mme Adeline had left in the drawer of her dresser, was gone.

Naturally, it was firmly on the *Père Noël* character that Robillard devoted the most time, aiming question after question first to Mme Adeline, who had hired the man; to Clémence, who had shown him to the boot room so that he could change into his costume; and to Mme Schaeffer, who had paid him and shown him the door.

A dozen witnesses swore the man did not leave the sitting room during his performance and save the time he took to dress and undress, at no point was he left alone.

Of the others, little was learned that was not already known.

Mme Vadeboncoeur, the companion, let slip at one point that she carried a torch for M. Comtois, he of the fiery socialist tendencies, but any suggestion that the two might have acted in concert to steal the jewel were swiftly quashed. Comtois, for all his radical leanings was, like his sister, in receipt of a healthy allowance, and even if Mme Vadeboncoeur's love was reciprocated (he assured us in terms that brooked no argument that it was not) he would have had no need to steal the family heirloom.

The priest, Gaudin, was priestly poor and seemed happy to be so.

The doctor, Ozanne, was possessed of a flourishing practise; the business of the merchant, Cartier, boomed by all accounts; and neither of those two gentlemen's wives seemed to want for anything or have any earthly reason for purloining a piece of jewellery, no matter how admired the trinket might be.

As for the servants, they had all worked for the family since the couple were first married, twenty years previously and M. Boisseau swore he would trust each of them "with his life".

The questioning was long and at times tempers became frayed, and it was after six o'clock in the evening when we finally bade our hosts — now Robillard's clients — adieu. As for the great detective himself, he put a brave face on things but I, who knew him so well, could tell how perplexed he was by proceedings.

As soon as the shops and offices opened again the next day, I accompanied Robillard to the offices of Dufresne & Fils Cie, theatrical agents, to make enquiries about the *Père Noël*, still the only serious suspect. Our enquiries were dealt with by the *fils*, who at first scoffed at Robillard's request. Did monsieur not realise how many bookings for *Pères Noël* were received at this time of year? Every out of work actor, whether he was qualified to call himself by that title or not, registered for work as a *Père*

Noël. But when he read the name on the card Robillard handed him and realised the esteemed company in which he found himself, the young clerk showed more civility and went to consult a thick leather-bound ledger which lay upon a table to the rear of the office. He made some notes on a scrap of paper and handed it to Robillard.

Marcel Revenant
60, Rue du Mont-Dore, 17 Arr

'This is the address he gave. But be aware that some of these fellows do not wish it known where they live. You're as likely to find the address to be that of a convent as a lodging house for third-rate actors.'

And so it was to prove. Not a convent, as it turned out, but a milliner, who, he told us with a fair degree of indignation, made hats, and did not rent rooms to members of the theatrical trade.

Over the following days my friend continued his enquiries, but his efforts threw up no new information. He questioned the owners of every jeweller and pawn shop in Paris, but no one owned up to having seen or heard of the missing gem. By now, M. Boisseau had been forced to record the loss with the police, who were, not surprisingly, disgruntled at being viewed as the port of last resort, and consequently were unwilling to share anything they might find with Robillard.

As the weeks went by, I saw less and less of my friend, and when I did see him, I grew more and more concerned about the state of his health and, frankly, the state of his mind. It was looking very much as though his unblemished record was in jeopardy, and the prospect was telling on him. M. Boisseau, seemingly having given up on Robillard, had entered negotiations with his insurers, and with the police having failed to turn up anything, it looked like all parties were ready to call a halt to the search for Krishna's Eye.

I did not see my friend again until March. Having not heard from him for over a month, I called on his lodgings on the Rue Thérèse, in the hope that I might convince him to accompany me on a circuit or two of the park, but what I saw when I entered his rooms left me wondering whether he was in any fit state to do anything. He had lost weight and the dressing gown he had wrapped around himself hung in swathes. His hair was lank and unkempt, and the bristles on his chin were an indication of a man who had all but given up.

I stayed for an hour or so and tried to distract him by talking of the news of the day, but he was uninterested. When I finally stood to leave, I shook his hand. Gone was the authoritative grip of previous times, and as I left the building, I had an uncanny sense that I would not see my friend again, and I was to be proved correct.

Sitting here in the reading room, newspaper in my lap, I remember how my friend once, when in his cups (which I am happy to say was an infrequent occurrence) spoke in the bitterest terms of how his profession had brought him fame, but his successes had failed to bring him any great fortune, and as the spectre of his twilight years crept over the horizon towards him, he feared that which he had to look forward to. He had gazed out of the window at the cold, wet streets of the metropolis and told me how he longed to be somewhere far away, somewhere warm, where the air would no longer chill his bones.

At the time, I had thought no more of the exchange, putting it down to a surfeit of champagne. I now remember that conversation as though it were yesterday and when my eyes landed upon the death notice in the newspaper this morning I knew at once to whom it referred. It was the elusive actor who had played the *Père Noël* whom we had been unable to find on the Rue du Mont-Dore all those years ago. Unable then, or subsequently, because he had never existed.

One day in May, Robillard's landlord, M. Roget, had called at my rooms, informing me that my friend had left the premises a month past and had not returned and as the rent was overdue, he felt he had no option but to find a new tenant for the suite. Given that he had now found someone suitable, would I be so good as to gather up M. Robillard's remaining belongings? Robillard had spoken from time to time about a brother who had gone to sea, and having no idea where that man might be, or even if he was still alive, I resolved that I was now the nearest thing to family he had, and so I agreed.

Robillard had rented the rooms furnished and there was precious little of his own that was worth keeping. So, with Roget's assistance, I divided his belongings into two piles: one to go to the rag and bone man, and one to the poorhouse.

I kept one souvenir for myself. As I checked the top of the wardrobe for any remaining items my hand encountered a parcel, covered in brown paper and tied with string. Even as I unwrapped it, I was sure of what I would find. A *Père Noël* suit. In that moment, all became as clear as crystal to me. Robillard's game was up, not that he cared anymore. Indeed, I have often wondered if he left the suit there for me to find.

Robillard had told me previously that M. Boisseau paid him a small retainer to advise on matters of security. In so advising, he would have been aware that Madame did not keep the jewel in a safe. He even told me once that he had made a point of recommending to her that not to do so was asking for the thing to be stolen. Knowing Madame's preference, his first step would be to register with Dufresne's posing as a hungry actor. Through his profession he had, of course, mastered the art of concealing his identity, and this rôle called for a triple disguise: first, the clerk at Dufresne's must not remember him as a down-at-heel thespian when he later returned as the famous detective seeking the elusive M. Revenant; second, the good servants of Maison Boisseau must not recognise him as the trusted family advisor when he arrived on Christmas Morning, prior to his performance; and third, and most daringly of all, as *Père Noël* himself, in front of the family and their guests.

Upon his arrival at the house in his first disguise on Christmas morning the maid Clémence, busy with her duties to the guests, would have noticed nothing untoward about the stranger on the step and would have left Robillard in the boot room to make ready for his act. He was familiar with the layout of the house; it would have been the work of a trice to ascend the stairs, pocket the gem, and return, ready to entertain the children. So long as Mme Adeline did not choose to return to her boudoir to complete her dressing during his show, he was safe.

As I look once again at the notice in the paper, I find my disapproval of his actions softening and I cannot remember my friend with anything but fond admiration.

Died, Papeete, 24th December 19——. M. Revenant, gentleman.

He had longed, he said, for warmer climes. I trust he found the Society Isles more to his liking than the cold and rain of Paris.

As for the stone, it next showed up some years later, adorning the breast of the third wife of a Turkish Pasha. The Pasha refused to divulge from whom he had purchased it or how he had come by it, and a long and bitter battle for its custody ensued. Indeed, I am told it is still being waged in the courts to this day and, so far, the only beneficiaries of the struggle are the lawyers.

And so, I settle back in my chair and call for the waiter to bring me a glass of champagne. It is early for me, and the man's cocked eyebrow lets me know he thinks so, too. But I care not. After all, how often is one permitted to enjoy the opportunity of toasting the world's greatest detective and its greatest thief at the same time?

A CHRISTMAS SUSAN: PART III: THE GHOSTWRITER OF C. Y. COMB

ANTONY DUNFORD AND WENDY TURBIN

DECEMBER 24TH, 2026

EVEN FOR A PRIVATE DETECTIVE, THE DAY BEFORE Christmas should be a time to enjoy the finer things in life. An active avoidance of forced jollity, a pair of comfy PJs, an ancient film of Poirot, and an unlimited supply of Cadbury's Creme Eggs because Easter gets earlier every year and a hard-working woman has to take the positives where she can.

Sadly, the vision of such comfort and joy was snatched away from me by a client with deep pockets and an unreasonable attitude to time off.

My previous good behaviour: trailing her husband to his office, the bowls club, the library and the local arts centre holding a Beatrix Potter display, had been all for naught. I had a flash of hope when the exhibition director turned out to be a glamourous sophisticate with eyelashes worth batting and legs for days, but sadly my target just strolled around the exhibits as if he were truly interested in Mrs Tiggywinkle and the gang. I hadn't caught him in flagrante. In my client's eyes, Wiseman Associates had, thus far, failed.

In vain did I suggest he may be innocent of the charges.

'He's got a twinkle in his eye the Star of Bethlehem would be proud of, and it shouldn't be there. Mark my words, Penny Wiseman, he's only this excited when he's getting his end away!'

Then came a gift-wrapped piece of frank information overheard via 'a friend' which had incensed my client but offered golden opportunity.

Alf was planning an awayday.

I tried to demur. Surely there were more convenient places to fornicate than Bognor Regis?

'Maybe it's where they met or something. What do you care? Just follow him and bring me back the proof! There's a Christmas bonus in it for you.'

So I set off after the errant Mr Jingle, following the tracker signal in his car. One hundred and forty-six miles around the A12, round the M25, down the M23 I parked in a compound more prison camp than leisure resort if the cracked concrete and barbed wire topping the fences were any indication.

This would not be my first choice for a bit of lustful lip-synching under the mistletoe, but chance would be a fine thing. Not with him though. My client's husband is a portly florid-faced man who would suit a blue-striped apron. I could more easily imagine his beefy hands wielding a blade to sever the spinal cord of a pig, than causing a shiver of ecstasy down a lover's spine. Still, it takes all sorts.

Putting all thoughts of liquorice aside, I headed for the central building, following the signs for reception which had been decorated somewhat alarmingly in view of my recent thoughts. Blood-spattered fingerprints adorned each one.

Joining the throng inside the foyer, I picked up the brochure for the event.

The organisers had done a semi-alright job in theming the Bognor Regis Crime Fiction Festival. Much had been made of the "i" that had been inserted in Bognor to create BogNoir, and everywhere there were logos where the B-o-g-N-o-r were in a normal black font, and the i was made to look like a slash from a blade, bloody and oozing. On my festival pass, it looked more like spilt pasta sauce than a mortal wound, which was rather comforting, but who would bring their mistress to an evening of blood and gore?

My stomach rumbled. I virtuously ignored it. Heating bills. Staff costs. Office overheads. A little Christmas bonus could make the season merrier, if only with an extra crème egg or six.

With Alf's image fixed firmly in my mind, I scanned the growing crowd wondering if crime festivals were of particular attraction to the loftier literary folk. What with the six-foot plus brigade out in force, the prevalence of tall novelty hats of seasonal variety, and the possible resurgence of the beehive as a hairstyle choice, I was on a hiding to nothing. The latter might be explained by a Classic Crime of the sixties being advertised in the Glitterati Lounge but the knowledge made no difference to my chances of success.

Christmas bonus – humbug! I needed sustenance before my blood-sugar fell from grouchy to plain mean. I went in search of a refreshment stall.

This was less straightforward than I had hoped. What looked like it might be a map of the venue turned out to be a promotional poster for headline author C. Y. Comb's latest novel, *The Brutal Murder of Mr Perker*, the fifth Huffam and Weep mystery. As police procedurals go, they're better than most but I was already on a mission. I resolved to ask the way to the nearest food source, before checking on the various simultaneous panels that seemed to be on offer for Alf Jingle. Perhaps he was the Butcher of BogNoir hired to add to the fun. Low blood-sugar can cause concentration issues. Time to get some food, then I'd go back to the hunt.

Not much use if my quarry was snuggle-bunnied with his

illicit love in one of the chalets in the grounds but I was obliged by my dwindling bank account to give it my best shot.

I took a breath, ready to accost an elderly gentleman in a smart suit who seemed to be directing pedestrian traffic with some success as folk were filtering out of the foyer in different directions, but before I framed the question, something caught my eye.

A rabbit.

It sat patiently by the entrance to one of the event halls. Rising up on its haunches, it twitched its nose and stared straight at me. A rabbit. It was also, undeniably, a ghost.

I've been seeing the dead since childhood so this wasn't the shock it might have been, and usually they turn up for a reason though even the human ones aren't obliging enough to tell me what they want. This one regarded me with deep black eyes that looked almost friendly, but still, a ghost's a ghost. A bit of a shiver there, deep down.

And there was something about this rabbit. Something that made my stomach rumbling fade from my immediate priority as it continued to stare in my direction. I nodded, prepared to wait until it did something useful. After a moment it stood up on its hind legs and sniffed the air, then turned to show off its white bobtail. It hopped once, then looked back over its shoulder.

Useful.

I stepped towards it, whereupon it set off at some speed, lolloping into the main event hall and down the aisle in the direction of the stage. Despite my niftily deployed elbows, I lost sight of it in the crush. At a halt and causing a hazard to late-comers, I took note of their annoyed hissing to claim an empty seat at the end of a row. The flier on the chair introduced the panel the audience was about to see. The shortlisted authors for the Richard Adams Memorial Prize for children's crime fiction were about to be interviewed. Didn't he do something about rabbits?

The ghost I'd followed had made it up the stairs onto the stage. Now it sat quietly in front of one of the five chairs, waiting. I cleared my throat to disguise my stomach's rumbling and tried to be patient.

'Are you hungry?' On the chair next to mine a small girl of eight or thereabouts held out a bag of sweets.

'Thanks,' I mumbled, taking a sherbet lemon.

On her other side sat a woman who looked vaguely familiar. She addressed the child. 'Well done, Fozzy.'

Who names their child after a muppet? I may possibly have misheard.

The man in the next seat along leaned across the woman and muttered something to the child who listened attentively. Then she turned back to me. 'I'm perfectly alright,' she said, 'so you mustn't worry, but it's best not to take sweets from a stranger.'

I tried not to choke as the lemon went down the wrong way and nodded. 'Right.'

The man who'd issued the warning was half of a couple holding hands. Ram-rod straight, with sensible haircuts and a stern cast to their faces, they both leaned forward as the lights began to dim. Off-duty police or undercover, and trying to pass for normal? If so, I've seen it done better but I glanced around, wondering where trouble was most likely to come from.

The muttering of the crowd faded as a woman walked onto the stage.

'Good afternoon, ladies and gentlemen, and welcome to this, the penultimate panel of BogNoir 2026. My name is Robin Stevens, and I shall be talking to the four authors shortlisted for the Richard Adams Memorial Prize for unpublished works of children's crime fiction. If you'll give a big BogNoir welcome to—'

Robin introduced the four authors by name, and they stepped onto the stage in turn and took a seat. The third of the four was Alf Jingle, and he took the seat next to the ghost rabbit.

I fumbled for my phone and hit video.

Susan held her breath every time Alf Jingle spoke. Fuzzy was excited too, though she possibly didn't understand why. Dawn and David, there to humour Susan, watched politely.

As a child Susan's bedroom had looked out over a grass bank that was riddled with rabbits. She spent hours watching them. She imagined them talking to each other, going out to work, burning the dinner.

Then her father had read her *Watership Down*. She'd been too young to hold the whole story in her head. She'd fixed on two things. The beginning, when the warren was destroyed, and the Black Rabbit. The Black Rabbit had haunted her dreams from then on. As she had grown older, she had convinced herself that the only result of fiction was to make your worst fears real.

Susan, as C. Y. Comb, had been invited to judge the entries for the Richard Adams Memorial Prize for unpublished works of children's crime fiction. Alf Jingle's tale, of heartbreak and heart-mend through a stormy and violent childhood, where the plucky young hero takes their strength from three generations of pet rabbit, had finished the healing that being C. Y. Comb had started.

'And the same question to you, Mr Jingle. Did any personal experiences influence your story?'

'Thank you, Robin, they certainly did. Nothing like a personal experience for influencing a story, that there isn't. Impersonal experiences just don't cut it. I feel I would be letting my readers down if I let impersonal experiences fog my writing.' He blinked out at the audience.

'The heart of this story, the seed that germinated, was my pet rabbit, Saturday Blues. I didn't name her, you understand. She was gifted me when an old neighbour died. I was seven years old. I'd never been close to a rabbit before. Never been close to anything other than people and my granny's cat. And suddenly I had this rabbit and my dad said it was up to me to keep it alive. I was seven and swore I would keep Saturday Blues alive forever and ever.

'I know now that the natural lifespan for a wild rabbit is a couple of years, and an outdoor pet rabbit is just a little bit longer than that. My dad didn't say anything when I swore to keep Saturday Blues alive forever and ever. Perhaps he thought to leave me to it, to see if I tried to keep my promise. And, of course, to a seven-year-old, forever and ever is about a week.'

Alf waited for the chuckling to die down.

'I never found out how old Saturday Blues was when she came to me. She was full grown, but can't have been full grown for long, because she lived until I was sixteen. Through my formative years, you might say, and my life was very normal compared to the child in my novel.

'But I found myself imagining, only a few years ago, how much harder growing up would have been without Saturday Blues sitting in the corner of my bedroom nibbling on some dandelion leaves. I got to wondering how much easier a hard life could have been for someone else if they had a rabbit.'

Alf Jingle stopped talking, quite abruptly just as Susan noticed the woman sitting on the other side of Fuzzy was surreptitiously filming the event. The old Susan, the pre-C. Y. Comb Susan, would have arrested her on the spot, even if it was her day off. The new Susan let it slide.

To her left, Susan sensed Dawn and David were less than enthralled by the panel. Dawn had been more excited by their recent wedding than Susan had thought was warranted given the two of them had been cohabiting for years, until she'd realised that Dawn had chosen to take David's surname. This meant that her old nickname, DCI Squared, for Detective Chief Inspector

Dawn Charlotte Icarus, was no longer relevant as she became Dawn Sergeant.

Dawn's joy had been short lived as the very next week she'd been promoted to Detective Superintendent, the same rank as her husband. DCI Squared became DS Squared. Married to the other DS Squared. Mathematicians were consulted on how to refer to the couple. DS-to-the-power-of-four was discounted as too much of a mouthful. DS Squared Squared defeated the easy-referencing nicknames were supposed to provide. The nick had, in time honoured tradition, settled on a simpler moniker for the irritatingly happy couple.

The Smug Gits, or TSG for short.

The hour drew to a close, and Susan started to feel the rabbits in her stomach she always felt before being publicly scrutinised. She squeezed Fuzzy's hand to comfort herself more than the child. Fuzzy looked up at her and leaned her head on Susan's shoulder. The woman on the other side of Fuzzy had stopped filming and was staring at a space by the wall of the event hall. Susan rapidly categorised her as "nutter" and focused on getting into character as C. Y. Comb.

Despite my increasing hunger and the excited wriggling of the child on the next chair, I'd enjoyed the Richard Adams Memorial Prize panel. Alf Jingle had been pleasingly articulate and had even more pleasingly solved my case by explaining his presence at the festival. He'd evidently kept his writing hobby secret from his wife.

My prospects of a Christmas bonus made me feel seasonally cheery, almost sufficient to contemplate mulling some wine when I finally got home. If I stayed for the C. Y. Comb interview, the traffic might have died down on the M25.

I checked my watch. Fifteen minutes till it started. That gave me sufficient time to find sustenance to hold body and soul together. And to ponder further on the appearance of a dead man wearing tinsel in his hair, loitering by the wall in the event hall.

Fifteen minutes later and the burgers of BogNoir were seriously depleted. The burghers, on the other hand, were flocking in for the main event including one or two wearing mayoral chains of office. Marley's ghost could do some serious clanking with that lot.

I secured a seat on the aisle only two rows from the front, after a minor altercation with a pensioner bedecked with ribbons. Naturally I'd have given way at the sight of medals – I have some respect – but these were ribboned bows with Christmas tags attached. One bore the legend 'I love you C. Y.' which should come with a stalker alert. I think I did C. Y. Comb a favour.

The lights went down, the crowd hushed, and Peter James stepped onto the stage, the celebrity interviewer.

'Hello, BogNoir!' he called, gameshow style.

'Good afternoon, Peter,' about one in five of BogNoir responded, politely.

'My guest tonight needs no introduction. Her latest novel, *The Brutal Murder of Mr Perker*, the fifth outing of the crime cracking duo of Huffam and Weep, has been a world-wide bestseller since its release three months ago, following hard on the heels of its predecessors. Hailed by the critic in *The Sunday Times* as "even better than Peter James",' this drew laughter from many, 'C. Y. goes from strength to strength. Ladies and gentlemen, please unleash your finest BogNoir welcome for C. Y. COMB!'

There was much applause, and even a wolf-whistle or two from the geriatric old-timers in the front row. I'd forgotten C. Y. Comb was a woman. In fact, I'd been convinced C. Y. Comb was a man but as she stepped onto the stage, I realised this was the woman who had been sitting on the other side of the sherbet lemon girl in the Richard Adams prize event.

More surprisingly, the writer who walked onto the stage was followed by the ghost who had been lounging against the wall at the end of the row.

The applause died down, and Peter and C. Y. sat. The ghost stood behind C. Y.'s chair, grinning like a lunatic. He had taken the tinsel from his hair and was trying to drape it round C. Y.'s shoulders.

'Should I call you C. Y.?' Peter began.

'Susan is fine.'

From behind, I thought I heard a tearing of tag from ribbon and a muffled sob.

'Alright, Susan. Perhaps you could start by explaining the origins of C. Y. for any members of our audience who aren't familiar with the tale.'

Susan related a story of her partner who had penned the first C. Y. Comb novel. A vague remembrance of the flyleaf of the first Huffam and Weep entered my mind and the light began to dawn.

'Ian was known as Sharpie around the station,' Susan said. 'I was so naïve in those days. It was only after he died, I realised it had been a pun on his surname, Feltpen. After the Sharpie permanent marker. Patented in 1964, so I've never felt too bad I missed the reference. A little before my time.'

'Did you have a nickname?'

'I did, given to me by Ian. He used to call me Fifty. It was only after he died he told me why. It was a reference to *Fifty Shades of Grey*. He'd thought it would be hilarious to call me Fifty Shades of Brown, as my surname is Brown. Tragically, he wasn't always as funny as he thought he was.'

The expression of mock outrage on the face of the ghost standing at Susan Brown's shoulder was priceless. I let out a laugh. I hadn't meant to, and it wasn't too loud. A couple of people looked around disapprovingly, but by then I didn't care, because by then I'd realised what that meant.

Her ghost spoke to her! Most of my life I'd hoped to find someone who could communicate with the dead. Someone who could not just watch them and guess, but who could be a verbal conduit. There were a lot of con artists, but I'd yet to find anyone genuine who could do it.

Until now.

'Did you say he told you after he died?' Peter asked.

'Sorry, a figure of speech. I worked it out after he died,' Susan replied.

My hopes began to fade.

'And your colleague Ian, he got a publishing deal for the first Huffam and Weep novel, *The Murder of Sam Weller*, and then was tragically killed a few days later. Can you tell us anything about that?'

Of course. The author photo on that first cover, why I'd thought the author was a man.

Susan took a moment before answering and in that pause, I saw Ian Feltpen reach out his hand, as if to rest it on her shoulder. Susan raised her own hand as if to pat his. As if she knew he was there.

'It was a great tragedy. But Ian and his wife Fleur had been very thorough, and had prepared quite detailed wills, and Ian had left me the job of writing the other two books he had been contracted to Macmillan for. I wanted to do it, for him, and for Fleur, as they'd always been so kind to me. But the first time I sat in front of that keyboard with Ian's notes for the second book, I knew I couldn't do it. I just don't have his wit, or his generosity of spirit.'

Susan fell silent for an uncomfortably long time. Eventually Peter prompted her.

'But you have written four great books, sizzling with chemistry between John Huffam and Marjorie Weep. What changed?'

Ian Feltpen acted out a pantomime of pushing Susan out of the way, taking her place at the keyboard, his ghostly fingers flying over invisible keys. Then he beamed at the audience and took a bow.

'One night, when I was ready to give up completely, Ian's personality just came to me, and I started to think as he would have thought. After that, the stories flowed.'

There was a catch in Susan's voice. Everyone could hear it. Peter steered the conversation away.

Thoughts flew through my brain – how could I get Susan alone to talk about her ghost? This could be the best Christmas present ever. But even as plans coalesced, they shattered. The spirit of Ian Feltpen looked in my direction, waggled his right index finger and slowly shook his head.

'It's as if he never left,' said Susan.

'Such a beautiful thought,' Peter said, pausing for a moment. 'So, moving onto the novel. What was it that gave you the idea to have pasta sauce as such a dominant motif?'

The rest of the talk was standard stuff and I filtered it out, observing Ian Feltpen watch his friend perform. Then there was applause, the lights came up and BogNoir was over.

At least I'd solved my case.

I was stowing my purchases in the car boot when my phone rang. It was Mrs Jingle.

'Do you have the proof? Is it the woman from his work?'

'No, Mrs Jingle, it's a rabbit called Saturday Blues.'

Silence from the other end.

'Mrs Jingle? Are you there?'

'Don't tell me he's tried to pull that crap on you too? He's been saying that for months, that he's written a story about a rabbit, that he's sent it to a competition. What nonsense. He's a grown man. I don't know how he's done it, but he's tricked you. Who was he meeting?'

'If he's tricked me, he's tricked the judges of a rather prestigious competition, Mrs Jingle. I'll send you a video of his panel at BogNoir and I'll look forward to the bonus. Have a Merry Christmas.'

I clicked off the call and emailed the file.

As it swooshed off into the ether, a little party passed me, heading to the next row of parked cars. Susan Brown, a.k.a. C. Y. Comb, hand-in-hand with the little girl, was walking in step with the couple who had been sitting next to her in the Richard Adams prize event, the ones who law-breakers and PIs have a sixth sense for.

'We'll see you in the afternoon,' the woman in the couple said to Susan. 'What are your plans for Christmas morning?'

'Fuzzy is going to get up late and then we're going to read out our cards to her mummy and daddy before covering the living room in glitter and rolling in it whilst we open our present.'

'Only one?' the woman said.

'It's special,' Susan said. She put her hands over the little girl's ears and turned her head so she was almost facing me. 'It's a rabbit,' Susan mouthed to the woman.

The little girl caught my eye and smiled.

Her sherbet lemon had earned her a smidgeon of civility and my grin grew broader as I saw who was attached to the little group. The ghost of Ian "Sharpie" Feltpen, arm in arm with the shade of a young woman.

The police couple got into one car, Susan and the girl got into another, and after a few parting calls of "Merry Christmas", both cars drove away.

Their ghost writer friend waved until they were out of sight and then he turned and kissed his wife. A fragment of Cliff

Richard's *Mistletoe and Wine* drifted past on an arctic chill as they wandered off towards the Waltzers.

I headed home looking forward to losing myself in a tale of death and pasta sauce, and my brand new seasonal favourite courtesy of the gift shop – a Christmas stocking filled with Cadbury's Creme Eggs.

Comfort and joy, indeed!

Merry Christmas, everyone.
Antony and Wendy

ACKNOWLEDGMENTS

This time last year, somewhere on the M1, we came up with what we thought was a bright idea: 'Let's put together an anthology of Christmas stories by our authors and ourselves!'. We were amazed at how keen and productive our authors were when we told them about the project. Out of that idea came *Never Mind the Baubles* which arrived on our doorsteps, just after Christmas. Ahem. We had had such fun putting the book together despite missing the big deadline. We gave the anthology away to subscribers, not confident it was worthy of the big wide world. With a bit more experience to hand, this year, we decided to do it again (starting a lot earlier). This time we felt brave enough to offer it to the big wide world.

We would like to say a heart-felt humongous thank you to both our authors who have contributed to this book and those who would have done if life and day jobs hadn't got in the way. There's always next year – hint, hint! But the most important person in this project is you. Yes, you. You, the person who has bought this book. You, the reviewer who has offered to read and put out your thoughts online for other readers and reviewers. You, the lucky person who has received this as a gift. It is you who deserve our biggest thanks. If it hadn't been for you and the support you have given for our authors and ourselves over the last twelve months and beyond, we wouldn't be able to do this at all.

Merry Christmas!

REBECCA & ADRIAN

If you have enjoyed this collection why not download last year's
Christmas anthology for free?

You could also download our ever expanding Hobeck author
compilation *Crime Bites*. All you have to do is subscribe to
Hobeck Books to get *Never Mind the Baubles* and *Crime Bites* for
free.

Crime Bites includes:

- *Echo Rock* by Robert Daws
- *Old Dogs, Old Tricks* by A B Morgan
- *The Silence of the Rabbit* by Wendy Turbin
- *Never Mind the Baubles: An Anthology of Twisted Winter Tales* by the Hobeck Team (including all the current Hobeck authors and Hobeck's two publishers)
- *The Clarice Cliff Vase* by Linda Huber
- *Here She Lies* by Kerena Swan
- *The Macnab Principle* by R.D. Nixon
- *Fatal Beginnings* by Brian Price
- *A Defining Moment* by Lin Le Versha
- *Saviour* by Jennie Ensor

Also please visit the Hobeck Books website for details of our other superb authors and their books, and if you would like to get in touch, we would love to hear from you.

Hobeck Books also presents a weekly podcast, the Hobcast, where founders Adrian Hobart and Rebecca Collins discuss all things book related, key issues from each week, including the ups and downs of running a creative business. Each episode includes an interview with one of the people who make Hobeck possible: the editors, the authors, the cover designers. These are the people who help Hobeck bring great stories to life. Without them, Hobeck wouldn't exist. The Hobcast can be listened to from all the usual platforms but it can also be found on the Hobeck website: **www.hobeck.net/hobcast**.

@STREETREADS

All of the royalties from the sale of this book is going to go direct to Streetreads, a charitable initiative based in Scotland.

Streetreads takes books and stories to people affected by homelessness. Stories offer a great way to escape the realities of trauma and tough times, a chance to lose yourself in another world, to find solace, adventure, new horizons. They also help us start conversations and build the connections that are vital to recovery from homelessness.

But Streetreads is more than the books – here are just some of the ways that they connect with people through stories:

- Providing spaces to bring in storytellers and to create stories
- Connecting readers with the authors and writers
- Running classes and events helping people connect with their world, where people can listen, take part and create their own stories
- Providing audio books and the tech for people to listen to them
- Offering reading glasses to those who need them

- Offering EasyRead books, graphic novels and books in a variety of languages

Find out more by visiting the Simon Community Scotland website.

https://www.simonscotland.org/our-initiatives/streetreads/

BY THE CONTRIBUTORS

JUDI DAYKIN, *WAYLAND BABES*

'5 out of 5 stars from me – and will be going down on my Christmas list for the paperback.' Joe Singleton

The Wayland Woods in Norfolk – an ancient place where sound and silence, truth and myth, and life and death intertwine.

Some say that the babes of the woods still walk the Earth. To see them is a terrible omen. What could it mean to see the babes, feel their presence, and be lured deeper into the woods?

Five tales tell of five lives touched over five centuries by the so-called babes in the wood. If they beckon, will you follow?

ANTONY DUNFORD, *HUNTED*

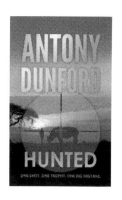

'In the Kenyan Savannah, Norwegian special forces veteran Jane Haven is one badass ranger you don't want to cross.' Jack Leavers, author of *Appetite for Risk*

Once a member of the world's first all-female special forces unit, the Norwegian Hunter Troop, Jane Haven is now helping her brother Kennet protect some of the world's most endangered animals at his Kenyan Wildlife Conservancy.

Drawn away from her vigil protecting Douglas, the world's last remaining male Northern White rhino, Jane returns to find a scene of devastation and murder.

Everything and everyone Jane cares for is affected.

But before she can track down the killers, Jane finds that she's the one being hunted.

LEWIS HASTINGS, *THE SEVENTH WAVE TRILOGY* AND *THE ANGEL OF WHITEHALL*

'One of the best thrillers, of all time just magnificent.' Surjit Parekh

Friends and enemies call him the 'Jackdaw'. He's Europe's most wanted man. Now he's ready to unleash the full power of his organisation, the 'Seventh Wave'. To what lengths will the Jackdaw go to get what he wants? There is only one man who can stop him. Former British cop John 'Jack' Cade is still recovering from the impact of a past encounter with the Jackdaw, but events force him to face his old foe again. Only one man can be victorious, and victory will only come at great personal cost.

This book is an absolute must... Buy this book!' London Crime

A young African woman's body is found slumped in a London side street. Her stomach slashed open, a single diamond hiding within.

An elderly sailor with just weeks to live harbours a dark secret that he has to share before he dies. The only problem. His memory is failing through dementia.

Former British police officer Jack Cade is the only man who can help unravel the mystery. Piecing together the fragments of information that the old man's fragile memory reveals, Cade unearths a scandal with links to the heart of the British Establishment.

LINDA HUBER, *DARIA'S DAUGHTER* AND *PACT OF SILENCE*

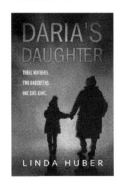

'I held my breath so many times and yes I did have to fight back the tears too on a couple of occasions. Brilliant, absolutely brilliant.' Patricia Gill

An explosive accident on the way to Glasgow airport leaves Daria hurt, bereaved and confused. Her daughter has vanished without a trace and nobody is telling her what happened. Evie's gone. That's all. Gone. What does Daria have left to live for?

Margie can't believe it. Bridie is hurt. Bridie needs her. They manage to escape the smoke, the noise and the confusion. They are together, that's all that matters. Everything will be better in the morning, Margie tells Bridie. And it will.

Will Daria ever be able to put the pieces of her tattered life back together after the loss of her daughter? Is it possible that things aren't quite as they seem? Can the unimaginable turn out to be the truth?

'What an emotional rollercoaster! Darkly addictive and packed to the rafters with secrets, I was flipping those pages, desperate to see how it unravelled.' Jane Isaac, psychological thriller author

Newly pregnant, Emma is startled when her husband Luke announces they're swapping homes with his parents, but the rural idyll where Luke grew up is a great place to start their family. Yet Luke's manner suggests something odd is afoot, something that Emma can't quite fathom.

Emma works hard to settle into her new life in the Yorkshire countryside, but a chance discovery increases her suspicions. She decides to dig a little deeper...

Will Emma find out why the locals are behaving so oddly? Can she discover the truth behind Luke's disturbing behaviour? Will the pact of silence ever be broken?

LIN LE VERSHA, *BLOOD NOTES*

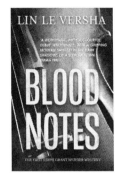

'A wonderful, witty, colourful "who-dunnit" with a gripping modern twist set in the dark shadows of a Suffolk Town.' Emma Freud

Edmund Fitzgerald is different. Sheltered by an over-protective mother, a musical prodigy. He enters formal education aged sixteen. Everything is alien.

Then there's the searing jealousy his talent inspires, especially when the sixth form college's Head of Music, begins to teach Edmund exclusively.

Observing events is the college receptionist, Steph, a former police detective who is rebuilding her life following a bereavement. When a student is found dead in the music block, Steph's sleuthing skills help to unravel the dark events engulfing the college community.

A B MORGAN *OVER HER DEAD BODY* AND *THROTTLED*

'A wonderful page turner that captivated me right from the beginning.' Misfits Farm

Recently divorced and bereaved, Gabby Dixon is trying to start a new chapter in her life. But Gabby is still very much alive. As a woman who likes to be in control, this situation is deeply unsettling.

Enter Peddyr and Connie Quirk. husband-and-wife private

investigators. Gabby needs their help to find out who is behind her sudden death.

'Another five star read from Alison.' Thriller Man

Scott Fletcher is dead – his lifeless body in a pool of blood. Sarah Holden's life is turned upside-down the day she is discovered with her fiancé's body. She has blood on her hands, but the screams do not come.

If she didn't kill him, then who did? The answer seems too easy. The likely culprit too obvious.

Peddyr and Connie Quirk, husband-and-wife private investigators, are brought in to unravel the tangle, prove Sarah's innocence and find the true culprit. As they are about to discover, the truth is sometimes much more than skin deep.

R.D. NIXON *CROSSFIRE*

'Without a doubt, one of the most exciting books I've read.' Shelley Clarke

Hogmanay 1987 and a prank robbery has fatal consequences. Five years later and the Highlands town Abergarry is shaken by the seemingly gratuitous murder of a local man. The case is unsolved.

Now in the present and ten-year-old Jamie, while on holiday in Abergarry with his mum Charis, overhears a conversation. To him, it is all part of a game. But this is no game and the consequences are far more serious than Jamie ever imagined.

Struggling PI team Maddy Clifford and Paul Mackenzie find themselves involved by a chance meeting. How deep into those wounds will they have to delve to unravel the mystery?

BRIAN PRICE, *FATAL TRADE*

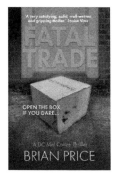

'A fast-paced edge-of-your-seat thriller from a major new talent. Gripping stuff!' David Mark, best-selling author of *Dark Winter*

Glasgow, 1999. Reaching the point of no return, Martina is ready to make her move. After years of being the victim, it's now time to turn the tables.

Mexton, 2019. DC Melanie Cotton's fledgling career is about to take an interesting turn. Freshly promoted to CID, Mel is excited by this disturbing and mysterious case – her first murder investigation as a detective.

S.E. SHEPHERD, *SWINDLED*

'Hard to put down. Totally engrossed from beginning to end.' Sarah-Jane Hill

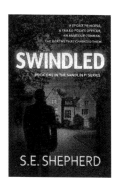

Beautiful, but a little spoilt, Lottie Thorogood leads a charmed life. Returning home from horse riding one day, she finds a stranger, drinking tea in the family drawing room – a stranger who will change her life, forever.

After a bad decision cut short her police career, Hannah Sandlin is desperate to make her mark as a private investigator. She knows she has the skills, but why won't anyone take her seriously? She's about to become embroiled in a mystery that will finally put those skills to the test and prove her doubters wrong. It will also bring her a friend for life.

Vincent Rocchino has spent his life charming the ladies, fleecing them and fleeing when things turn sour. How long can he keep running before his past catches up with him?

KERENA SWAN, BLOOD LOSS

'...in the same league as Ian Rankin and L J Ross...' Graham Rolph

With one eye on the rear view mirror and the other on the road ahead, Sarah is desperate to get as far away.

When a body is discovered in a remote cabin in Scotland, DI Paton feels a pang of guilt as he wonders if this is the career break he has been waiting for. But the victim is unidentifiable and the killer has left few clues.

With the death of her father and her mother's failing health, Jenna accepts her future plans must change but nothing can prepare her for the trauma yet to come.

Fleeing south to rebuild her life Sarah uncovers long-hidden family secrets. Determined to get back what she believes is rightfully hers, Sarah thinks her future looks brighter.

WENDY TURBIN, *SLEEPING DOGS*

'...a cracker of a novel' William Ryan, author of the Captain Korolev series and winner of Guardian Novel of the Year

Meet Penny Wiseman, a private investigator by circumstance, stumbling through adulthood and desperately trying to keep her late father's business afloat.

She's on the trail of her client's husband. He's guilty of hiding something, but is he having an affair? The case leads her to an intriguing series of mysteries and encounters, and not all are quite of this world.

Because, for Penny, seeing the dead is a fact of life, and when a teenage ghost wants justice, who else can the girl turn to for help?

There's one big problem – the dead don't talk.

MARK WIGHTMAN, *WAKING THE TIGER*

'A wonderfully accomplished debut... Wightman is a writer we can expect great things of.' Abir Mukerjee

Longlisted for the Bloody Scotland McIlvanney Crime Novel of 2021 and shortlisted for the Crime Debut of 2021.

Singapore, 1939 and a young Japanese woman is found dead on the dockside, her throat slashed. A distinctive tiger tattoo is the only clue to her identity.

Inspector Maximo Betancourt is working a new beat, one he didn't ask for. Following the disappearance of his wife, his life and career have fallen apart.

Once a rising star of Singapore CID, Betancourt has been relegated to the Marine Division, with tedious dockyard disputes and goods inspections among his new duties.

But when a beautiful, unidentified Japanese woman is found murdered in the shadow of a warehouse owned by one of Singapore's most powerful families, Betancourt defies orders and pursues those responsible. What he discovers will bring him into conflict with powerful enemies, and force him to face his personal demons.

All these books and the other books published by Hobeck are available from the Amazon website, the Hobeck website www.hobeck.net or they can be ordered via your local bookshop.

Printed in Great Britain
by Amazon